BLUE MEN AND RIVER MONSTERS

BLUE MEN & RIVER MONSTERS

FOLKLORE OF THE NORTH

A WPA collection

Edited by John Zimm   *Foreword by* Michael Edmonds

WISCONSIN HISTORICAL SOCIETY PRESS

Published by the Wisconsin Historical Society Press
Publishers since 1855

© 2014 by the State Historical Society of Wisconsin

For permission to reuse material from *Blue Men and River Monsters: Folklore of the North*, ISBN 978–0-87020–670–2 and ebook ISBN 978–0-87020–671–9, please access www.copyright.com or contact the Copyright Clearance Center, Inc. (CCC), 222 Rosewood Drive, Danvers, MA 01923, 978–750–8400. CCC is a not-for-profit organization that provides licenses and registration for a variety of users.

wisconsinhistory.org

Photographs identified with WHi or WHS are from the Society's collections; address requests to reproduce these photos to the Visual Materials Archivist at the Wisconsin Historical Society, 816 State Street, Madison, WI 53706.

Printed in the United States of America
Designed by Mayfly Design

18 17 16 15 14   1 2 3 4 5

Library of Congress Cataloging-in-Publication
Blue men and river monsters : folklore of the north / edited by John Zimm ;
foreword by Michael Edmonds.
    pages cm
  Includes index.
  ISBN 978-0-87020-670-2 (pbk. : alk. paper) — ISBN 978-0-87020-671-9
(ebook) 1. Folklore—Wisconsin. 2. Wisconsin—Social life and customs.
3. Frontier and pioneer life—Wisconsin. I. Zimm, John, editor.
  GR110.W5B58 2014
  398.209775—dc23
                              2014007545

♾ The paper used in this publication meets the minimum requirements of the American National Standard for Information Sciences—Permanence of Paper for Printed Library Materials, ANSI Z39.48–1992.

CONTENTS

FOREWORD

This book was conceived eight decades ago, during the heart of the Great Depression. In 1935, with nearly 10 million Americans out of work, Congress established the Works Progress Administration to provide jobs. When WPA director Harry Hopkins was criticized for giving work to writers and artists, he snapped, "Hell, they've got to eat like other people."[1]

Federal Writers' Projects were soon springing up around the nation. Each was charged with preparing a travel guide to its own state that captured the "native and folk backgrounds of rural localities." WPA editors encouraged staff to interview farmers, factory workers, immigrants, former slaves, Indians, and other Americans typically left out of traditional travel guides.[2]

In October 1935, WPA officials appointed Charles Brown to head the Wisconsin writers' project. As museum director at the Wisconsin Historical Society, Brown had been collecting artifacts and running archaeological digs for three decades. He knew old settlers and tribal elders all around the state who recalled oral traditions. Brown agreed to supervise the project if he could keep his museum job and have someone else oversee the new office day to day.[3]

Washington initially required writers' project offices in every city of ten thousand or more, "from which writers and investigators will comb the neighboring territory for color and historic information." In Wisconsin, large offices opened in Milwaukee and Green Bay, and by early 1936 about 140 staff around the state were gathering information for the proposed guidebook.[4]

One of Brown's first and wisest decisions was to hire Dorothy Miller, a thirty-nine-year-old single mother, to head the Wisconsin folklore section of the writers' project. Miller was the voice of "Miss Marjorie," a radio personality who broadcast short pieces each morning for a Madison department store. She had also worked in advertising and helped lead the Delphian Society, a women's group that ran adult education programs. The goal of her new WPA job was to locate "folklore that has been related from generation to generation and would eventually die out," unless she made it "blossom forth in its original form—in print for the first time."[5]

Miller quickly assembled a team of unemployed women to save the state's vanishing oral heritage. It consisted of several field interviewers assisted by two typists and various clerical staff; at any given time it totaled ten to fifteen workers. Although some men were also employed on the project, in her office memos Miller affectionately called them "my girls."[6]

Their wages ranged from $62.50 to $83.50 a month, on which some of them had to support families. WPA workers were often scorned by the public as freeloaders and repeatedly laid off when Congress or WPA administrators shifted funding priorities. Yet in the words of one Wisconsin staff member, "They bore poverty, opprobrium, and the recurrent strain of the quota cuts and shake-ups without losing their self-respect, their respect for one another, or their keenness for and belief in what they were doing."[7]

Miller and her staff began in the spring of 1936 by unearthing folklore hidden in obscure books, pamphlets, and newspaper files at the Wisconsin Historical Society. Then they drove around the state to interview elderly residents in Shawano, Rice Lake, La Crosse, Prairie du Chien, and Dane and Door Counties. Gregg Montgomery and Dorothy Potter appear to have been the principal field-workers, with Coryl Moran and Jane Olson also conducting some of the interviews. Three of the four had grown up working class; two were single working women like Dorothy Miller herself. In six months they talked to more than 300 people, who provided more than 1,000 folktales, 3,000 songs, 1,500 games and superstitions, and 9,000 proverbs.[8]

But that was just the beginning. Over the course of the entire folklore project (December 1935 through November 1937), they gathered "5,000 stories-songs-rhymes-riddles-epitaphs; 8,000 games, superstitions, customs, weather lore & sayings; and made 6 folklife maps." The project's file cabinets bulged with more than 5,000 pages of folklore.[9]

Although the material was largely collected from living people, it passed through several stages of editing. The field-workers' hand-written notes were recast into grammatical sentences as they were typed. Carbon copies were marked up by editors mainly interested in their potential use for the state guide. By the time final clean copies emerged, the speech of local informants had usually been rearranged and polished by the project staff.

In Washington, folklorist John Lomax congratulated the Wisconsin team for collecting "an amazing amount of good material. . . . The work has been carefully and thoroughly done." Miller broadcast shows about Wisconsin folklore on the radio and published fifty articles in newspapers around the state and national magazines. She provided two hundred folktales for use in the Wisconsin guide, sent exhibits to Washington in 1936, and organized Wisconsin's participation in the National Folk Festival in Chicago in 1937. She traveled as far as New Orleans to give presentations based on the material her "girls" had amassed.[10]

But apart from Miller's close-knit group, the Wisconsin writers' project fell apart. "The county and district units broke down almost immediately," editor Harold Miner wrote afterward. Only the offices at Milwaukee and Green Bay ("which had so far concealed its ineptitude by a great show of energy") survived the first six months. Miner recalled that they had merely assembled "a large accumulation of inaccurate and inane material, all elaborately filed and cross-indexed. When I left Madison, this mass of material was stored (for it could not be destroyed, since it was government property) in the attic of a condemned school building, and everyone hoped the rats would eat it."[11]

Miller, on the other hand, worked hard to see that the best of the oral tales were preserved in print. Within eighteen months she issued four pamphlets: *Wisconsin Indian Place Legends* (January 1937, 55 pages); *Wisconsin Circus Lore* (May 1937, 72 pages); *Wisconsin Mushrooms* (1937, 17 pages); and *The Fighting Finches: Tales of Freebooters of the Pioneer Countryside in Rock and Jefferson Counties* (1937, 31 pages). Between 125 and 200 copies of each were mimeographed, hand-bound by the WPA's Milwaukee Handicraft Project, and distributed to public libraries for free.[12]

Early in 1937, after Brown's wife died, he fell in love with Dorothy Miller, and on April 7 they were married while en route to a folk-lore conference. For the next decade, they gave lectures, wrote articles, published books, and traveled to professional meetings together, as well as parenting a menagerie of stepchildren and having a daughter of their own.[13]

Brown had never been able to give the Wisconsin writers' project the attention it deserved, and it was plagued by incompetent managers, administrative blunders, labor disputes, and bad press. In the fall of 1937, a disgruntled former employee publicly denounced Brown for hiring his own son and marrying a member of his staff. In a scathing letter to the press, the employee demanded to know how WPA officials "could be so exceedingly kind and generous with federal funds to one family already pretty well financed by the state of Wisconsin."[14]

Though his superiors had approved his actions, Brown resigned in embarrassment in November 1937. Dorothy followed him out the door. "Heading a Federal Writers Project in Wisconsin," he wrote to a colleague, "as I did for two years much against my own wishes and in addition to my other work and at a real monetary loss to myself, was a very ungrateful undertaking not properly or fully appreciated here or in Washington."[15]

Friends and supporters gathered around the Browns to create the Wisconsin Folklore Society. Operating out of their home, this private group issued twenty folklore booklets over the next decade. Much of their material came directly out of WPA files that the Browns carried off when they resigned. After Charles died in 1946, Dorothy published more pamphlets from the purloined federal files, and twenty years later, she donated what remained of them to the University of Minnesota.[16]

Most of the folklore project's records, however, were shipped to Washington in 1943 when the Wisconsin writers' project office shut down. Four decades later, librarians at the Wisconsin Historical Society ordered microfilm of the official records from the Library of Congress. Among the papers on the microfilm rolls were the hand-written and typed notes made from interviews conducted in 1936 and 1937 by Dorothy's field-workers.

These totaled hundreds of pages of stories, customs, jokes, music, maxims, and games shared by local residents around Wisconsin. The people interviewed ranged from Swiss settlers in New Glarus to Ojibwe elders beside Lake Superior. Some of the tales and customs they shared were brought from Europe, while others recorded oral traditions of life in pioneer Wisconsin or narratives of the state's American Indian peoples.

John Zimm has selected the very best stories and tales from these WPA interviews. After being transmitted orally for generations and put down on paper eighty years ago by Dorothy Miller's dedicated "girls," they are now available as a book for the first time.

---

1. Hopkins is quoted in Jerre Mangione, *The Dream and the Deal: The Federal Writers' Project, 1935–1943* (Syracuse, NY: Syracuse University Press, 1996), 4.

2. Arthur M. Schlesinger, *The Age of Roosevelt: The Politics of Upheaval, 1935–1936* (Boston: Houghton Mifflin Harcourt, 2003), 2; Michael B. Katz, *In the Shadow of the Poorhouse* (New York: Basic Books, 1996), 254.

3. "Chats with the Editor," *Wisconsin Magazine of History* 28, no. 2 (December 1944): 133–34; *Wisconsin Archeologist* 25, no. 2 (June 1944): 46–48.

4. "The Color of Wisconsin," *Wisconsin State Journal*, November 7, 1935, 11; Harold Miner, "Essay and Letters, 1941–1942," MS SC 1243, Wisconsin Historical Society Archives, Madison; "Register for the Records of the Writers' Program, Wisconsin, Green Bay District Office, 1936," Green Bay MSS 54, Area Research Center, UW–Green Bay, Green Bay; "Anti-Union Charge Tossed at WPA Here," *Wisconsin State Journal*, December 20, 1936, 1.

5. "Color of Wisconsin," 11; "Writers Dig Folklore from Hidden Vaults," *Wisconsin State Journal*, June 11, 1936, 5; *Capital Times*, July 25 and December 31, 1930.

6. According to Brown's 1943 final report on the Wisconsin writers' project, Miller's staff con-

sisted of Ann Brunkhorst, Ethel Hahn, Gregg Montgomery, Coryl Moran, Gertrude Mulick, Jane Olson, Dorothy M. Potter, Nettie Smith, Gertrude Sontag, Dawn Young, and Edna Zimmerman (Writers' Program, Wisconsin, "Folklore Project Records, 1935–1937," Wis. MSS IZ, Wisconsin Historical Society Archives, Madison).

7. Miner, "Essay and Letters."
8. "Writers Dig Folklore," 5.
9. Writers' Program, "Folklore Project Records, 1935–1937."
10. *Appleton Post-Crescent*, November 30, 1937; Lomax, July 17, 1936, in "Folklore Project Records, 1935–1937."
11. Miner, "Essay and Letters."
12. Copies have become quite rare, but all four are online at www.wisconsinhistory.org.
13. *Capital Times*, January 19, 1928; May 27, 1928; and July 25, 1930.
14. Miner, "Essay and Letters," 5–6; *Wisconsin State Journal*, October 29, 1937, 4; and November 29, 1937, 4.
15. Brown to Robert Halpin, November 10, 1937, Museum Curators' Correspondence, Series 972, Wisconsin Historical Society, Madison.
16. Ethel Falk to D. Brown, February 3, 1947; D. Brown to Charters, September 11, 1947; Charters to D. Brown, October 31, 1947; D. Brown to Charters, November 28, 1947, and March 19, April 29, June 18, and July 14, 1948, all in the W. W. Charters Papers, Children's Literature Research Collection, University of Minnesota, Minneapolis.

PREFACE

From stories of Huldrefolk, to detailed descriptions of ethnic feasts and customs, Federal Writers' Project researchers gathered a wide array of tales throughout Wisconsin. I have organized these into three sections. Part one, titled "Myths and Legends," is a collection of supernatural stories that convey the hopes and fears of those who told them. Part two, "Local History," shares stories about towns and villages throughout Wisconsin, of characters and homesteaders, shenanigans and mayhem. Finally, part three, "Daily Life and Customs," is a celebration of work, landscape, clothing, food, and Old World traditions imported to Wisconsin—in short, the things that enlivened everyday existence for people of many ethnic backgrounds. Together, these stories bring us from the world of the imagination, to community and, finally, to the individual.

The WPA workers who rambled about the state collecting stories were not professional folklorists. This leaves us with a few things to keep in mind while reading this book. WPA interviewers took liberties when writing down the stories they heard. Texts were edited and rearranged, presumably to improve the narratives at the expense of the original diction. Thus we cannot always know for certain whose voices we are hearing in these accounts.

Because the texts were already edited, I made further editorial changes while creating this book. Specifically, while unorthodox usages have been maintained for the most part, with variations across selections, I corrected punctuation and spelling occasionally when necessary to clarify meaning or to avoid possible misreadings. Additionally, in the original documents, some of these accounts had titles that were fitting, while others did not. Those with no title were given ones that seemed appropriate, and other titles have been changed to better reflect the contents of the stories. These editorial changes have been made silently, without being noted in the text.

Another thing to keep in mind is that throughout the first part of the text, nonstandard names and spellings for mythical beings common in European folklore have been retained. Notably, the Hasgaardsreia that make their appearance in part one are more commonly known as Asgardsrei. My objective here was not to standardize or correct, but to present what WPA fieldworkers recorded and how they recorded it.

Some of the language used in these accounts is, by modern standards, insensitive. Conspicuously hackneyed dialogue, for example, is used in several accounts involving American Indians. Instances like these have been included here not to offend, but rather to accurately represent what WPA workers recorded when they made their rounds across the state. Throughout the text the term *Winnebago* is used to refer to the tribe now known as the Ho-Chunk. Translated to "People of the Stinky Waters," *Winnebago* was a term given to the Ho-Chunk by their native neighbors and subsequently adopted by the United States government when dealing with the tribe. In 1993, the tribe reclaimed its traditional name, Ho-Chunk, which means "People of the Big Voice" or "People of the Sacred Language."

Where possible, the names and places of residence of interview subjects have been included with their respective accounts to give the stories context. Quite often, one or both of these pieces of information were unavailable or unclear and could not be included. Notably, the authorship and location of the lumberjack stories in part two were not recorded clearly, thus none of this information could be included for that chapter.

The artwork in this book was produced under the auspices of the Federal Art Project, which was a part of the same Federal Project Number One that birthed the Federal Writers' Project. In the same way that the writers' project gave work to unemployed writers, the Federal Art Project supported unemployed artists. Thanks to this program, many in Wisconsin's art community were able to create, even while the private sources of funding that artists normally enjoyed dried up during the Depression. While artists used a host of different media in their creations, the images printed throughout this book are mainly block prints. Artists such as Frank Utpatel and Beryl Beck created these prints by carving the designs on pieces of wood, cutting away areas that were to appear white in the print while leaving lines or black areas untouched. Once the carving was completed, ink was rolled over the block and the block pressed to a piece of paper, creating the finished product. The stark and uncompromising block prints, portraying varied subjects at times with great simplicity or great complexity, beautifully capture the spirit of the complicated Depression years.

These accounts paint a charming picture of a diverse population. Whether a supernatural tale, a bit of local lore, or the customs surrounding daily life, these are very personal accounts. Interviewees felt these stories were important enough to treasure in their memories and share when researchers came around and knocked on the door. These stories originally survived by word of mouth, yet as written documents they have outlived their original tellers and endured the Great Depression and the tumultuous years between then and now. Considering all they have been through, it is a great pleasure to present them in print for a new generation to cherish.

MYTHS AND LEGENDS

Federal Writers' Project researchers who traveled throughout Wisconsin in the late 1930s uncovered a wealth of myths involving preternatural beings and phenomena. Interviewees spun yarns about helpful little elves and mischievous bluemen, ghosts and witches, animals that terrified locals and others that helped, while prophecies, portents, and gifts from higher powers abounded.

Many of the mythical beings depicted in these tales were imported from Europe, where they had appeared in Old World legends for centuries. Most familiar to American audiences are trolls, dwarves, and elves. Lesser known are the Hasgaardsreia and Huldra, or Huldrefolk, two types of underground people said to be the disowned children of Adam and Eve. Ghosts appear to have haunted the old country as well as the new, while witches and wizards were also imported from Europe by immigrants to Wisconsin.

Yet many of the stories writers' project researchers recorded were distinctly American in origin. Raconteurs shared stories of terrible river monsters haunting Wisconsin's waterways; of medicine men, tricksters, and characters populating the Wisconsin prairie in olden times; and of dreams and prophecies, ghosts, and talking animals appearing in undefined times in the state's past. Also present are stories from Wisconsin's lumbering and lead-mining days, two of the more colorful eras in the state's development made richer by the legends woven about them.

These stories reveal the fears and hopes, dreams and beliefs of the diverse people who shared their mysterious and entertaining tales during the depths of the Great Depression.

Elves, Bluemen, and Other Mythical Creatures

The Elf Home
Told by Elfreda Zweifel, New Glarus

A little boy under a tree one September evening, which was dark and dreary, playing that he saw the stars. He then heard the wind rattling in the leaves and it got darker and darker. He heard a deep sigh from the woodlands, and became so frightened that he started running on a path through the woods. As he ran he thought of all kinds of horrid things, became more excited and ran further and further into the woods and off from the right track. He thought about his father, mother, brothers and sisters and said to himself, "God help us, little one, if I was only there."

Again there was a deep sigh from the woodland. Running in his fright the little boy finally came to a little elf's home and found himself in the midst of a group of the little people. "Tell me, tell me you beautiful little maidens: who heaves with deep sighs in the woodlands?" A fair little elf smiled a queer little smile, patted the little boy on a red cheek and said, "Don't cry pretty boy, even if you get lost and scared so badly, but sit here on the grass among the flowers of June. Dry your tears and I will tell you who heaves those deep sighs. When night is drowning near over land and sea and the sun is setting and the waves go to rest under the island, and all the pretty stars are shining, the sky becomes mirror-like and clear, a host of good angels float through the air and cry silver tears over the earth for the sins and misdeeds of the day done by the people of the earth during the day."

"Thanks to you, my elf queen, I'll never forget, and now I am afraid to go home. I am very poor. I have no earthly goods and praise the Lord and never for my sake shall there be so deep the woodlands."

Elf Gifts

Told by Elfreda Zweifel, New Glarus

There was a child sleeping in the woods when some elfs discovered him, gathered around and decided to bestow some gifts upon him. They each touched him with a wand and gave him their gifts. One gave him knowledge, another that praise and flattery would never affect him nor glory or fame, and the third gave him a childish, innocent heart. All of this came true and was a part of the child until he died an adult.

Hasgaardsreia—Yudestad

Hasgaardsreia is something peculiar to the Scandinavian countries—perhaps especially in Norway. On Christmas Eve the underground folk seem to get together in flocks, or considerable numbers, and go from place to place. And as they move about they make much noise. Some describe them as hilarious and jolly, others say they indulge in howlings and screechings as they travel about. It is generally conceded that all kinds of fairies feel themselves under a certain ban—non-Christian and condemned to be shut out from heaven. Learnedly and solemnly, through centuries, so-called Christians have discussed the status of fairies as to the question of final redemption and heavenly felicity. Perhaps most of our ancestors inclined to the belief that fairies will eventually be saved in a manner similar to so-called humans. And fairies perhaps join in this hope. But as centuries drift by and their status seems unchanged, they have become restless. It is at Christmas that they express their dissatisfaction mostly. Therefore on Christmas Eve all decent and normal humans try to be at their homes early in the evening. But humans are subject to accidents, carelessness, and some to bad habits—such as drunkenness—and some do not reach home in seasonable time. If they are away, they are liable to encounter Hasgaardsreia on their way home. A man in a community unavoidably on Christmas Eve, was coming home late, when he met Hasgaardsreia. To prevent trouble, he lay down by the road, stretched out his legs and arms. Lying thus supinely as the mob came by, one after another remarked, "There lies a cross." Fairies avoid crosses.

I never heard that Hasgaardsreia ever injured anyone severely—but usually those they encountered were badly harassed and half-scared to death and sometimes weak persons were never quite right again after they had met Hasgaardsreia. Perhaps there is in Norway no superstition more common than the belief in Hasgaardsreia. . . .

In conclusion I will tell you a story about Hasgaardsreia.

> *"In the days that are forgotten.*
> *In the unremembered ages."*

There lived in the parish where my mother was born a farm-house known as Yudestad. Among all the farms in Norway there is no more beautiful name than Yudestad in Bygstad parish. On this farm in the days that are forgotten lived a man with his wife and children. Legend tells us he was not a rich man—rather poor but comfortable and beautifully situated. Except for one thing, he and his family might have been happy. But there was a shadow over his home which neither his ancestors nor he had been able to disperse. Like all good Christians he regarded Christmas as the sacrosanct holiday of the year—for this was the day when Christ was born to atone for the sins of the people who had lived on earth and all those still unborn. Therefore this family, living on Yudestad, had a right to rejoice, except for the fact that through many long years the occupants had to vacate their home on Christmas Eve, for every Christmas evening the Hasgaardseia claimed the use of this house for a feast. Wise men, good men, and holy men had been consulted, begged, and importuned to prevent or banish the underground people in the form of Hasgaardsreia, which affected this place. But to no effect.

Once more the glorious day was near. The family, in the falling shadows, was huddled in their primitive home getting ready to vacate the house when an old man suddenly opened the door and came in, bidding them the unusual courtesies of the occasion. As for instance: "God's peace be with this house and its folks. Happy Christmas and a good year." Indistinctly, the family mumbled from habit a kind of response. Then the old man, leaning one of his hands on a gun he carried, made this startling request. "I have come a long way, am very tired and hungry; please may I stay with you tonight?"

But for a moment neither wife nor husband made any reply. The old man, fearing his request was to be denied, continued:

"I do not need to mention the sacred occasion of this hour in which I have met you, nor the many solemn injunctions which He, whose anniversary we are about to celebrate, has left behind for our instruction and salvation. He was all goodness, kindness, charity and hospitality."

As he looked around he found the wife and all the children were crying and the husband's eyes were misty with tears.

Then the husband spoke and said, "God help us, stranger! We are compelled to leave our home this evening. Therefore we cannot entertain you."

Then he explained that he and his ancestors before him had for years been compelled to give up their home every Christmas Eve to Hasgaardsreia.

The old man listened to one of the strangest stories he had ever heard.

"But," he answered, "if you grant me permission to stay here, I will take my chances with Hasgaardsreia." This permission was granted, and the family left immediately. After they had gone, the old man looked about, laid off his outer garments and prepared for bed.

The house was of the common type, one single large room with a long table in the center of the room—probably twenty or twenty-four feet long. In one corner of the room a hearth built of rocks, perhaps seven feet or more high. This was called the "oven" in olden days. This so-called hearth or oven was used as a fireplace. As nearly as I can recall, it had an opening about three and a half feet wide, four and a half feet deep, and maybe five feet high. At three o'clock p.m. during cold weather this space was filled with wood. When the wood had been reduced to coals, various kettles were suspended on cranes or supported on andirons where many kinds of food were prepared. I have forgotten to mention that this so-called fireplace had no chimney. Therefore the smoke from the fireplace which naturally was produced all came out in front and filled the house. To get rid of the smoke there was an opening in the center of the roof known as "Ljoren." When the smoke had cleared away, the "Ljoren" was covered by a trap-door in the roof. From the trap-door hung a very substantial pole, the lower end reaching to about six feet above the floor. Old time houses had no ceilings. While the wood was burning, the front door was opened to permit escape of smoke. The fireplace was naturally built in by very substantial stones. The foundation may have been three to three and a half feet built up solidly from the floor. This foundation projected in front of the fire-box maybe two feet. This was the real hearth. Then over the fire-box were wide massive stones.

Therefore on top of the fire-box or oven was a good place for sleeping—though rarely used for that purpose as it was too hot until late in the night. This oven, or fireplace, was very frequently called "Rauk-ovn"—"Rög-ovn." Those at fashionable houses were also very commonly called "Rauk-hus" or "Rög-hus."

It was on top of "Rauk-ovn" that the old man in this story elected to sleep. Here he lay down with his gun by his side to wait for what would happen. As Hasgaardsreia never move about until it is real night, the old man had a good rest before there were noises about the premises. Then he heard at first a murmur of voices in several keys, as if there were men, women, and children. But as the noises came nearer he heard laughter, hummings, and even songs. Then as the crowd neared the house there was a hubbub and babble of sounds increasing in intensity but rather like subdued excitement. Old-time homes never were locked, so the latch was lifted and in a minute or two the room was filled to the limit. At first there was only a torch or two to light the room; in a few minutes there were more than a dozen torches and a lot of rush-lights carried by children.

One big fellow, who seemed to be a leader, circled the room while he seemed to sniff all about. Then he called loudly, "I smell Christian blood."

But several replied, "It's only a cat or Christian dog you smell."

This seemed to quiet all suspicion, and the women began at once to set the table. And when they had finished, the "Long Table" was loaded with such a variety of dishes and foods as the old man had never seen before during his long life. Dishes of gold, silver, crystals, carafes, beakers, goblets, chalices, decanters, cruses, bottles, and demijohns, all carved and ornamented. Many vessels were set with gold, silver, and jewels. Of foods there were too many to describe. On the floor and around on benches were casks, kegs, and even barrels, containing ales and liquors of various kinds.

As the old man watched the arrangement of seating the men and women around the table, he noticed they followed the customs usually observed by Christians. The more important and most richly and gaily dressed were seated first beginning at the head of the table and so on down to the end of the table. Most of them were richly appareled, with gold, silver, and beautiful gems.

At the head of the table sat a great big, fat fellow with three heads. After they had eaten for some time, a big man who sat on the right side of the three-headed monster rose and commanded attention. Then he raised a big goblet or beaker and said, "Now let us all 'skaal'* to—" I have forgotten the monster's name.

All the people with goblets in their hand rose, when suddenly from the top of the "Rauk-ovn" came a voice. "Yes, I have a skaal too, for the three-headed king of 'Yudestad Noset.'"

Then from the old man's gun sped a silver bullet which hit the monster squarely in the middle of his head. This caused the greatest haste and consternation while the banqueters fled from the house,

---

* *Skaal* is a term used as a toast in various Scandinavian cultures, meaning "cheers."

8

where they left all their treasures, never to return to "Yudestad." From that time forth, the owners of the home lived in peace and great prosperity.

I have told this story as it was told to me by Mother and other neighbors while I was a boy. I am conscious of the fact that I have not told it as effectively as my mother told it first to me. One reason is that my mother told the story in greater detail and used many words and phrases I have forgotten. Besides, there are many idioms used in our country, which cannot be expressed in English. But you have the substance of a once popular tale in our community.

The Curious Shoemaker's Wife
Told by A.H. Becker, location unattributed

[Gnomes] were small elf-like men who would come around during the night and do the work for artisans and tradesmen. They were seldom seen at work.

One time a shoemaker's wife was determined to get a peek at the gnomes while at work. She devised a plan, to put peas on the stairway (their pathway), hoping they would fall, then she would be awakened and have a look at them. The plan was carried out and she did get a glimpse of the gnomes. They felt so mistreated that they never returned.

Rebekka and the Bluemen

When I met Rebekka at Alvern, in June 1909, she was about eighty years of age. She was still mentally and physically active. Forty-two years had passed since I parted with her when I started for the U.S. I recalled that she was very superstitious when I used to meet her when I was a boy. Therefore, when I visited at Alvern in 1909, I took some pains to ascertain whether she and her neighbors still were superstitious. In answer to my general questions, she told me that the "underground people" were less plentiful than they used to be. And

"Farm at Night," wood engraving by Frank Utpatel. A longtime resident of Mazomanie, Wisconsin, Utpatel was one of the state's most accomplished engravers and printmakers. He illustrated books written by another notable Wisconsinite, August Derleth. WHi Image ID 79711

she added that she thought the reason was, they had better preachers now than formerly. "I remember," she said, "that those hills below your home were a great place for 'Huldrefolk'"—a general name for all kinds of fairies. As a sample of various experiences she had had, she told me this story:

"When I was about fifteen years and preparing for Confirmation one day one of my friends and I were up in the woods above our home herding sheep and goats. My friend was also preparing for Confirmation, so we both had our hymnbooks and catechisms. As we were studying our books, suddenly a 'Blauman'—Blueman— came directly towards my friend. I realized at once, he was after my friend, so I jumped up and began to walk around my friend and repeated the Lord's Prayer. I repeated it three times. This stopped him, but he kept near us. We gathered our sheep and goats and started for our home—but would you believe it, he followed close to us till we got close to home."

I heard many stories about "Bluemen." My grandmother—mother's mother—was a very devoted woman—deeply religious. One day she was sitting on the roof of the cow-barn just at the edge of some woods. In those days all our buildings were covered with turf. First were boards, then birchbark, and the final covering was grass-covered turf. Every farm home had a cattle-barn outside of the fence where the cattle were stabled when evening came. It was on one of the barns or stables, as Grandmother was watching that the cattle did not stray, she saw one of the Bluemen. He was a fine-looking man, neatly dressed in blue. Grandmother was not disturbed at all, for it was well-known among all humans that fairies never harmed anyone unless they had been mistreated by humans. Besides, fairies were fond of cattle and wanted even to look after cattle to keep them from getting sick. In fact fairies were, as the Irish called them, "Good Folks."

Of course Bluemen sometimes kidnapped pretty girls and married them. Perhaps while on this subject I had better tell the story of the "Fairy Crown," which hundreds in our neighborhood wore when they were first married. Among others, Mother wore this crown when she married my father. After Father died Mother married again while still in Norway. But under a universal custom, brides were not allowed to wear any kind of crown except when they were brides the first time. The fairy crown belonged to some family in the community who loaned the crown to the expected bride or to her folks. According to custom she wore the crown when she started for the church to be wedded and carried it until the wedding celebrations were finished. This might be from a day up to a week in olden days. Rose, Mother, and I attended a wedding which lasted three days. But the bride did not have the fairy crown.

And now to the story:

A young girl had been kidnapped and was not seen for some time. Perhaps she was too young or stubborn before she wedded her Blueman. At any rate, the day she was to be married, she asked for the privilege to step out for a minute to see the outside—the "Christian world." Out from the cliff, hill, or mountain she stepped with all her gay apparel including a golden crown. Just then a hunter with his gun came along and saw the bride with all her adornments. And being a man with a quick wit, he at once took in the situation. She had evidently been captured and was now about to be married to a Blueman. He carried a loaded gun but realized at once that a leaden bullet shot over her head would not break the charm by which fairies held her. A hundred years ago nearly all men carried silver buttons on the vests and coats. So he cut off a silver button and put it in the barrel of his gun on top of the leaden bullet, then fired over her head and the spell was broken. He took the girl home to her folks with all her ornaments. But the crown is the only ornament now known. Mother was the only one who wore that crown that I have heard of. Undoubtedly many wore it, but I was a young boy when I left Norway in 1909. If my brain was not so muddled, I could no doubt find out about the Fairy Crown and make a good story of it.

Originally pure myths became very real sometimes.

Tomte Nisse
Unattributed storyteller, Westby

Among the interesting beliefs and stories which the Norwegians have brought to Wisconsin from the homeland are those which tell of the *tomte nisse*, household dwarfs. These small, bearded men wearing tippet capes are supposed to assist in work about the peasant home. At night it is customary to set out a bowl of porridge or other food for the household elf on the doorstep or in the kitchen. In return for this kindness they wash the dishes, sweep the kitchen, mind the fires, and perform other useful tasks for the housewife. Sometimes they also assist the husband about the barn.

One old farmer set aside in his fields each year a small fenced enclosure where he planted wheat and vegetables for the use of the fairy folk.

Of Trolls

In Sweden the Trolls are a part of the daily part of the old people the same as they are, or were, of the Norwegians. There was a mound in the middle of a field in which a group of Trolls lived. All around the hill the ground was ploughed and the Trolls could not travel over ploughed ground. They were able only to go on their little paths, which had existed for years. These particular Trolls had a pipe on their hill which was quite coveted and valuable. Its use the narrator was unable to tell me and I am trying to get this information from someone else. A farmer one day had the nerve to try and get that pipe. He rode up on horseback, grabbed the pipe and was able to make off with it as he rode over the ploughed ground [where] the Trolls could not follow him.

The Water Man
Told by Stephen Kliman, location unattributed

There is no doubt that Satan and his minions have great power. They can grant any wish, but you must pay with your immortal soul. You may desire a certain girl, or to be wealthy, or to wreak vengeance on a neighbor. At midnight of the full moon you go to the crossroads, draw a circle with chalk and sit within it. Apparitions, in the form of devils or wild horses or black knights appear. If you are afraid or start to run, they will slay you. If you courageously stay within the circle, Satan arrives and you sign your name with your blood in his black book. He grants your wish. But when you die Satan claims your soul.

Now the Water Man is not a devil, but he will try also to get your soul. He is not a ghost, for there are villagers who have actually seen him. My grandfather, who transported timber on the river, talked and walked with him. He told me that the Water Man looks like any other man. He dresses in a long cloak, slit into tails. You may recognize him by the water dripping from his handkerchief thrust into the slit tails.

His castle is situated in the deepest part of the river. His family consists of three generations. They can be seen walking on the water at any time save the ringing of the Angelus during the noon hour. Then they lurk in the castle and woe betide the boy who is swimming there at the time. For the Water Man ties a hair from a horse's tail around his big toe, drags him down and drowns him. He seizes the boy's soul, and thrusts it into an earthenware pot mounted on a tripod over a big open hearth. The soul boils for a year.

You are incredulous? Here is proof: Each year the merchants from all over the country hold open market in the village. It is quite an event. Everyone attends. The Water Man is there, too, to buy earthenware pots. Hard-headed merchants do not trade with wraiths.

And for further proof there is the tale of the girl who went swimming at the forbidden time, sank, and supposedly drowned. She found her way into the kitchen, inquisitively poked among the pots on the hearth and lifted a cover. Out flew a soul. She uncovered all the pots and released other souls. Then she too escaped.

And there was the immodest woman who in an open meadow brazenly removed her footwear and bathed her foot in a shallow pool. Not two foot deep was it, yet the Water Man tried to snare her big toe with his horsehair. But the woman screamed and ran away.

So it is no wonder that the belief in the Water Man is very deeply rooted. As deeply rooted as the conviction that certain trees and plants have supernatural powers. No secrets, for instance, are ever told under willow trees, particularly during the night, because the souls of women go to sleep in willow trees. And you know the weakness of women with secrets. Besides, a willow twig makes an excellent whistle, and when the whistle is blown the secret comes out.

Ghosts

A Family Ghost Story
Told by Allie Churchill Sweeney, location unattributed

There is a "ghost story" in my family that is one of the most interesting ones I have ever heard. I do not know how current it was outside the family. It was somewhat taboo in the family—but I have heard it often from my mother, who was certainly intrigued by it. My father was skeptical and, I believe, a little annoyed that he should have been a witness to the ghost. I am going to tell it to you—but I do not know whether it is grist for your mill.

Here it is:

Sometime during the seventies, a cousin of my father's living in Maiden Rock, Wisconsin, lost his wife under very pathetic circumstances. She died in child-birth, leaving several small children. She was not told that she would die until about an hour or so before her death. This distressed her greatly. She said that had she known there were so many things she would have liked to talk to her husband about, especially about plans for the children. She felt she could not forgive the doctor. She died mourning for her children—full of anxiety and distress for them. She seemed to have no realization of death in relation to herself.

A sister, Belle, came to stay with the husband and children. I have forgotten whether Belle was the father's sister or the mother's. But I know that she was a young girl—not twenty. There was a maid, or housekeeper—but I do not remember hearing anything about her in connection with the mysterious occurrences.

I believe the first thing that happened was that as Belle was playing the melodeon and the children were singing in the evening

16

Belle saw the mother for an instant, standing in the doorway look-ing at them. Belle said that the mother looked so natural in a brown housedress she had often worn that for a moment she forgot that it could not be the mother—forgot that the mother was dead. Then she decided that it had been her memory and imagination that seemed to see the mother. But a few nights after that the vision came again. Only this time the oldest little girl was singing, turned around and gazed earnestly at the doorway. Belle did not stop the song. But the next day she asked the child at what she had been looking in the doorway while they were singing. The child answered—as simply as Wordsworth's little maid—"Mama." Belle said, "Did you ever see Mama before?""Oh, yes," little Sadie answered, "many times."

Belle: "How was Mama dressed?"

Sadie: "She had her brown dress on."

Belle was getting behind with her sewing for the children. One evening she was surprised to hear the sewing machine running in the sewing room on the second floor. She felt sure it was the mother. This continued for some time. Once a neighbor came in and said: "I saw you were sewing late last night. As we were going home from the school entertainment we saw you busily at work at your sewing machine." (I should explain that the main street in Maiden Rock is on the side of a very steep bluff. To reach the houses on the west, or lake side, of the street, one had to descend stairs from the sidewalk. The second stories of the houses were on the level that a first floor would normally occupy.) Belle said nothing. She, too, had heard the sewing machine after she had gone to bed.

Soon after that the children were taken sick—measles, I think it was. My father was practicing medicine in town some distance away and his cousin asked him to come and take care of the children. So my mother and father came to stay a few days until the children should be on the road to recovery. They were very ill, especially one child who my father feared might not get well. About midnight Daddy left the children with the nurse and went to bed. Soon, my mother was awakened by a sharp rap upon the bedroom door. When she opened

17

"Shack in Fall," drawing by Berton Beebe. After only a few months of working with the Federal Arts Project, Beebe received a scholarship to attend the Layton School of Arts in Milwaukee. WHi Image ID 53592

the door, however, no one was there. My mother had heard Belle's stories, so she wondered. After a while it came again. Mother did not get up. The rap came again more loud. It awakened my father. He called, "Who's there?" and got out of bed, but found no one at the door when he opened it. He put on slippers and trousers and went down to the sick room. The nurse was dozing and all was quiet. No one had rapped on father's door. Everyone in the house was in bed.

Father was always sure that he must have been dreaming. Mother was sure that there had really been three raps on their door that night. But no explanation was ever made of any of these things.

After three or four years, the father married again—a good woman who was a wise and affectionate mother to the children. There was some criticism of the father because the stepmother had been the housekeeper, but apparently the real mother was satisfied because the little brown ghost was never seen or heard again.

Belle and the children were the only ones who saw the mother after her death. The father never did. Neighbors saw the light in the upper window and heard the sewing machine—but thought it had been Belle. Father and mother heard the raps. Belle and the children were never afraid. And they never doubted that it was the mother. They simply accepted it as a fact of experience and did not try to understand how it could be. As I understand it, the matter was not known of or discussed outside a few members of the family.

The Spirit of the Dead

A friend of Wilson's, while working on a road, found some beads, arrowpoints, and tomahawks. These he took home for souvenirs. At night they rattled, indicating that the spirits of the Indian dead, who once owned them, were angry. So the next day, he buried them so he would have no trouble with the dead.

Old Lady Lake
Storyteller unattributed, Hayward

Near Hayward is Smith Lake, to which the Chippewa Indians gave the name of "Old Lady Lake." The story of how the lake obtained its name has often been told.

Some Indians who were traveling north over a trail had in their party an old Indian woman. She was very infirm and they thought that she would not be able to stand the hardships of travel. When they reached the shores of Smith Lake they made her as comfortable as possible and left her behind to die. No one ever knew what became of her. For many years Indians traveling over this trail saw, or thought they saw, the spirit of the old lady near the shores of this lake and so the lake was called by them "Old Lady Lake."

The Fire Ball

One evening when I was about eight years old, my sister, Ethyle, and I were in front of the house picking flowers. All at once she called my attention to a ball of fire floating around the trees on the other side of the river. Naturally the first thing we both thought was that someone was trying to send some evil to our house, and we were terrified. The thing was a fiery red thing that looked about six inches in diameter, and it seemed to stay above the tree tops all the time.

Fascinated, in spite of our fears, we stood and watched the ball, wondering what harm it was bringing. After a short time, my sister ran into the house to tell the folks, who all trooped out to see what all the excitement was. I stood where Ethyle had left me, thinking how pretty the thing was, floating around all by itself. But suddenly, just before the others came, it disappeared, and although we all watched for a long, time, we saw it no more. I never discovered what it was, and to this day wonder about it.

The Yellow Canary
Storyteller unattributed, Cassville

George Foeheringer's mother, Mrs. J. G., is very superstitious. Some years ago on her old home a yellow rose bush bloomed at the end of the porch. A very dear friend and next-door neighbor died. Shortly after her death a yellow canary was seen continually flying about the yellow rose bush. Mrs. Foeheringer insisted that that was her friend and neighbor who had died and come back in the form of the canary. The canary acted as though it knew her and was very tame. She believed that those who led a good and righteous life on this earth died and came back in the forms of birds, whereas if they were horrid and mean in their life they became pigs and hogs after death. Some seven to eight years ago Mr. & Mrs. J. G. Foeheringer had their golden wedding anniversary and the relatives wanted to celebrate but Mrs. Foeheringer absolutely forbade it as she said that if a couple celebrated their golden anniversary one of them would die shortly. There was no celebration.

For years, in fact as long as any of the many old inhabitants of Cassville can recall, there have always, with but few exceptions, been a series of three deaths in the village. If one person dies, two more always follow within 10 days or two weeks of the death of the first. Just before I arrived there was a death and since then two more have died within that time of the first.

The Story of Red Mike

"Curses come home to roost," says Fr. O'Connor to O'Flaherty, in a stern voice; "an' it's ye that'll suffer Mike O'Flaherty, an' no one here. Get ye gone at once, or I'll put the word on ye." Whereupon Red Mike replied surlily [sic]: "I'll go when I choose, Father O'Connor!" The priest then drew a crucifix from his breast, saying to O'Flaherty that even if he were in league with the devil he could not withstand that. Mike gave a howl like a wild beast, and turned and ran down the glen as fast as he could. The old piper, King, was crossing the moor that night, and who should he see but Red Mike, dancing and shouting like mad and screaming in mortal fear. The old piper called out to him, "Mike, Mike," but O'Flaherty paid no attention to him, but kept on screaming and shouting out, "My time's up! My time's up." He then started to run and took one great leap, and disappeared in the ground as if he had jumped into the sea. Nothing more was seen of Red Mike in person, but his ghost often appeared in the swamp in the form of a light (will o' the wisp) and in Ireland the place is known as Red Mike's Rest.

A Haunted Castle

Told by Mary Saxer, Belleville

Mrs. Saxer can remember the old decayed and mouldering ruins of castles near her home [in Switzerland] which she and the children of the neighborhood were afraid of because there were ghosts in them. They would often think that they saw the white woman. The story was that many, many years before, the wife of the owner of the castle had been killed by her husband and her ghost still walked.

The Devil Will Take Me

Told by Anna Baumann, Monroe

It was firmly believed that if someone had wronged another and the wronged one died they would come back and haunt as a ghost the one who had harmed them.

There was a Swiss man in this country who was always swearing and his pet phrase was "the devil will take me." One day he was grubbing out some stumps and he got hot and mad as one simply could not be budged. A friend of his had approached unseen and unheard into a clump of bushes nearby. The Schweizer finally swore profusely ending with his pet phrase. The friend said in a low voice, "Now I will take you." The poor farmer thought for sure that it was the devil and shouted, "Oh no no no I meant take the stump," and away he ran.

There is a story about an old castle which is now in ruins in Switzerland near the former home of Mr. Baumann. Many years ago a man had been given what we would call the contract for building the castle and according to the agreement it had to be done by a certain time or he would not be paid for any of the work or material he had put into it. As the day drew near on which it was to be completed the man realized that he could not possibly get it done. It made him very sad to think of what he was going to lose and he decided to quit then rather to continue and lose that additional work too. A man came to him and assured him that he could finish that castle for him by the day it had to be done if he would give him his soul on the day it was completed. This was the devil. The man consented rather reluctantly. The work progressed by leaps and bounds and the castle fairly flew together. When they were almost done the contractor regretted his bargain for on the following day, at the completion of the castle, his soul would belong to the devil. He told his predicament to an old woman who was a friend of his. He told his story and said that the work had to be done by the crow of the first rooster, which was always about three a.m. The woman said she thought she could fix it for him so the next morning she went out to the chicken coop and stirred up the chickens long before three. The rooster roused himself and crowed. The devil had planned the work to be finished at three when the rooster usually crowed, and when he did crow before that hour the castle was incomplete. The work was so nearly done though that the owners accepted and paid the man but the devil could not claim his soul.

Witches, Wizards, and the Spells They Cast

The Hexemester

You have probably read that a normal child at the age of five has learned more than an ordinary student learns in four years of college. This statement may be an exaggeration. I was twelve years of age when I left Norway and since that time I have had approximately seventy years in which to survey and reflect on the fairy lore, demonology and theology which I had acquired up to the time I left Norway.

For the first time in my life I have really taken an attentive and comprehensive view of what I had learned about the subjects I have mentioned up to the time I left Norway. This retrospect has really astonished me because of the quantity as well as the quality of learning I had acquired in my childhood, especially when I consider how extremely limited were my opportunities. I further realize that all my acquirements pertaining to the unseen things, such as God, devils and almost innumerable beings which were supposed to affect my destiny here and hereafter, were without any efforts of mine. I was simply like a piece of wax capable to receive impressions only. Thus every child, from a palace to the poorest hut, goes forth to make its journey through life. And after all, perhaps, Lo, the poor Indian or the Hottentot enters the gate of the unseen world as wide as any.

On the farm next to ours was a stone which had evidently rolled down from a small mountain years and years ago. It was as big as a small house. In it was a cleft almost in the center from top to bottom. The upper part of the cleft was big enough to admit a small boy. Naturally, ignorant people were apt to wonder how that stone came, for it was some distance from the mountain. Next, they wondered how came the stone to split?

Legend has it that on the farm or nearby lived a Hexemester—wizard—by the name of Hexemester Knudt. I have not learned what harm he did but in course of time he was arrested to be tried and executed. On the west of this farm lay Gaula, the biggest river in Sondfjord. In conveying Knudt to court the officers had to take him past the big stone, then across Gaula. In passing the stone he spit on it and remarked, "I will leave a mark on this stone the people will never forget." And in a minute the stone split in two. We of a wiser age behold the stone and easily conclude neither man nor beast could have brought it there, but also deduct the mountain may have quaked and sent the stone whirling until it split.

Hexe Kari

Hexe Kari was a witch who lived on the west side of Gaula. I was not told what farm she lived on. But in the course of time she also was arrested to be taken to court. Court for years had been held near where Gaula enters Sondfjord. Therefore, Kari was naturally conveyed along the main valley road which follows the river. When she was passing a small natural meadow which lies between the river and the road she asked the officers to remove her cap for a moment so she could once more get a view of her native home. Her request was granted and she got a glimpse of the little meadow and remarked, "Never again shall flowers bloom, nor grains and grasses grow in this meadow." And to this day not a spear of any vegetation is ever seen to grow on the meadow which Kari cursed. Wider observation has taught us there are many areas that are absolutely unproductive because they are impregnated with certain acids.

David Hagen

In my early youth I heard of David Hagen, usually referred to in a low tone of voice, for David was still living not far from Sande in our parish. It was usually explained that David in his younger years was a sort of "Dare Devil," fond of pranks and unpleasant mischiefs. Some spoke of him as liable to come to some bad end, though there seemed nothing to prove he was vicious or criminally inclined. The probability is he was simply a very vital young man with a super-abundance of activity and energy. He was fond of dancing, athletics, and ventures spiced with risks and dangers. He delighted to plague all who showed excessive piety, and took particular pleasure in show-ing his contempt for supernatural beliefs. He frequently asked for the privilege of meeting some pretended agent or representative of the unseen world. Then in usual course came a Pentecostal Sunday. It happened to be a beautiful day when most of the adult popula-tion in the parish turned out. In leaving the church in company with several of his young friends, someone remarked: "Well, tonight the church will be filled by a different crowd." This gave David a chance to express his skepticism and to deride those such as believed in "Witches Sunday Nights." After some good natured discussion per-tained to witches and other supernatural beings, one of the company said, "David, I will bet you a good fiddle"—David was a good fiddler and often entertained at dances and other gatherings—"you daren't attend church tonight." David at once accepted the challenge. So he went to church and concealed himself in the belfry. After that David was a different man. He was no longer the exuberant young man his neighbors had known. He rarely smiled and never laughed. At dances and other jolly gatherings he was absent, and even at church he was seldom seen. His splendid body seemed to shrink, his energies to waste, and his mind listlessly lost interest in nearly everything around him. Concerning his experiences in the church, Pentecostal night, he said little to anyone except the man who had challenged him, and he was reticent about telling what he learned from David. David's epi-sode must have occurred while my mother was a child, for she spoke of David as an old man when I first heard the story.

Witches in Switzerland

Told by Mr. and Mrs. Fred Hefty, Belleville

In the 17th century in Switzerland there was a girl who had frightful pains and finally died. The people thought that the pains were given the child by a local woman who was considered a witch. The woman was tried in court and convicted and burned at the stake.

An old bachelor lived in one part of a duplex in a village from which Mr. Hefty comes from in Switzerland. In the other half of the house lived a young couple with their two children. The old man was obsessed with the idea that the young wife was a witch and he finally set fire to the house and burned it to the ground in hopes that he would burn her too. They all escaped alive, but lost their home and everything in it.

It was believed that if a witch came to the door of the barn and looked at the cows, or a cow, the cow would become bewitched, would not give milk and would not calf anymore.

A cow was sick and the owner went to the door of the barn and saw a witch standing there. The witch grinned and the cow never calved after that.

It was believed in Mr. Hefty's town that there was a woman in the town who turned into a black cat and went in the other houses. Black cats were always avoided and believed to be bad luck.

People would often have nightmares and they would firmly allege that they were conscious and that the witches were after them, that they had seen them coming through the key hole and all such things.

One of Mr. Hefty's brother's cows was sick and he sent for a man from quite a distance to break the spell cast by the witch on the cow.

It is firmly believed there that if someone comes to the door of the barn the door must not be opened. They cannot bewitch the stock unless they can see it. If a man comes and begs for something to eat and you do give him something he will harm your stock, but if you refuse he will immediately get a pain somewhere. He will have a lame leg, a sore eye or some such visible ailment. People in the community who are lame or obviously deformed are looked upon as witches for this reason.

If anyone openly disliked someone else and they became sick it was accepted that the person doing the disliking had a poison and bewitched him or her or them.

In Zurich there is a huge home full of plants from which are made teas to cure hundreds of different ailments. You can pick out your plant, have it dried and make your own tea. People from all over the world send for different species of these herbs.

If the woman of a household is scared of witches she buys a certain root and hangs it, or them, over the door and that prevents a witch from harming anyone in the household.

If someone is bewitched they can break the spell by saying the names of the Father, Son and Holy Ghost. . . . Mr. Hefty's brother always says that when he leaves the barn. . . .

There used to be a large number of snakes on one of the Alps and [these] were the continuous source of trouble to two farmers who lived there. One day a poor traveler came, went to one of the houses and asked for something to eat. He was turned away without a morsel of food. He went to the other home and there he was given all that he could eat. Everyone was sitting around the table and during the conversation the farmer lamented the fact that there were so many snakes on his property, and that he was losing so much stock dying from snake bites. When the poor stranger left he banished all the snakes from the property of the man who befriended him onto that of the one who had refused to give him food.

Witches in France

Told by Mrs. Shepard, Belleville

Mrs. Shepard's parents came from St. Germain, France.

Some old friends of the family would come and tell witch stories when she was a child. This old man told of the time that he and his wife were going someplace in France. They were calling on a neighbor and were walking. They came to a woods and the husband asked his wife to wait a few minutes, and he disappeared into the trees. A few seconds later a large wolf came out and started chasing the woman. She ran and yelled for her husband at the top of her lungs. The husband did not answer nor make his appearance. Finally the wolf stopped in his pursuit and went back to the woods. In a few seconds the husband appeared and in his mouth were red threads which the wolf had torn from the underskirt of the woman as he had chased her.

Witches could take the milk from cows without even going in the barn or being near the animals. The churns would go busily about making butter without anyone being near them.

A witch lady gave an old lady an egg for her grandchild. She opened the egg and made the sign of the cross over it and it turned into ants, all of whom crawled away.

Children were never supposed to accept anything to eat from a witch, for it would have ill effects upon them.

Witches had the power of assuming the shape of animals and pursuing people.

Strange Things in McFadden Springs
Told by Constant and Gustavus Lamboley (brothers), Belleville

One of their [the Lamboley family's] first homes was at McFadden Springs. The former owners had buried some of their family in a small plot near the springs. A later tenant swore that the witches played nightly around the pool, that he saw a huge dog dragging a chain after him wandering about the place, and that he often saw a man without a head go around the house.

In those early days these newcomers from France who never saw wild animals before thought that the wolf's howl and yelp, the owl's hoot and the song of the cricket were all attributable to the witches.

One newly arrived Frenchman went to call on a neighbor and a skunk got in his path. He had never seen one before and was not afraid of it. The animal was tame so he kept pushing it along with his hand. Every time the odor got worse he would give it another push and keep asking, "What is that?"

It was commonly believed that people would turn into rabbits and wolves and all manner of animals. One was reported to have turned into a sheep, for a man had a sheep and was trying to carry it to market and it kept getting heavier and heavier until he had to quit. He attributed the increase in weight to the fact that the animal really was a witch. The witches would meet on the Sabbath. It was believed that they turned into different animals and traveled in that disguise to their meeting place. A man was out hunting one day and saw some rabbits going by one at a time all towards the same direction. He stood there perfectly amazed and seemed unable to lift his gun to shoot them. They seemed not in the least perturbed or aware of his presence. Finally the last rabbit, who was a little lame and hence slower than the rest, stopped, looked at the hunter and asked, "Did you see the rest of my comrades go by?"

A neighbor woman bewitched a cow one time so that it did not give milk and was sickly. The owners of the cow were told to go to the barn between 12 and 1 at night, take the cow out of its stall and pound the manger. They did this and the next day the woman who had done the bewitching was all black and blue.

A Bad Neighbor

Told by Mrs. John Hoerler, Belleville

There were once two neighbors who disliked each other bitterly. A particularly hated B's daughter and she him. The girl became very ill and the people thought that a ghost might have harmed her in some way. Finally one friend of the family said that they thought it was A who had put a curse on the girl and he told B what he should do to counteract this curse and to cure the girl. He was to pound three big nails in a hole in the side of the barn. The neighbor, if he was guilty, would then come and holler for help for he would be suffering physically. B did as he was told and A came hollering to him for help. The daughter got well and A became very ill and died.

Medicine Men and Supernatural Cures

Owl Medicine

Storyteller unattributed, Spread Eagle

Robert Wilson's father was once hunting with a Midiwewin man.* In sleeping in a hut the first night they were out, they heard the hooting of an owl. The second night the Midi man recognized this as the manifestation of another medicine man in the form of an owl. The third night they went out to shoot it, but it escaped.

In two days Wilson felt a pain in his leg brought about by the medicine of the Owl Man. Examination showed a great hair growing from it. This the Midi extracted. By his advice Wilson shot in the general direction of the owl when it again returned. They went to the place and there found only a ball of feathers. Within this was a bark medicine bag. This proved that the owl was a person possessed to magic powers.

Snake Medicine

Storyteller unattributed, Hayward

The lakes of this region abound in local legends, the following being strongly based on fact.

Years ago a Chippewa Indian left his home at the Lac Court Oreille lakes near Hayward on a journey to Chequamegon Bay, at present Ashland. Upon departing an old Indian woman gave him a packet of snake "medicine," the powdered root of an herb, with

---

* The Midiwewin, also spelled Midewiwin, is a traditional religious society of the Ojibwe and other Great Lakes Native American tribes. Its rituals aim to improve physical and spiritual health and ensure longer life. Practitioners may be known as medicine men or medicine women.

instructions on its use. There were then known to be many rattle-snakes and other snakes in this country. The Indian tramped all day through the dense forest and at the approach of night built a small camp fire in a clearing. Before lying down to rest he took the packet of "medicine" and strewed its contents in a circle about his camp site; then wrapped in his blanket, he went to sleep. The next morning he awoke to find a number of large snakes (ginebig) lying with their heads at the edge of his "medicine" circle. They had tried to get at him when he slept but had been unable to cross the powerful medicine. Thus his life had been preserved. In later years this Indian always cultivated a few plants of this snake medicine in his garden.

The Wonder Child

Storyteller unattributed, Spread Eagle

An Indian family of known location in Canada was to have an illegitimate child. So the mother planned to destroy it soon after its birth. She took it into the woods to chop it in pieces. Then it spoke, telling of a great calamity to come in five years—the destruction of all North America. To prevent this, the child said for everyone to hang a feather from his house. The child was killed by its mother. Many people heeded the warning which it gave.

Cure of a Sick Child

A sick girl was placed at the end of two lines of Midewewin members. They passed a beaver skin (medicine bag) over her closed outstretched hands. When opened, there appeared in her hands some medicine bag objects—small black beans. These cured her of her illness.

The Mouth That Moved

An old Indian often went to visit a couple who had three little girls. He was well liked by all of them and sometimes joined in their games. So one day when he gave them some candy all took a share joyfully.

That night one of the children became deathly sick, and strangely, her mouth went to the side of her head, almost touching her ear.

At once the medicine man was called. He looked at the child and said she had been poisoned by food. He gave her two little flat pieces of iron to wear around her neck. Then, putting a blanket over her, he poured some hot herb liquid over two hot rocks and had her sweat.

Under his care the little girl was cured, and her mouth went back to its normal place. Today she is happily married and hardly remembers the terrible experience.

Escape from the Sioux

One time when a band of Ojibwa was traveling in the winter, the members noticed a war party of Sioux coming toward them just as they arrived in the center of the lake. The Ojibwa had old people with them, so it made it difficult for them to escape by ordinary means. One of the old men (probably a medicine man) set up a white cloud around the party which made them invisible to the enemy, but through which they themselves could see the Sioux. By this means they were saved.

The Killing of Oneidas

A band of Ojibwa, who were traveling near L'Anse, Michigan, were attacked by Oneida Indians. All were killed but a small boy. This boy wept for several days. One day when he was looking for food, he saw a bag in the crotch of a tree. He did not touch it and that night cried himself to sleep.

"North Shore," woodblock print by Beryl Beck. Beck was an instructor in the art department of the Superior State Teachers College, now the University of Wisconsin–Superior. This print is from *Superior Wisconsin in Woodblock*, a book published by the WPA in 1939. Jim Dan Hill Library, UW–Superior

On the fourth day when he came near the bag, a voice told him to take the bag and travel west toward the country of his people. He got along alright, always finding food and protection when needed. When he came to "Honest John's" Lake, he saw a fleet of canoes. The canoemen first thought him to be one of the "Little People" of Marble Point.* When he explained to them who he was, they took him and cared for him for several years.

Now came a war party of Oneida who far outnumbered the Chippewa. They saw that they would be defeated. Only the small boy had a plan, and this was adopted, leading to the death of all of the warlike Oneida. They were the same war party who had killed their own people. Only one boy was spared. His ears and nose they cut off and sent him back to the tribe. The Chippewa boy became a great medicine man.

Recovery of a Drowned Body

After a drowned Indian boy's body had not been found for several days, a medicine man—John Sky—was called upon. He chanted for a long time in his lodge which shook so violently that hand bells on its outside rang.

Coming out at last (at 9 o'clock), he said that the Great Spirit had told him that it would communicate the location of the body in the morning.

The following morning some men went in a canoe to the spot designated. They took the boy's clothes and some tobacco and passed them under the canoe three times and without getting them wet. Later in the day some boys were fishing in this spot and brought up the body.

---

* Ojibwe tradition contains stories of little, powerful people living on Marble Point in Iron County on the south shore of Lake Superior. Marble Point got its name from the perfectly round rocks, resembling the once-popular children's toy, found on the shores there. Among the stones on the beach, rocks have also been found resembling miniature humans. For more information, see Linda S. Godfrey, *Monsters of Wisconsin: Mysterious Creatures in the Badger State* (Mechanicsburg, PA: Stackpole Books, 2011), 72–74.

The Medicine Man

In a wigwam on the Bad River, some time ago lived an old Indian named Ne-bwa-kaud. He was known to the tribe and many outsiders as one of the greatest medicine men of his time. Many Indian wars he served, curing both friends and foes.

In later years when hunting, fishing and other sports of the reservation were opened to outsiders, there came many men from the cities to enjoy their vacations. On one of these trips was a doctor who had been in poor health for some time. While on this trip he was very sick, but refused to be taken to the Indian Doctor, saying the spell would soon pass. But at the end of a week he was no better, so he consented to go.

On arriving at the Indian's wigwam, the white man was told to lie down on a couch made of furs and robes. He was then examined and the Indian said his illness was cancer. The white doctor refused to believe this.

The Indian told him he could be cured and began to gather up many little bags of herbs and other medicines which were hanging from the sides of his wigwam. He then sprinkled some powder on the open fire in the center of the room and sitting on the floor started to sing in a low voice, casting a spell over all. At once the wigwam started to move back and forth as the old Indian sang louder and louder his weird songs. After a long period of this he came out of his coma. Then mixing the medicine into a poultice, [he] applied it on the white man's chest, bidding him not to touch the application and to come back in three days.

The white doctor left, having very little faith but much surprised at the strange doings. The three days went by and to please his friends he went back to the doctor for another treatment and again the strange spell was cast and everything danced and moaned. These treatments went on for the six weeks of vacation and one could notice the great change in the sick man and when the hunters left for the city, the white doctor begged to stay on through the summer. When fall came he was cured and returned to Chicago where many of his friends failed to recognize him.

The man was so pleased with his newfound Indian friend that he sent him a thousand dollars in silver as a present, for the Indian had refused to take anything for his services.

As the years went on, the hunters often brought their sick friends to the medicine man, and as he became more feeble the white men begged him to sell them at any cost his secret of curing cancer. The Indian always refused, saying that it was handed down to him through many generations. So when he finally passed away his knowledge was buried with him because he had no son.

Love Medicine

Odanah Indian stories collected by Bessie Bentley, Ashland

The boy went to a neighboring Indian village to see the games. As he was passing a crowd, a girl he knew spoke to him, so he stopped to talk. During the conversation, she hit him on the back of the neck and he, thinking it was just in fun, playfully jostled her and left.

The next day he went home. Almost at once his neck began to pain him, and a big lump formed for no reason at all. And he thought constantly of the girl—he wanted to see her again—touch her hand—talk to her. This he thought queer, for he hardly knew her.

He was supposed to go with a group of Indian dancers from Odanah to the Chicago Outdoor Show. But he couldn't bear to put this distance between himself and the girl who suddenly became so dear to him.

So back he went to the town where she was. After seeing the girl, a strange peace came over him. But his neck was still sore. So he decided to see if the medicine man could help him.

The old man gave the boy a little buckskin bag of herbs to wear around his neck and told him to return the next day. The following day the boy was told to lie face downward in the medicine teepee. And the man blew towards him clouds of smoke from the fire, upon which he had thrown a handful of ground herbs. Then with a knife the doctor opened the angry looking lump on his patient's neck and pulled something out of the wound. It was a stickpin.

The boy got better and returned home. He never again thought amorously of the girl, but often wondered where she had obtained his tie pin.

She died soon afterwards. The medicine man said that after her love medicine had failed to work, she could live no longer.

Wab-shay-aw's Medicine

Odanah Indian stories collected by Bessie Bentley, Ashland

There used to be an old Indian named Wab-shay-aw living in Odanah. This old man always carried a cane and a small buckskin bag and was known to be a medicine man.

Often he would go to Duluth to visit some of his relatives and while there would always stop at my grandmother's house to visit.

One day she told him that she had been greatly bothered lately by headaches. He seemed much concerned about this and offered to cure her. So he opened his little sack and took out a small brownish object that looked like a piece of cinnamon bark. He told her to grind this into a fine powder, then heat some bricks and put the powder on them, leaving it until a great cloud of smoke arose. Then she was to cover her head with a blanket, put the bricks on the floor (in a pan), and lean over them, inhaling as much of the smoke as she could stand. So she followed his directions. To her surprise and joy her headaches left, and she was never again troubled by them.

Za-ba-dees Foiled

Odanah Indian stories collected by Bessie Bentley, Ashland

There was an Indian girl in Odanah who had two suitors—a pagan and a Catholic. She married the Catholic because her parents liked him. But the pagan would not give her up, so she went to a distant village to rid herself of his attentions.

The pagan followed her and one day stole a lock of her hair. She became childishly simple then for no apparent reason and did such foolish things that her friends sent for her husband. But she did not know him and grew steadily worse.

At last the medicine man was called in. He immediately said she had been poisoned. He cut a little slit in her flesh at the base of her skull and put into it some herbs.

Immediately she regained her lost senses and became normal, and the next day her friends found a wooden knife coming out of her left upper arm. They found a few strands of hair around the tip of the knife.

She returned to Odanah and never was bothered again, living to a ripe age and rearing a large family.

The Future of the Great Power

Old Turtle possessed the great tribal medicine powers. These were only topped by special medicine men.

Old Turtle communicated with an Indian in Canada, telling him he had invested it in him so it would not be lost. This power is so great that nothing can withstand it.

One man in Odanah is said to possess it, but he is too young and will only be able to use it in the future.

Animal Stories

The Terror of the Rock
Storyteller unattributed, Janesville

The Winnebago Indians say that when their people and the Prairie Indians (Potawatomi) encamped on the banks of the Rock River, there lived in that stream a huge and terrible water monster. This water demon the old people describe as a long-tailed animal with horns on its head, great jaws and claws, and a body like a big snake. It ranged over the whole length of the stream from its mouth to the foot of Lake Koshkonong. It preyed upon both animals and men, seeming to prefer one no more than the other. Hapless deer that went to the banks of the river to drink or walked out into the water were seized and swallowed by the monster, horns and all. At the fording places of the river this demon especially hunted for victims. Indians crossing at these places were dragged down out of sight beneath the water and were never seen again. Canoes in the river were sometimes overturned by its limbs or a slap of its tail and their occupants submerged and lost. Only a few people ever saw this water monster, but its presence in the river was known by the churning and boiling of the water.

In the springtime its movement in the river broke up the ice and heaped it against the river banks. Its dens were in the deep places. There it slept and devoured its victims. Some Indians believed that there were several of these water monsters in the Rock River. Offerings of tobacco and various articles were cast into the river to appease their wrath when they were angry. These preserved the lives of many people.

"Wild Life—Deer," woodblock print by John Liskan, from *Superior Wisconsin in Woodblock*

JIM DAN HILL LIBRARY, UW–SUPERIOR

When the Indians ceased to camp in numbers along the Eneen-neshunnuck (river of big stones) after the white men came, these water demons also left the river. Some Indians thought that they established dens in the Mississippi River where they are today.

The Waupaca Water Monster

Ma sheno mak was a water monster with the form of a giant fish, who overturned canoes, caught unwary swimmers and fishermen, and dragged his victims to the bottom of a lake or stream, and there devoured them. He was responsible for the disappearance of many Indians. Ma nabush was at last appealed to by his people, and he determined to destroy the monster, if possible. Locating his lair, he allowed himself to be swallowed.

In the body of the huge fish he found his brothers, the Bear, the Deer, the Porcupine, the Raven, and the Pine Squirrel. All had been made captive and swallowed like himself. Ma nabush had his sing-ing stick with him, and he began to sing his war song and to dance. His brothers joined in the dance. As they danced round and round in his body the monster began to reel. As Ma nabush passed his heart, he thrust his knife into it once and then three times. Now the big fish began to quake and to reel more and more violently. Ma nabush now said, "Ma sheno mak, take me to my wigwam." Then all became unconscious. When Ma nabush awoke, the monster was dead. He cut a big hole in his side, and through this he and his brothers escaped to their wigwams.

Indians say that in the old days a favorite lurking place of this giant fish was in McCrossen Lake. This water bore a bad reputation, because when a wind was blowing from the east or the west through either of its entrance channels, its navigation by canoe was dangerous. This some white canoeists also know. Ma sheno mak was always on hand to seize the unfortunate.

Suamico
Storyteller unattributed, Suamico

A Menominee Indian Village was very early located at Big Suamico (Mato Sua mako—Big Sand Bar), at the mouth of a river and along the Green Bay shore. This site is famous in Menominee Indian folklore, mythology, and history.

A great manitou came on earth and chose a wife from among the children of men. He became the father of male quadruplets. The first born was called Nanaboojoo, the friend of the human race, the mediator between man and the Great Spirit; the second was named Chipiapoos, the man of the dead, who presides over the country of the souls; the third, Wabosso, as soon as he saw the light, fled towards the north, where he was changed into a white rabbit and under that name is considered there as a great manitou; the fourth was Chakekenapok, the man of flint, or firestone. At Big Suamico Nanaboojoo had various adventures. He taught the people how to make stone hatchets and arrow and spear points to assist them in their hunting and in protecting themselves against their enemies of other tribes.

At Little Suamico (Suamako sa—Little Sand Bar) the Menominee also formerly camped.

Dells of the Wisconsin
Storyteller unattributed, Wisconsin Dells

A well-known Winnebago Indian legend of the Wisconsin River says that its bed was formed by a large serpent which long ago began to move southward from its home in the northern forests. As it crawled, the smaller snakes in its path fled in various directions, thus forming the beds of smaller streams tributary to the Wisconsin.

When this large serpent neared the present Dells of the Wisconsin large masses of rock barred its way. There the rock was rent and broke by thrusts of its great head and twists of its powerful body, leaving them in their very picturesque present day shape.

43

Namekagon
Storyteller unattributed, Namekagon Lake

The word *Namekagon* means "place where there are many sturgeon (or trout)." A local Chippewa legend of Lake Namekagon tells of a monster sturgeon which once inhabited this beautiful Bayfield County lake. This fish was so large and powerful that it could overturn the birch bark canoes of the Indians by rising up under them or with a slap of its tail. After a number of Indians were drowned in this manner, Winneboujou, the giant Indian culture hero, was appealed to. He came and waded out into the water and after a fierce struggle killed the monster by striking it with his club, the trunk of a tree. For a long time afterward the lake was red with the monster's blood. It bothered the redmen no more.

Winneboujou once rode another monster fish down the Namekagon River.

The Monster Sturgeon
Storyteller unattributed, Fond du Lac

Lake Winnebago was believed, by some Indians, to be inhabited by a monster sturgeon. He ranged over the entire large lake. This fish had a great appetite for elk and deer and would catch them as they swam in the waters of the lake or crossed from one bank to another of its tributary streams. These it bore beneath the water and devoured, horns and all. After many such kills the great sturgeon was found by some Indians, floating on the surface of the water near the shore. He was dead. In searching for the cause they found the branching antler of an elk protruding from his stomach. He had swallowed a large elk and had been unable to digest its horns. Thus Lake Winnebago was freed of a greedy water monster.

Untitled woodblock by John Liskan, from *Superior Wisconsin in Woodblock* Jim Dan Hill
Library, UW–Superior

How the Rabbit Got His Nose Split

A tribe raised a good corn crop, but the rabbits came and began to eat it up. The Indians were unable to stop their depredations. Finally, they hit upon a plan.

A flat stone was found. On this was placed a small stone with a point sticking up. This stone was scented with a perfume attractive to rabbits. The rabbits came to smell it and in doing so, struck their noses on the sharp point and split them. The rabbits kept coming to smell the stone, and now all have split noses.

The Sacred Hawk

Chickee and I were taking the mail from Ashland to Duluth late one day in December. It was hard going and we were still far from camp when a terrible snowstorm overtook us. There was nothing to do but try to reach the cabin. Luck was with us, for Chickee's instinct guided us aright, and though we were almost frozen, we were at least sheltered during the blizzard.

For two weeks we were unable to leave the little house, and by the end of that time we were almost dead from starvation. Our rations had been for one week at the most, and it was only through rigid economy that we had eked out the scanty supplies to last eleven days.

Both of us knew that remaining where we were meant certain death, and we also knew that tramping in our weakened condition would probably mean the same, but we decided that the latter choice was better, so we started.

There was nothing but miles of snow in every direction—where could we find food? Going along, cautiously, in hopes of startling some small game, we made little progress. I was too numb to think and knew the end was near when Chickee suddenly grabbed my arm and pointed. I looked and glory be! It was a rabbit. With his hands shaking, he took careful aim, fired and—missed. I had all I could do not to cry out.

We went towards the place where the animal had been—nothing there. Way ahead I could just see it disappearing and all my hopes were shattered. No food, and we were too weak for further effort.

Suddenly I heard a queer noise and looked toward the left. A large hawk was swooping downwards—it landed on something below that was hidden from our sight. Running, or rather stumbling, to it, we saw our rabbit dead at our feet. We ate the meat raw and got enough strength to continue our journey until we were rescued.

To my dying day I will believe that the hawk was impelled to come to our aid by a Higher Power.

The Window of Wauchesah
Told by John V. Satterlee, Menominee

Little Hill or Little Mountain is a high mountain of solid rock on the Peshtigo River. Its Menominee Indian name is Wau-che-sah. Surrounding it is a region of small forest openings and barren plains. The Thunderers, coming from their homes in the west, set fire to these plains by the flashes of lightning which issued from their eyes. And they keep the region burned over as they desire it to be.

At the beginning of this hill and ledge there is a small lake, a deep fountain of clear cold water.

This lake the Indians believe to be a window of the mountain. In the lake there is the den of a great White Bear, the king of all bears. Through this window the bear observes what is going on in the world and keeps an eye on his enemies, the Thunderers.

The Spirit Raccoon
Storyteller unattributed, Madison

Many centuries ago two Winnebago hunters near the ford of the Yahara (Catfish) River at Lake Monona saw in the sandy soil the tracks of an animal, unmistakably those of a raccoon. They were of unusually large size. The hunters followed them to a wooded point on the eastern shore of Lake Mendota, at present known as Maple Bluff. Here the raccoon had found a hiding place in a hollow log. One of the Indians fitted an arrow into his bowstring and was about to shoot when the animal called to him in human language and besought him not to shoot. It informed him that it was a "spirit" animal and that a dire calamity would befall him if he killed it. The Indian wisely desisted. The other hunter had no such scruples. He said that he did not care whether it was a spirit raccoon (which he did not believe) or not; he was going to kill it, as he was very hungry. So he shot and killed the animal. He skinned and cut up the raccoon, then built a fire and roasted its flesh. Of this he ate heartily, his friend refusing to partake of this feast.

The day being warm, the two Indians lay down under a tree and slept. After a while, the Indian who had eaten the flesh of the "spirit" raccoon awoke. He was very thirsty and descended to a large spring once located at the base of the bluff. Kneeling at its rim, he began to drink its water. The more he drank, the more thirsty he became. Finally, his thirst became so intense that in desperation he waded out into the lake. As soon as the water rose above his middle, his dreadful thirst ceased. It returned again the moment he ventured into shallower water or tried to go ashore. In the lake he was obliged to remain until night came, and he then sank into its waters. He was transformed into a fish. His hunter friend stood on the lake bank but was unable to help him.

For many years Indians camping near this bluff have heard after dark, in the deep water, the splashing of a great fish—the unfortunate Indian—followed by the beating of a war drum and the singing of his war song.

From this legend Lake Mendota obtained its Indian name, *Wonkshekhomikla*, "where the Indian lies."

There is another version of this story in which the "animal" discovered in a hollow tree was a catfish instead of a raccoon.

Bear Story

Told by Robert Wilson, location unattributed

Robert Wilson's grandmother and father were out on a hunting trip. The father had to leave for several days. During this time, something came for three days and nights and scratched on the door. Seeing that it was a bear, the woman lighted a candle, beat the bear, and told him to go. The bear promised her everything if he could stay in the hut. She finally drove the bear away. As it departed, the bear took the form of a man. She was pretty sure that she knew who he was.

Swedish Horses

Told by Elfreda Zweifel, New Glarus

Years ago one of the kings of Sweden went out for a ride on his favorite mount. He was followed by enemies and finally found himself at the top of a cliff overlooking some water. Seeing that he had no other way of escaping and this way was almost sure death he patted his mount and then urged him to jump in. The horse did and swam to the other shore where there was a very green pasture. There is still to be found in that pasture the copper hat with a plume on a stick which was put there to commemorate the event. . . .

A story goes to the effect that a wheel snake, the equivalent of our hoop snake, grabbed onto his tail and started after a man on horseback and did its best to strike him. The man and horse jumped a stone wall and the snake struck it and cracked all to pieces.

Prophecies, Dreams, and Supernatural Gifts

A Prophetic Legend

Three brothers each had a wonderful dream of a divine mission they should fulfill. Each secretly decided to do his best. So the first brother left home, going towards a great forest many miles away.

After a long journey he arrived at a little wigwam on the edge of the woods. Stopping to rest, he was welcomed by No-ko-mis (Old Lady) and given a lovely lunch gotten from a magic handkerchief. He then told her that he was going to the woods to build a giant cradle. She directed him to the best tree for his purpose and he was soon at work chopping it down. He did not notice that all the chips that fell were tiny cradles. And when the whole tree fell with a crash, there lay before him an enormous cradle. He was terribly disappointed, for he had really planned to make an airship and had lied to the old lady.

Meanwhile, the second brother had started his journey and had arrived at the same witch's hovel. After a repast from the same magic handkerchief he told his hostess that he wanted to make a boat, so she directed him also. When his tree fell it turned into a gigantic boat. He too was disappointed, for he had also wanted an airship.

The third brother had also left home, and arriving at the witch's hut had also eaten with her. While eating, he told her that he wanted to make an airplane that could do wonders, but first he must find the right material. The witch liked the boy because of his frankness and told him where he could find what he needed. And she gave him the magic cloth for a parting gift. He then went a great distance over hill and dale and set to work on the designated tree. The chips flew high and wide. After some time he sat down to rest, and looking around him was surprised to see that all the chips had turned into little airplanes. He jumped up and began to chop again, with great zeal, and soon the giant tree fell to the ground. After the dust had settled, the boy saw to his amazement a beautiful airplane. He ran up to it and began to look at all its parts to find out if he could operate it.

Getting into the driver's seat, the lad started out to find his passengers described in the dream. These he found and took: a woodsman who could chop down more trees in one day than three other men; a hunter who could shoot three arrows, hitting the first two before they all landed; a runner who could travel so fast that nothing could be seen but a dust cloud in his wake; a man who could hear what was being said miles away by putting his ear to the ground.

The five then started towards the king's palace where they planned to enter the games. And first the runner started in a contest against the fastest woman sprinter in the country. Soon the two were out of sight and the four had high hopes for their friend's glory. But a long time passed and neither racer came into sight. So the man with the sharp ears put his ear to the ground. Springing up quickly he said, "Why, the boy is asleep; he has been doped by the woman." The hunter then selected his swiftest arrow and shot in the direction indicated by the woodsman, waking the boy at once.

They were in despair, however, for the woman was seen in the distance, and all knew she would win the race. But suddenly, the woodsman pointed, and looking they saw a cloud of dust coming rapidly towards them. And just before the woman crossed the line, in came the boy. The friends rejoiced, and so did the people, for their coming meant a new regime.*

---

* Coming after this story in the WPA files is this explanation: "Meaning: 3 boys—Boy Scouts; Woodsman—modern mfg. methods; East—civilization going east; Dope—drugstores; 4 passengers—seasons; Sprinter—modern athletics; man with sharp ears—telephone; King—new methods of governing."

A Dream That Was a Warning
Told by Mrs. Gregory, Madison

A young mother of three small children living in Illinois dreamed that on their journey into Kansas, where they were going to establish a home, they crossed a stream and she saw branches underneath which her older children had to stoop to pass; when they came into the clearing she realized that the babe in her arms was missing. The dream probably troubled her somewhat as she had dreamed something similar three times. On their journey westward the little tot somehow was run over by a wagon wheel and killed. Later when they passed the scene she had seen in her dream she frantically realized that her dream had been a warning.

Death Foretold
Storyteller unattributed, Holy Hill

Father Andrew Ambaum, a native of Switzerland and a priest in St. Joseph's parish at Dodgeville for over fifty years, had a great fear of automobiles. Besides his own parish he served two out missions known as Pancake and Pleasant Ridge. To reach these missions every fourth Sunday he was in the habit of hiring a driver and an old horse and buggy to convey him the fifteen miles.

About eight years ago the Reverend Father started on a trip to Holy Hill. He made the journey by train as far as Milwaukee, but from there he was compelled to complete his trip by car.

While driving along, the kindly old priest asked the driver, "In case we meet with an accident, would you be prepared to meet your maker?" The man replied that he had driven the road for almost twenty years without an accident. "Well," said the priest, "if we do, we shall have to meet Him the best we can."

They had gone but a few miles further when an accident occurred. Father Ambaum was severely injured. He was rushed to a hospital, but died without regaining consciousness.

The Magic Lodestone

Storyteller unattributed, Spread Eagle

In this wooded region of northeastern Wisconsin, says an old legend, there was a mysterious lodestone which was so highly magnetized that it drew to itself all objects made of metal. It was so powerful that the Indians feared it, believing it to be inhabited by a malignant spirit. It was thought to have fallen from the sky or to have been cast down by the Thunderers. Even men were carried away by it, and its neighborhood was avoided by the Indians. When passing over a trail near this stone a Dakota war party on its way to attack the Ojibwas and armed with metal weapons was said to have disappeared until only one man was left.

The belief in this lodestone was such that in later years some white lumber cruisers claimed that their compasses would not work properly or at all in this region. Lumberjacks believed that their axes, saws, and pevies mysteriously disappeared when left in the woods. Some people believed the devil was responsible for the frequent disappearance of tools; others thought that all were drawn to the magic lodestone. Search has been made for this stone but it has never been found. Some Indians still believe in it.

O'Meara's Discovery

Storyteller unattributed, Linden

One night in October, 1857, O'Meara, an Irishman, camped on the bank of a stream near Linden. While preparing a brush bed he stubbed his toe on a stone. He became angry and threw the stone across the stream. Next morning he happened to look where he had thrown the stone and discovered a lead outcrop. He went to Galena and soon after returned with a friend, Morgan Keogh. The two men erected a rude sod shelter, now called Keogh's Grove, and engaged in digging for lead ore.

Having little knowledge of the science of mining, these early miners were called "suckers" because they did their digging so near the surface and in such a haphazard fashion. Their diggings were known as "sucker holes." Their idea of blasting rock was to burrow a hole a few feet in the ground and toss in a quantity of powder and then set it off by pouring red hot coals on the powder. Only the bravest man of the miners would take coals on his shovel, empty them, and run as fast as he could before he was hurt. Often casualties resulted.

Ma-coonse (Little Bear)

Ma-coonse lived with her two sisters and their parents in a wig-wam far out in the woods. The time was nearing when the two elder ones would have to depart for Odanah in search of suitable husbands. The little girl begged every day to go along on this trip, but no one heeded her importunities, and when the day for departure came she was left behind, tied to the door post of the wigwam.

After walking a long way one of the sisters heard someone calling to them from behind, and turning she saw Ma-coonse running as fast as she could towards them. Much against their wishes they decided to let her stay with them. So the three kept going along the trail to the village.

It was almost evening when they came to a wide river, on the other side of which was Odanah. How to get across? They had no canoe and the stream was too wide to swim. It was indeed a problem, and they were about ready to give up when suddenly Ma-coonse pointed to a tall pine tree growing on the bank and said, "Watch me." She pushed the tree with all her feeble might, and strange to say, it began to lean slowly towards the opposite bank. And all of a sudden it fell with a mighty crash, making a beautiful bridge to the other shore. So they all crossed.

Ma-coonse then said to her wondering sisters, "Soon we will come to the wigwam of the devil woman. You must not eat anything that she offers you until you see me do so." Remembering this, both girls were soon refusing wild rice, although the sight of the delicious food made them realize their terrible hunger. On the sly the little girl had shown them hidden snakes in the middle of the cereal. Next, they were offered a bowl of blueberry sauce, but seeing Ma-coonse pass it up, they did the same and were mighty glad they had when they later saw frogs in the fruit. But the old woman tried no more tricks, and when they were offered steaming corn meal, all three girls ate to repletion.

By this time evening had come and they prepared for bed. Ma-coonse was to share the old woman's bed, while the two sisters were to go with the devil woman's daughters. Soon everyone was apparently asleep; but the little girl knew that the crafty witch was only pretending. So she did the same, and was soon rewarded by hearing her bedfellow breathing regularly in genuine sleep. Then she arose, and quietly going over to the other bed, deftly shifted the positions of the four occupants. Then she returned and slept. It seemed like hours later when she was roused; keeping perfectly still, she watched the devil woman softly tiptoe to the other end of the room, holding something in her hand that caught a tiny gleam from the opening in the roof as she went across the room. Then she felt the hag again beside her.

Very early the next morning Ma-coonse called her sisters and they sneaked out after one horrified look at the daughters of the devil woman. For they lay with their throats cut.

Just as the girls got out of the door they heard a terrible volley of curses. And they knew that their treacherous hostess had discovered her mistake. They wasted no backward looks but hurried towards safety as fast as they could.

That evening they neared the town just at nightfall. Seeing a light, they were guided towards a tiny wigwam whose owner welcomed them. He told them that the king had offered anything in his kingdom to the person who would get the sun away from the evil devil woman, who had taken it because she had been tricked into killing her own daughters.

Ma-coonse immediately said she could do it, but refused all offers of soldiers, money, weapons, taking only a large quantity of salt. Her reward was to be the king's oldest son.

Ma-coonse journeyed quickly to the wigwam of the devil woman and crawled to the top. Inside she could see the witch's dinner cooking, so she poured the salt she had brought into the pan below. She was soon rewarded by seeing the old woman going towards the brook. At once she jumped down and let the sun out of the house. He joyfully went into the sky and once more the world was beautiful.

After giving the king's oldest son to her oldest sister for a husband, Ma-coonse began to cast about for a suitable mate to give to the other girl.

Her chance soon came, for the king again offered a large reward to the person who would defy the devil woman for another prized possession. This time the desired object was a horse that had to take only one step to reach any destination. Again the girl went, taking some salt and the promise of the king's second son if the venture proved successful.

When she arrived at the devil woman's abode, she did the same things as before, with the same results, so she was soon on the back of the beautiful horse. It took one step up to heaven and then one step to the door of the king's home. And so the two sisters were happily married.

And Ma-coonse was given the third son. Everyone thought the results of the girls' journey were wonderful. But it soon was plain to be seen that the husband of Ma-coonse did not love his bride. The poor girl was very sad and told the young man that he should make a big fire of basswood and throw her into it. The young prince did so joyfully thinking that he was at last rid of the ugly girl. When the fire burned down he was amazed to see something rolling in the ashes. And before him arose a beautiful woman. He immediately wanted to embrace her, but she pushed him away.

Church Bells

Told by Elfreda Zweifel, New Glarus

Last year on her trip to Sweden Mrs. Zweifel met a man on boat about whom she later learned a very interesting story. He was a Swede named Carl Peterson who went to the south seas and there married a native girl. His wife loved him greatly and even wore the native dress of his country for him. She had two sons and then died. Later he made a trip to his native country and there met and married a Swedish woman. She went to the islands with him and mothered his two boys, learned to ride and shoot and in every way learned the ways of the new country. Mr. Peterson many times went on long trips and while absent upon one of these his wife learned from a doctor that she had very little time to live and that if she ever intended to see her native country again she had better leave immediately. When he returned and found her gone he followed but she had died when he arrived. The servant girl in the south seas heard the church bells ring very distinctly on the day and at the exact time that Mrs. Peterson died in Sweden.

Charley Big Knife

Charley Big Knife, Chippewa weather prophet of the Huron mountain country, delved deeply into Indian lore and came up with a prediction of another old fashioned winter—a cold one.

Acting on his own forecast of "big snow and plenty cold before next moon," Big Knife, his wife, and their two children made their fall trip to Marquette for winter supplies two weeks earlier than usual.

"Bear, muskrat, beaver, mink, loon and wild goose all say cold winter, and no tell 'um lie," reported the Indian, who claimed that his weather prophecies have not missed fire in 40 years.

"Goose go south two weeks ago," he continued. "Muskrat build house hurry-up and bear come out of swamp to look for place to sleep. Everything no good."

Other indications he cited were thicker fur on forest denizens, earlier appearance of snow buntings and prolific honey gathering by wild bees.

And, as if those danger signals were not foreboding enough, Big Knife purchased extra blankets, a hot water bottle for his wife and a plumber's blow torch. He said he would use the torch to thaw out his traps and possibly himself. "Everything plenty bad," he remarked as he set out on the return trip to his Yellow Dog river home. "Gitchi Manitou (the Great Spirit) on war path, he punish white people for talking all time about election."

Origin of the Winnebago

A Sioux woman and an Ojibwa man fell in love and were secretly married. When this was learned, they were both ostracized by their tribes. They had to live alone, and from their offspring grew the Winnebago tribe.

The Red Banks

Storyteller unattributed, Green Bay

In the beginning Earthmaker created four men. These four brothers were Kunuga, Henanga, Hagaga, and Nanyiga. These first four he made chiefs of the Thunderers. He opened the heavens in order that they might see the earth. He gave them a tobacco plant and he gave them fire. The earth was to be theirs to live upon. And the four brothers flew down to earth and landed in the branches of a tree. This place was at Within Lake, at Red Banks on the shore of Green Bay. They then "lit" on the ground and began walking toward the east. There they selected a camp ground. There they started the first fire. One brother went to hunt for food. He took the bow and arrows which Earthmaker had given them and he killed and brought back a deer. Not having any cooking vessels, they roasted the meat over the fire on sharp sticks.

At this camp ground the Thunderers were joined by other clans. These obtained fire from them. The first to join them were the War clan people. They came from the west. Then came the Deer clan, the Snake clan, and the Elk clan. The Bear clan, the Fish clan, the Water-spirit clan, and the Buffalo clan followed them. All of the other clans came. Together they formed a tribe, the Hochungara (Winnebago). They began to intermarry. The men of the upper clans married women of the lower clans. They cut poles and stripped bark from the trees and with these built wigwams. From clay mixed with slippery elm bark they made cooking vessels. They formed a village. The members of the upper clans were the chiefs. They organized a council lodge in which the members of each clan had their place.

In the beginning the Thunderers were very powerful. They made the valleys and the hills. They planted the tobacco plant and with its crushed leaves, which they threw into the fire, they made offerings to Earthmaker. And Earthmaker gave to the Hochungara his blessings.

Miracles Don't Happen
Storyteller unattributed, Grafton

Miracles don't happen. At least that's what they say in 1937 and what they probably said way back in the early seventies in the little town of Grafton, perched along a small river in an obscure corner of southern Wisconsin.

It was the behavior of that little river one Sunday spring morning some sixty-odd years ago that led later to vehement debates between the rationalists and the believers. For the rationalists maintained that the so-called miracle was a phenomenon resulting from an abrupt but natural weather change; the believers as stoutly affirmed that death and destruction were averted only by deep faith and stubborn religious observance.

Spring, as a rule, came gently to the countryside. The snows disappeared gradually; the rains fell with quiet benevolence. But this particular spring followed a winter of raging blizzards, a sudden thaw, and turbulent downpours. Fields were inundated, roads were mud-bogged, and the placid, shallow little river became a raging torrent tumbling down the side of the hill on the edge of the town.

The little wooden bridge was strong enough in normal times to bear the wagons that brought the farmers in to town to trade and frolic and to worship. But now, as the river's waters rose higher and higher and the brush and small trees uprooted by the violent storms came down and lodged against the pilings, the frail structure threatened to break from its moorings and temporarily separate village from farming community.

The farmers did not know this on the Sunday morning when the waters were at their height. Though the wind lashed their bodies and the rain drove stinging needles into their faces, though the mud-churned roads put incredible hardship on man and horse and wagon alike, not one family failed to start the long trek for church in the village. That was their upbringing and they did not question it. Simply because it was inconvenient to travel you did not miss Mass, for thereby you committed a sin. And in those days you did not commit sin light-heartedly.

When they reached the river they halted their horses, got out of the wagons, grasped the children firmly and fought their way to the bridge. But there they stepped short. To cross that shaking, quivering span was to court suicide, and suicide was another sin. Either way they were damned.

Meanwhile, the villagers, who were more worldly than the farmers, had looked out upon the lowering skies, had heard the shrieking wind, had seen the blinding rain, and decided to a man that these were acts of God absolving them from church-going and so had turned over in their beds for another forty winks. Only the priest was in the sleepy little church on the village bank of the river. He looked with rueful tolerance upon the empty pews and made ready to say Mass without server and without worshipper.

His vestments on, he gazed out of the window across the bridge and beheld the group of farmers who feared to come forward and dreaded to go back. He hesitated not a moment. Here was the church, there were the church-goers. The church-goers could not come to the church; he would take the church to them.

In his sacred robes embroidered with loving care by village lady and farmer wife, carrying chalice and altar cross, the priest left the quiet sanctuary of the church for the violence of the storm, stepped upon the swaying bridge, and (it seemed to the fear-stricken group on the other side) walked across it with firm, erect tread, though the rain beat at his robes and the wind bore down upon him with furious malevolence.

Still on the bridge, he stopped and started the ritual of the Mass. A brave soul came forward, took the cross, and made the responses. Their voices were lost in the clamor of wind and rain, but so familiar were the farmers with the service that they followed it without the help of sound.

There came the supreme moment of the Mass, the holy sacrifice, when a cry went up from one in the group. All eyes save the priest's turned to the crest of the hill. A huge tree came plunging down the side and on toward the bridge. Certain destruction loomed for the two men and the bridge when that tree should strike. But the priest seemed unaware of imminent death. With unhurried calm he raised the chalice high. The wind rose to a shrilling pitch, then died to a thin whisper. The rain, no longer lashed to driving sheets, settled to a monotonous downpour. The river's waters, once a raging cauldron, ebbed to a steady lapping. All this occurred in but a moment of actual time, yet an eternity of human experience.

But there was still the tree. Ironically, it remained a menace, though the storm had abated. Its headlong rush was checked, but still it came inexorably forward. The group on shore, torn between religious duty and craven fear, knew not whether to bow in reverence or flee the spot. Spiritual training prevailed, and eyes were lowered. Abruptly, then, the tree veered, turned its full length across the stream, and came to rest on either bank, damming the waters behind it. And at last, while the priest still held the chalice aloft, the bridge stopped its shuddering tremors and settled to its old security.

Natural phenomenon? Miracle? Which?

A Tree Spirit

Storyteller unattributed, Sugar Bush

An Indian woman was once gathering maple sap for the making of maple sugar. She was very old and not very successful in her undertaking.

One day when this old woman was emptying her bark buckets, a tree spirit appeared. The next day when she again visited her sap troughs she found a lump of maple sugar adhering to a cut she had made in the bark of the tree. The tree spirit told her to take this lump and mark her kettle with it near its rim. Whenever she boiled sap in this kettle it would rise to this mark no matter how little sap she had in it. Now the old lady always had an abundance of maple sugar.

There were innumerable places in Wisconsin where the Indians and the white settlers made maple sugar in past years. Wisconsin once was one of the greatest maple sugar producing states.

LOCAL HISTORY

Much of the material amassed by WPA field-workers in the 1930s centered not around mythical creatures and preternatural occurrences; rather, interviewees told of the lives they built in Wisconsin, of the notable people and beautiful places found throughout the state, of the struggle to build towns and the characters—jokers and mischief-makers, bandits and counterfeiters—who agitated otherwise quiet communities. Interviewees found these episodes significant enough to treasure them in their memories and to recount them when field-workers visited seeking stories. In this way, the stories that follow tell us as much about the interviewees as they do about the people and places of whom these stories were told.

What did Depression-era Wisconsinites find noteworthy, significant, or memorable enough to warrant sharing? Those interviewed told of building a life in Wisconsin, whether on a farm or in a town, of the beginnings of various communities, and of the notable occupations early settlers engaged in. While farming and logging were common, Wisconsin also had its share of circuses in the nineteenth century, of which many anecdotes were repeated.

Not surprisingly, interviewees readily shared stories about their neighbors, spinning yarns and creating legends about the famous and infamous alike. In addition to telling of the Wisconsin days of John Muir, narrators also shared tales of counterfeiters, robbers, murderers, and hermits, among others, whose names may not be well known but who were noteworthy all the same.

This, then, is a people's history of Wisconsin, a collection of stories, anecdotes, and reminiscences recounting what Wisconsinites found interesting and memorable during the time they were helping shape Wisconsin's growth and development.

Notable Places and People

Rainbow Falls

Told by Mrs. Angus Lookaround, location unattributed

Rainbow Falls may be found today on the well-publicized trail off of Highway 47 about three miles south of Neopit. This spot was officially opened to the public by Roy Oshkosh, son of the late Chief Reginald Oshkosh. He built near the highway a log lodge and trading post with refreshment counter, and provided picnic conveniences and parking space. From this point through a heavy pine forest, he cleared a long trail down to Rainbow Falls. On this trail, thousands of people walk every season to view the grandeur of these appropriately named falls. While one must needs go uphill to see Smokey Falls at its grandest, one walks down a circuitous rock- and root-encumbered path to Rainbow, and, to see its famed scintillations best, walks as far down as possible and looks back and up to the tumbling waters with their prismatic spray. The densely forested shoreline curves, deeply and more deeply, into the pine wilderness until one feels that there is a special mystery about Rainbow of which the forest alone can tell. Visitors marvel at these falls and go on to view other scenic spots, enthusiastically proclaiming the beauties of the Menominee Reservation.

However, before the white man knew it existed, the Indians came to Rainbow Falls; and for a reason quite different from that motivating the average traveler. They would come and sit silently on the rocks and listen, sit silently longer than it is customary for most persons to sit in silence. For Rainbow was one of the Great Spirit's "talking waters." It had a message for the Indians. They knew it. They knew they needed it. Rainbow was one of the hallowed places. Many Indians resent today the presence of curious "outsiders," as they call the tourists, at those natural sanctuaries of theirs. In the tourist season, the native Indian will not visit Rainbow Falls. Neither will a worshipper seek the sanctuary of a cathedral if he thinks a party of tourists is there to study its architectural style. He will wait, until he is alone, to pray. Nevertheless, the non-Christian Menominees find a time when they can visit Rainbow Falls undisturbed for the same inspiration that their fathers found there. Even the modern Christian Indian, now and then, is able to put aside the veil that constrains his eyes from perceiving what the Old People saw, and he, too, comes down to those "talking waters" and takes into his soul the eternal message. Regardless of garb and education, the Menominee Indian is at heart as Indian as his forefathers were, though, due to the influence of the outside world, frequently he is reluctant to acknowledge it. Rainbow Falls has lost none of its meaning to the strictly native Menominees. "It will always be the same," they say, "no matter how many strangers look at it."

When you visit Rainbow Falls, try to realize a little of its significance to the Indian. And listen for the voice of the Falls and discover what message it has also for you.

Big Eddy Falls

Told by Mrs. Angus Lookaround, location unattributed

One must travel north from Keshena five miles on highway 55, then north one eighth of a mile down a winding road to the Wolf River, to find Big Eddy Falls. Thundering over its holders and eyeing southward, Big Eddy Falls is magnificent. One may sit on the greensward nearby or upon the great granite rocks, and sense all that wonder, wild music, and magic. Many picnickers and tourists have done so. But they do not know about that greensward on moonlight nights, that greensward that stretches so gently from the forested slopes to the rocky banks of the Falls. The Indians will tell you that the spirits of happy children come there to dance and play when the moon is high, that they scamper on the cool grass and flit out on the rocks, dip their dainty toes in the spray and laugh and sing. There are Indians who will tell you that they have seen them. And many will tell you that they have heard their laughter in the moonlight. Maybe that is why so many people like to spread their picnic cloths upon that greensward and listen to the Falls.

Smokey Falls
Told by Mrs. Angus Lookaround, location unattributed

Among the northernmost falls of the Wolf River, as it flows through the Menominee Reservation, are those called Big and Little Smokey. The wooded road that connects them with the outer world branches off from Highway 55 about ten miles north of Keshena and winds upward to the high banks at the bend of the river where these sonorous rapids come tumbling down with a stupendous roaring. Recently this place and its environs were commercialized. Indians have cleared paths and picnic spots, built foot bridges, and set up souvenir and refreshment stands to cater to tourist trade. The river itself and the mighty upper and lower falls remain unchanged, however, and flow along during the lonely icy winters and the hot vacation days of summer with the same intrepidity as in those far off times when none but Indians knew the whereabouts of them.

Indians, always aware of the spirit world, tell the story of Smokey Falls in this wise: The beauty of this place attracted the Great Spirit. He came to sit in a rocky cavern unseen beside the falls and smoke his pipe. If you follow the paths and walk out on the narrow bridge and down onto the rocks, you will see the smoke of his pipe. It comes in puffs from the secret cave and floats out over the falls like a fine mist. Certainly, the Great Spirit is there smoking his peace pipe. No, you cannot see him. But you can see the smoke of his pipe. See it, floating on down the river, clinging to the rapids, disappearing at last among the trees of the forest? The Great Spirit loves the river and the "talking eaters."* He sends out his smoke over it. So Smokey Falls came by its name.

Platte Mounds
Storyteller unattributed, Platteville

In the summer of 1827 General John H. Rountree and a friend, both from the Fever River near Galena, made a prospecting tour of the lead region in Grant County. As they saw the Platte Mounds at present Platteville in the early morning, they thought they were one of the most beautiful sights in nature. They climbed to the top of one of them and viewed the surrounding country. It was a wide and lively prospect but an unbroken wilderness.

It was the Fourth of July, the birthday of our national independence, and they were in particularly good spirits. They cut their names and the date on the rooks of the mound. It was a hot day and they wanted water. So they left the mound and set out for the north. They followed an Indian trail. They had their blankets with them and were prepared to prospect for mineral. They camped near Wingville. Then they turned west, traveling through the present town of Fennimore, camping the second night at a fine spring. The next day they passed by where Mt. Hope now stands. All this was then a wild, but most beautiful, region. They returned home by way of Beetown.

General Rountree later became the owner of one of the most profitable lead mines located where Platteville now stands. The early Indians are reported to have used the Platte Mounds as a signal station, lighting fires on its top with which to [send] smoke signals to their encampments.

---

* "Talking eaters" likely means humans.

Potato Lake—Indian Potatoes

This large lake in Rusk County is said to have been named for the arum-leaved arrowhead (wabasi, or white potato), a water plant, the root of which the Chippewas, as well as other Wisconsin Indians, use for food. To the Chippewa especially the corns are a most valued food source. "They will dig them if they cannot get them more easily. Muskrat and beavers store them in large caches which the Indians appropriate. They are white inside, sweet, and quite starchy. For winter use the potato is boiled, then sliced and strung on a piece of basswood bark fiber and hung up overhead for storage. They also use the fresh corns, cooking them with deer meat and maple sugar. Some of the potatoes are kept over after cooking and the maple sugar is thickened until they might almost be called candied sweet potatoes." They may also be roasted in the ashes of a fire.

An Indian woman once took some of these potatoes from a beaver cache. The beaver was a powerful spirit. When she reached her wigwam the corns had become a tumbling mass of small mud turtles. She threw them away.

Portage

Portage is the birthplace of Zona Gale, famous writer. She received her education at the University of Wisconsin and Wayland Academy. Her earlier years were spent in newspaper work in Milwaukee and New York. Her first book, *Romance Island,* was published in 1906. Her best-known work, *Miss Lulu Bett,* as dramatized was awarded the Pulitzer Prize in 1920. Her girlhood home is preserved in Portage.

At Portage was located Fort Winnebago, a frontier fort constructed in 1828. Here Jefferson Davis, president of the Confederacy, served as an officer. Several of the fort buildings remain.

The Indian Agency House, built in 1831, has become a historic house museum maintained by the Wisconsin Colonial Dames. This was the home of Mrs. John H. Kinzie (Juliette Magill Kinzie), author

"Wisconsin Point," woodblock print by Beryl Beck, from *Superior Wisconsin in Woodblock*

of *Wau-Bun, The Early Day in the Northwest,* of which six editions have been printed.

Radisson

In 1654 Pierre Esprit Radisson and Medart Chouart Sieur de Gros-seilliers, daring young adventurers, following in the wake of the Frenchman Jean Nicolet, set forth from Three Rivers in Canada to discover the great lakes they had heard the Indians speak of. They wintered among the Potawatomi in the Green Bay region.

In the spring of 1655 they ascended the Fox River, portaged across and entered the Wisconsin, spending four months on the trip. They may have reached the Mississippi.

In the spring of 1659 the same men, with other fur traders and a band of Huron Indians, skirted the south shore of Lake Superior in their canoes and learned of the Indian copper mines. Late in the autumn they entered Chequamegon Bay and built a crude fort near the site of Ashland. This was the first white habitation in Wisconsin. They visited the Huron village near the headwaters of the Black River. They wandered into the Mille Lac region in Minnesota, meeting the Sioux Indians.

In 1660 they built a fort at Oak Point, east of Ashland. That year they returned to Three Rivers, after making four journeys to the Iroquois and to the Northwest. Later they transferred their allegiance to England and were among the founders of the Hudson Bay Company.

Prairie du Chien—Preface to Evangelism

At the first annual meeting of the Old Settlers of Crawford County at Prairie du Chien in 1873, the Rev. Alfred Brunson told this story of his arrival at the Prairie as a missionary to the Indians in 1835.

"On reaching the south bank of the Wisconsin River, the road came to an end. But seeing a house on the hill on the other side, I hailed, and soon a flatboat came to ferry me over. On the boat I inquired, 'Is this the Wisconsin River?' 'Sees bitts,' was the answer. This I understood to be the ferriage. I then motioned to the water and asked again. The answer was, 'Oui, M'sieu', Wisconsin, Wisconsin.' 'How far to Prairie du Chien?' 'Sees mile,' was the answer. I felt as if I had got to the end of the world and the jumping-off-place.

"The first man I met on the Prairie was staggering his way home on the Wisconsin bottoms. I inquired for Samuel Gilbert. 'Is he your brother?' was the answer. 'No, except in the Lord,' I replied. 'Oh, may be you are a missionary?' 'Yes, I profess to be.' 'Well,' said he, 'Sammy Gilbert is a good man. If it wa'nt for him and I this Prairie would sink.' I concluded that if he was all that saved the prairie it must be in a bad fix. I afterwards learned that he was a backslider, but still believed that he was one of the elect, though, as he said, he had swallowed two thousand dollars worth of whiskey."

Father Inama's Shrine
Storyteller unattributed, Roxbury

In a farm pasture one mile west of Roxbury are the ruins of a Catholic mission church and monastery built by Rev. Fr. Adelbert Inama in 1846. Only the ruins of the good priest's brick-lined wine cellar and a few stone heaps and earth mounds and depressions remain to mark the site of the father's pioneer venture. This church was the mother church of all of the surrounding country.

Father Inama was born in Tyrol in 1798. As a young man he joined the Norbertine order. Following his ordination he served for some years as professor of Greek and Latin at Innsbruck. In 1842 he decided to come to America as a missionary priest. He was sent by Bishop Martin Henni, Milwaukee, to Roxbury, arriving in November, 1845. Count Harazthy of Sauk City donated one hundred acres of land for the erection of the church and monastery; a German missionary society gave the necessary money.

The Father was an indefatigable worker and traveled hundreds of miles on foot through the forests and over prairies in carrying out the work of his church. In 1852 his mission consisted of five separate centers—at St. Norberts at Roxbury; St. Martins at Martinville; Pine Bluff; Lyndon in Juneau; and Sauk City. In carrying out his life's work Father Inama brought the rites of his church not alone to Catholics, but to non-Catholics as well. He baptized Lutherans, Quakers, Methodists, Presbyterians, and others who came to him for this Christian rite. Even Indians of the Sauk Prairie came to him to be baptized. He was looked upon by all creeds as a beloved churchman. He has been called the "Four Lakes Apostle."

It was from this little chapel and monastery, later destroyed by fire, that Father Inama carried on his work. In February, 1853, there were three priests, one student, and five lay brothers at the monastic colony. His parishioners were too poor to contribute much to the support of the venture, and after an impressive beginning the colony languished.

Father Inama died in 1879 and was buried in the St. Norbert's church cemetery at Roxbury.

Nelson Dewey
Storyteller unattributed, Cassville

At Cassville the State of Wisconsin has acquired for state park purposes the early farm home of Nelson Dewey, governor of the state from June 7, 1848, to June 5, 1852. This estate stretches for a mile or more along the bank of the Mississippi River and contains a residence, cattle and horse barns, and other interesting structures.

Nelson Dewey was born in Lebanon, Connecticut, December 19, 1813. He came to Wisconsin Territory in 1836, settling at Cassville, where he found employment. In 1837 he removed to Lancaster, the county seat, where he engaged in the practice of law. His legislative career began in 1838, when he was elected to the Wisconsin House of Representatives, where he continued until 1842, being speaker of that body in the session of 1840. He was a member of the council from 1842 to 1846.

The significance of his administration as governor lies in its pioneer character. He is described as a plain, unpretending, democratic citizen, of excellent talent, much originality, and the highest integrity of character. After 1855, he dropped out of public life. His private fortune, once large for the time, was lost. He died at Cassville, July 21, 1890. All of the old residents of Cassville knew and liked Nelson Dewey. In that town there still stands the old Dennison House where the governor boarded during the last years of his life and where he and his cronies played cards and told stories.

Abraham Lincoln

Storyteller unattributed, Port Washington

In September, 1855, Abraham Lincoln went to Port Washington with the idea, it is stated, of establishing himself in the legal profession in that city. While there, he stayed at the Wooster Harrison house. A tablet marks this place.

Lincoln made three visits to Wisconsin in the years 1855 to 1859. On October 30, 1859, he delivered an address at the State Fair at Milwaukee, and after his speech he gave Henry Bleyer, a young reporter of the *Milwaukee Sentinel,* the sheets of his address. One of these pages Lincoln had written in pencil on the arm of his seat on the train on the way to Milwaukee. The young reporter kept the sheets of the address for years. While attending a national convention of colored leaders in the East he generously gave away—not knowing their value—all of the sheets except the one written in pencil. A tablet marks the site of this Lincoln speech.

Weyerhauser Loses His Fur Cap

In 1887 Holland and Barker of Chippewa Falls had a camp putting in Weyerhauser timber on the Jump River. One evening a blind man drifted into camp. He was an old woodsman, who while working in a quarry the summer before had lost his eyesight by a premature blast. He also had cancer of the throat and was going around through the lumber camps trying to raise money enough to have the cancer properly treated.

Shortly after supper Frederick Weyerhauser with three other lumbermen and a teamster drove into camp. While they were eating supper one of the lumbermen of the camp, Al McCaulley, told the blind man to go in and ask the "brase collars"* for some money.

"All right," he said, "I will." He was gone about a half hour. When he came back Al asked him if they had given him anything. "Yes," he answered, "they helped me."

"How much did they give you?" McCaulley asked. At first the old man would not tell. However he finally admitted that Weyerhauser had given him twenty-five cents—five cents apiece for each member of his party.

When Weyerhauser had entered the camp he had worn a sealskin cap valued at twenty-five dollars. In the morning after breakfast the cap was missing. The sleeping shanty, dunnage sacks,** cook shanty, ox hovel, horse bars, and blacksmith shop were all searched but the cap could not be found. Weyerhauser left the camp wearing a big woolen scarf and a little hat about as big as a dollar.

A week or ten days later the cap came into dinner—Al McCaulley was wearing it.

Frederick Weyerhauser, who was called the "lumber king of the world," operated on the Chippewa River and its tributaries and logged and sawed four hundred million feet of white pine timber in one year. He had many jobbers and contractors and walking bosses and when you figure it out, actually employed about twenty-five men to the million feet to do the work.

There surely was an army of lumberjacks in the great forest of pines. It employed as many more to drive the logs down to the saw mills, separate them at Chippewa Falls and Beef Slough, make them

---

* Perhaps a term, like "muckety-mucks," for supposedly important people.
** Bags in which belongings were placed, similar to a duffel bag.

into great rafts, and deliver them down the Mississippi River to his many mills.

The Hodag
Storyteller unattributed, Rhinelander

Eugene S. (Gene) Shepard of Rhinelander, a former lumber cruiser, was one of the greatest practical jokers the state ever knew. One of his most famous creations was the Black Hodag (Bovinus spiritualis). This ferocious beast of the North Woods, according to its discoverer, lived in the dense swamps of his home region. He found a cave where one of these hodags lived. With the assistance of a few lumberjacks he blocked the entrance with large rocks. Through a hole left in this barricade he inserted a long pole, to the end of which was fastened a sponge, soaked with chloroform. The hodag, rendered unconscious by the drug, was then securely tied and taken to Rhinelander, where a stout cage had been prepared for it. It was exhibited at the Oneida County fair. An admission fee was charged and a considerable sum of money earned. Later, Mr. Shepard claimed to have captured a female hodag with thirteen eggs which she had laid. All of the eggs hatched. He taught the young hodags a number of tricks, hoping to exhibit them for profit, but all died before they reached maturity.

The hodag had horns on it, large bulging eyes and terrible horns and claws. A row of large sharp spikes ran down the ridge of its back and long tail. Colored picture card views of this animal can be obtained at Rhinelander. The hodag slept leaning against the trunks of trees. It could be captured by cutting down these trunks. It was a rare animal of limited range.

Shepard was the author of many other outstanding practical jokes. At one time he claimed he had discovered some perfumed moss in a swamp and took a group of school teachers who were at a summer camp to see it. It had previously been soaked with a jug of cheap perfume. The teachers all sent home samples of this wonderful moss. Once when his potato crop produced many small potatoes he took them to the county fair and sold all at a good price as rare Indian potatoes. One year he conducted a matrimonial bureau in his home town, listing all of the marriageable girls and spinsters. This attracted men to the town from everywhere.

He was the author of a book of Paul Bunyan tales which became widely known.

John Muir's Inventions
Told by Harry W. Kearns, Hickory Hill

Mr. Kearns' father bought Hickory Hill from the McReaths, who had purchased it from John Muir's father. Mr. Kearns senior, now deceased, knew many of the stories of John in his invention stage and delighted visitors with the relating of them but he died and his son has taken so little interest in them that he recalls very few of them. . . .

John put locks on the barn door which no one but himself could unlock. One fall day a group of men were thrashing on the farm, helping his father, when a bad rainstorm came along and they tried in vain to gain entrance to the barn to protect the grain, horses and themselves. No John, no admission to the barn. They waited until John came home and let them in.

Many of the weird locks on the Muir farm outbuildings were ingenious contrivances of spools, wires and rope and could only be assembled and operated by their inventor.

Mr. Muir was a hard task master and little time was granted John from the irksome jobs of grubbing etc. to devote to his studies or inventions, and the Scotch father refused permission to use light at nite but granted it for getting up as early as the lad wished in the morning to study and invent. Most of these two occupations were indulged in in the basement where neither noise nor light would disturb the paternal family head.

The present home at Hickory Hill includes the old Muir home, for Mr. Kearns built brick around the Muir frame home and added a couple of rooms in the rear—hence the basement, pantry, living room, kitchen and upstairs bedrooms are exactly as they were in the original Muir home.

Many years ago when John Muir and his brother David were grown men they returned to Hickory Hill and reminisced about their early days there. David asked John if he recalled the time they had to water the oxen when they were looking at the old well in which John nearly died, and which he had built. John replied that he would never forget it, for a chain was used to pull the buckets up and his hands were covered with blisters. It seems that on the occasion they were talking about their father, at the end of the day's labors, had told the boys to give the oxen all they would drink and they drank 70 pails of water! . . .

John spent many hours in the cellar working on a clock which he was going to put either on the top of the house or the top of the barn so that it could be seen from anywhere on the farm. The clock never reached its proposed station of duty and what has become of it Mr. Kearns does not know.

Mr. Muir built his farm in the middle of his property so that no one need waste time getting to any point of it to work.

In the winter time there were often huge snow drifts through which the Muir sisters had to wade and trudge to school, and many times this was impossible. Their father would not have a path cleared for them for that was a waste of time and no money was derived from it. Some of the neighbor boys however took compassion on the two of the weaker sex and dragged brush over the path obliterated by the snow making the way at least passable. The Reed boys were the gallant young gentlemen and Mr. Kearns says that they later married the girls but I have not verified the accuracy of that statement.

An old miner by the name of Duncan came through the Muir property one day when John was down in the well working. His father commented to Duncan that he hadn't heard from John for quite some time, but he did not seem perturbed. Duncan, having had experience in mines knew that he must have been overcome by fumes, immediately ordered him hoisted up. When John arrived unconscious at the top of the well he was nearly dead from inhaling the poisonous fumes.

The Muir Farm

Told by Mrs. Tom Duffy, Near Old Muir Home

On the farm John had perfected an invention which dumped him out of bed at the correct time in the morning. His sisters scoffed and laughed at it so he, unbeknownst to them, placed the invention under their bed and the following morning when they should have been getting up they found themselves not very lightly deposited upon the floor.

Muir's Family

Told by W.C. English, Portage

Everyone was much surprised when John Muir married, for it was taken for granted that he was a confirmed old bachelor and would remain so to the end of his days. The woman he did marry was the daughter of a doctor in California who was very interested in herbs and medicinal plants, and he had many acres planted with varieties from all over the world. It was through his interest in these botanical specimens that Muir met his wife. His proposal was typically Muirish for he said that his life's ambition was to explore the glaciers in Alaska and that he was going on the government boat which was being out-fitted for that purpose and would sail soon, and if that boat left the day before they were to be married he would leave on the boat. The woman didn't mind and they were married and the boat did not sail until a year after they had married and only a short time after their first child was born.

When John Muir's children reached school age he did not want them to go to school—he wanted to teach them himself, and he did teach them, but only the things he wanted to, such as botany and zoology and left out such bothersome things as mathematics.

His older daughter attended a graduating exercise of the local high school and was greatly impressed by what the students got from the school and what they knew. She went home and told her father that she was going to high school and his reply was that she couldn't, for he wouldn't let her and he would not give her a cent for such foolishness. She became obstinate too and said that she was going and didn't care whether he gave her the money or not, for her grandmother had left her enough so that she could, and she did and graduated.

Professor Frost of the university found the site of the school in which John Muir taught while going to the university about 10 or 12 years ago near Oregon. He planted a tree there to mark the spot.

Muir in Prairie du Chien
Told by Mrs. D.H. Johnson, Prairie du Chien

Mrs. D.H. Johnson, widow of Circuit Judge D.H. Johnson, who was at one time a resident of Prairie du Chien, where for a number of years the judge was editor and publisher of a newspaper, wrote some years ago for a newspaper an article on John Muir which might be added to those collected from Portage.

"In September of 1860 the Wisconsin State Agricultural Society's fair was held at Madison, and it was there I first saw John Muir. He came with two clocks and a thermometer which he, a rather clumsy looking boy, had invented. I remember distinctly only one of the machines, and that was a hickory clock shaped liked a scythe to symbolize old Father Time. The pendulum was a sheaf of arrows, whose ceaseless movement typified time's flight. It was hung upon a branch of an oak tree, and on the snath* was inscribed the motto, 'All Flesh is Grass.'

"Muir and his invention were the chief objects of interest in the Fine Arts Hall at the fair that year. Crowds of people continually flocked around him and made him explain the contrivances. The

---

*The handle of the scythe.

clock was so constructed that it indicated the days, weeks and months of the year, and other virtues which I heard of later. . . .

"John Muir came to Prairie du Chien expecting to work in the shop of a Mr. Wiard, the inventor of an ice boat to ply between Prairie du Chien and St. Paul. But John soon found that Mr. Wiard was too busy to give much instruction. Even the ice boat never had a chance to make a success. So John looked about for some place where he might work for his board. Mr. Pelton offered him the position of shore boy at the Mondell house, and he gladly accepted.

"One of the vacant rooms of the hotel was fitted up and finished with a cot bed, a light stand, a stove, etc., and we were summoned to see the working of John's wonderful invention. It was the identical clock which we had seen at the fair, which would at any hour at which John might set it give an alarm, scratch a match, light a candle, light a fire in the stove and finally tip the bed up so that the occupant would find himself on his feet. These performances were a never-failing fund of amusement to the household. John was an efficient and conscientious shore boy, but all his spare time he devoted to his studies.

"There were quite a choice number of intellectual people in the house, and we had weekly gatherings in the parlors, where one after another read aloud some choice bit of literature of his own selection, and interesting discussions would follow. John came to the readings, but I do not think that he ever volunteered to read. I remembered that we had a very nice entertainment on Thanksgiving Day of that year. After a bounteous dinner in the big dining room the tables were cleared away and we had a series of games. 'Blind Man's Buff,' 'Hunt the Slipper,' 'The Needle's Eye,' etc., were all played with zest, till someone proposed a game called 'Pig,' which was played by all joining hands except one, who stood in the center of the ring blindfolded and held a stick or cane in his hand, which he extended to anyone in the circle whom he could reach. The person reached was expected to make a noise or audible grunt at the end of the stick, and if recognized by the person in the center was compelled to change places with him. It was quite a jolly game, and there were quite a number of wrong guesses, which made much more merriment for the party. John Muir did not join in the game, and soon retired greatly disgusted. Afterwards he said that he could have stood the foolishness of most of the party, but there was one man, a Mr. Port, who was a colporteur and agent for the American Bible Society—a rather stout man and very grave and dignified on ordinary occasions—whom he thought ought to be above such foolishness. To his surprise Mr. Port entered into the game as fully as any of the most frivolous members of the party. As a distributor of the Bible, John had set him on a pedestal, and he felt that he had fallen from his high estate, so he left the room in disgust and freely expressed his opinion of the whole performance."

Pioneers and Homesteaders

Midway

Told by Myrtle Olson, Midway

The history of the Midway community is an interesting one. Nearly a century has passed since the first white men made their homes in that community. In spite of many difficulties and hardships, the pioneers progressed, and we owe them much for our present advancement.

The first schoolhouse was built of logs. These were placed very similar to rails, on the old rail fences. Between the logs was a layer of clay, which added to the warmth of the building. There were only three small windows on the north side and the schoolroom was not sufficiently lighted. It was a very small building and the enrollment was too large for its size.

In 1882 a new schoolhouse was built. This was a fairly good school and had been in use until 1927, when it burned. Then another school was built. This is a very nice school with all the modern conveniences, such as electric lights and running water. This schoolhouse was built a short distance from where the old one was.

In the pioneer days much enjoyment was obtained by spell-downs* in the school. Many schools would compete with each other in much the same way as our schools do now in speaking contests. The Midway school was hard to beat, and many times its scholars spelled-down the teachers from other schools.

The form of entertainment in the pioneer days was very different from that of today. There were no movies, or anything of

---

* A spelling contest much like a spelling bee.

the sort. The kinds of entertainment were limited. They had corn-husking bees, at which the farmers would all get together at each other's homes and husk com. Then they would tear the husks into small strips, and put them in sacks. This was exchanged for furniture. After their work was completed they had lunch, and a social hour. Another form of entertainment was the kraut bees. The farmers helped each other put up big barrels of sour kraut which was shipped to the north and exchanged for lumber. They also had social hours after their kraut bees.

Farming was the chief occupation. They raised a number of sheep and cattle. From the sheep they got wool for making many of their clothes. Some of the women wove cloth and made suits for the boys. The girls all were expected to be able to knit at the age of eleven. They made their own stockings of bright colors, which was fashionable at that time. Instead of going skating in the wintertime, as girls do now, they had to stay at home and knit.

The first church services and Sunday School classes in Midway were held in an old warehouse. After this burned down, they had church in a blacksmith shop, owned by a man named Lockman. People walked for miles to attend Sunday School. The first church in Midway was built in 1882. Rev. Morgan was one of the first ministers.

Game was plentiful in this community. There were partridges and wild pigeons. The wild pigeons came in big flocks, but today they are so scarce that the government offers large sums of money for them. There were also many fox and wolves. A big black bear was killed in a field near the schoolhouse, by one of the first teachers in Midway.

Indians were very numerous in this community. Large bands of them settled near the schoolhouse. One day last week a skeleton was found in a field where a tribe of Indians had lived. This skeleton is believed to be that of an Indian. There was much danger of Indians in the pioneer days. Sometimes a whole band of them came to the houses when the men were not at home, and they would help themselves to anything they wanted. Indian massacres were quite common. One day a band of Indians came to a home where only the children of the household were at home. They peeked in through the windows at first to see who was at home. It happened that this family had a large dog tied up on the porch. The oldest child untied him and the dog chased the Indians away. They were very much afraid of dogs, so most of the farmers kept a dog for that purpose. There is an Indian grave in a field near the schoolhouse. This Indian had been found dead in the road by one of the farmers.

There were many hardships that the pioneers had to live through. Their means of communication were poor and the only means of traveling was by ox-teams. But in spite of hard times they progressed rapidly and have set a good example for future citizens.

The "Green Farmers" from Manchester

Storyteller unattributed, Mazomanie

In 1845, a large number of Englishmen, members of the British Temperance Emigration Society, came from Manchester and settled in western Dane County—some of them on the site of the present town of Mazomanie. Most of these gentlemen were without farming experience. They were what is called "green," and many an amusing tale is still told of their early experiments in agriculture.

One man procured a quantity of seed corn, prepared the ground and had most of it planted when he found that he had made a mistake. He had planted an entire ear of corn in each hill.

Two of the others were about to clear the timber off a piece of ground when a heavy snow fell. It snowed hard for several days until the snow lay about six feet deep in the woods and a hard crust formed on it. When the weather settled the men began their clearing. They worked on top of the crust, chopping or sawing down the trees and hauling away the logs. In the spring the woodland presented an astonishing appearance, the stumps of the trees standing six feet above the ground.

In one locality one of these Englishmen-farmers was postmaster. It was his custom to carry the mail in his high stovepipe hat. When the neighbors called for their mail he removed his hat and let the letters fall to the ground. After sorting out the mail for his customers he replaced the remaining letters in his hat and the hat on his head.

One of the immigrants, a man named Crother, seems to have been a better agriculturist than the others. On taking over his claim, he was very much dissatisfied with it. He said it was nothing but a "miserable sandy prairie that would not grow white beans." He therefore abandoned it and bought better land. This quite disgusted the officers of the society. Some of them sent word back to England that Mr. Crother had left a nice farm and gone off and settled in a swamp. But Mr. Crother prospered on the good land he had obtained, and in after years when his old friends visited him he would say, "Well, let us go out and look over my swamp land."

The Seston Family

Told by Inez Seston, location unattributed

Miss Seston's grandfather, William Seston, came to America from Bolsover, England, in the year 1845 with a family named Gillets. He first came to Springfield with his wife and two children and stayed there a year. The family then went to a log house one mile north of Marxville where he and his wife kept house and ran the farm for a family named Davis. The men of the Davis family had gone on a hike to Pikes Peak, these being the days of speculation in land.

One day the Davis cows strayed and while down in what is now known as Halfway Prairie looking for the beasts Mr. Seston saw the place he wanted to buy. He told his wife about his find and her laconic reply was, "Well, we have 50 cents." He told Mrs. Williams, an old lady who also lived with the Davis family, of his ambitions to buy the land and she said, "Well, you know if you haven't the money, I have," and coolly counted out the necessary $45 to buy the tract of 40 acres. That very day Mr. Seston started out for Mineral Point, the U.S. land office, to file his claim. He walked all night and arrived at the land office at 8 o'clock the next morning.

When he returned Mrs. Williams said, "Forty acres ain't much. You better get the next forty too. And you had better hurry back because someone may get ahead of you." She handed him an additional $45 and he started off again for Mineral Point. Before he got to the land office he was taken ill with the ague but continued doggedly on his way to the land office and got his papers. As he was leaving the office he saw his neighbor, Mr. Ford, entering. He had come to file a claim for the same forty that Mr. Seston had just bought.

William Seston built a small log cabin on his new land and in May 1852 moved in with his family before the new home could boast of a floor, doors, windows or even the spaces between the walls chinked. Here it was that Lewis Seston, the father of Inez Seston, was born. He weighed only three pounds at birth. At the time the baby was born, Squire Lewis, a surveyor, was laying a road between Ft. Winnebago and Mineral Point, and had asked to spend the night at the Seston cabin. On being told of the event which had happened in the night Squire Lewis said, "I want to pay for his first suit of clothes, but on one condition—that you name him Lewis. He is needed to help clean up the country." When the boy was old enough for his first suit of clothes those from Squire Lewis arrived—The suit was a Scotch plaid with kilts.

During the Civil War, a mother's club in the town of Berry planted an evergreen tree for every boy who served from that community. The trees were planted in a row on Mr. Seston's "80." Tags with the name of a boy were placed on each tree, but now though the trees still stand, the tags have grown into the bark. There were about 25 trees planted at that time.

Berry Haney was the first mail carrier between Cross Plains and Sauk City, and the township of Berry gets its name from him. Halfway Prairie, which is just below the present Seston home, was so called because it was the halfway station where the mail carriers of those days stopped to change horses, or to have their meals, or to stop overnight as the case may be. The mail route between Ft. Winnebago, at Portage, and Sauk City, The Dells and Spring Green came through

Halfway Prairie, as did the mail route from Milwaukee to Mineral Point. . . .

A temperance society back in England promoted a great colonization project through which many families were swindled on their purchases of Berry and Mazomanie lands. Officers of the Temperance society were no doubt honest, but some of their agents and employees here were far from honorable.

The temperance society had purchased a large tract of land in Berry. This was sold by contract to English emigrants before they left the old sod. The contract promised that out of each forty acres there should be a certain number of acres of plowed land, but it was so worded that the men who were employed to plow land for the temperance society hit upon a trick of making a furrow six miles long.

Using oxen for motive power, this meant a great saving in time, as it was not necessary to make many furrows six miles long to get the required number of acres as per contract. The new settlers were stung, of course, but with the other party of the contract across the wide Atlantic and the unscrupulous plowmen here being irresponsible, there was nothing to do about it. Technically, the contract had been carried out.

Oxen were valuable animals in the earliest pioneer days. Mr. Seston tells about trading "the best riding horse in the country" for a yoke of oxen. He liked the horse better than the oxen, but he needed the oxen in his business of breaking new land and for heavy pulling otherwise.

Horses were not considered equal to oxen for general farm work in the early days. The oxen made a steady pull, while the horses were too quick, too jerky, for the early pioneers.

Rudolph McChesney
Told by Joseph McChesney, Dane

Mr. McChesney's father, Rudolph McChesney, hired himself out before he had become of age, chopping wood and doing odd jobs.

By his hard labor he was able to buy himself a horse, harness, wagon, and an axe. He continued working hard then until he was able to buy himself free from his mother. He then left his home in Oswego, N.Y., and took one of the first steam vessels on the Great Lakes to Wisconsin, which had a national reputation as being a veritable Eden. He settled in Rock County first. This was in the year 1848.

Rudolph's mother was granted 160 acres of land as a widow's pension. In those days those granted government land could choose it wherever they wanted. So sight unseen and by the reputation Wisconsin had gained through hearsay, she took 40 acres near what is now the village of Dane and the remainder in Marathon County. The 40 acres near Dane proved to be very fertile, while that in Marathon was timber and not fit for cultivation. She never came to Wisconsin to live. On her death she willed the 40 acres to her son Rudolph and the timber land to a daughter. Rudolph then settled on his small tract of land and began buying additional acres.

It is believed that before Rudolph McChesney came to Dane there was an Indian village on his property. It is known that there was a flint mine on the property that was worked by the Indians, and many interesting Indian relics have been found around there.

In the year 1866 Rudolph McChesney built the house in which the McChesney family still live. He dug the stones from the surrounding hills and hauled them to his farm.

At the time Rudolph first came to Dane everyone was a pioneer and suffered the hardships of poverty. Many built log cabins because sawed lumber was too expensive to get. Rudolph soon began rafting lumber down the Wisconsin River to Okee where it was hauled to various settlements. He would take neighbors with him to fell, saw and raft the lumber. For their pay they could have either money or lumber. He worked up quite a business for himself and helped many other pioneers get a start.

Rudolph was in the habit of sticking lumber into his rafts that was not the usual thickness or length of ordinary boards used for building purposes. The object of these strange boards was soon learned by needy neighbors. It seems that at the time of a death in the neighbor[hood] some people would be too poor to even buy lumber for a coffin. So when a neighbor died, old Rudolph would work all night making a coffin out of the boards he brought for that purpose, and the next morning the bereaved would find a sturdy, well-built coffin outside their door so that the deceased might have a respectable burial.

Dane School

Told by Joseph McChesney, Dane

In the year 1870 the first railroad was built through Madison to Baraboo. The station agents at that time spent many long and not too busy hours in their stations. Agent Taylor at Dane would become very lonesome at his job so he began inviting young men there to visit and keep him company. Soon he began teaching them their three R's, and it was not long before some of the boys had gained enough education from him to hold station agent jobs elsewhere, and also other jobs that required a little education.

History of Sour Creek

Told by Manley L. Mahlum, Sour Creek

Sour Creek, a small prosperous country which in the middle of the nineteenth century was the scene of a few log cabins scattered throughout the locality, has steadily increased to the various modern farm homes of today. This small tract of land is located in the northern part of La Crosse County, lying partly in the towns of Farmington and Holland. Previous to 1867 the part now called Farmington was known as the Town of Jackson. This land, the same as other, belonged to the government and was a vast wilderness.

As far back as can be remembered the first homesteader in this locality was Ole Anderson. His brother selected this tract of land for him and another brother. In the fall of 1855 Ole purchased it from the government. He, like other pioneers, came empty handed and was compelled to borrow money to pay for his homestead.

His own story, as related to another to show some of the hardships he met with and also his success, runs like this: He borrowed money from a party in La Crosse paying him 40 percent interest. This shows the scarcity of money at that time. To meet his debt he worked in the woods during winter, and spent the summer on the river. While working there, he had the misfortune of breaking his collar bone, and evidently was unable to work for some time; still he managed to save enough to pay for his land within one year. . . .

Mr. Anderson's good example of taking up a homestead was soon followed by others who were equally anxious to establish a home of their own. One of these was Dave New Comb Jr., who purchased the farm owned by Palmer Mahlum, most of Even Mahlum's and a portion of Odell Brenson's. He erected his cabin on that part of his homestead now owned by Palmer Mahlum. . . .

Some of our ancestors were not homesteaders but instead early settlers. We also find that a number of these homesteaders stayed for only a short time, selling to these early settlers who on the whole remained for a longer period to see the progress of the community. . . .

Ole Larson, a Civil War veteran, purchased his farm from Mathias Johnson. Mr. Larson's life was not all pleasure. Besides experiencing many hardships in the army, he had yet to meet with the most heartfelt sorrow. Only a few days previous to Christmas in the year 1881, death entered this home and claimed Mrs. Larson, leaving him with a large family, the youngest being only ten months old. The next year, Mr. Larson sent to Norway for his sister to help care for the family. With the aid of his sister and children, he managed to operate his farm for many years. Some years later a son became the victim of the dreaded disease diphtheria. Advanced in age, Ole sold his farm to his only remaining son, L. C. Larson. This farm is now owned by Mr. and Mrs. Adell Evenson, Mrs. Evenson being a granddaughter of Ole Larson. . . .

We will note that in this part called Sour Creek, we can still find three of the old log cabins erected in the early days still standing, not merely standing, but are the dwelling houses of three families. Although some improvements have been made, the original log cabins are the same. They are Palmer Mahlum's, Albert Mahlum's and Ole Seeberg's homes.

The household furnishings of the pioneers were very simple, only what he himself was able to manufacture. Benches made out of planks took the place of chairs. Often small planks were carried home from the river to be made into some piece of furniture. The tables were also homemade. The beds were made with straw or corn stalk sticks. To illuminate their homes, they lit a strip of cloth placed in a saucer filled with grease. This method of lighting up the homes was soon improved by the use of homemade tallow candles. A few years later kerosene lamps came into use.

The implements in use were also very crude. The sleighs were homemade. The wheels of the wagons were cut from large logs with tires shrunk on. All the work was done by hand. The grain was seeded by hand, cut with a cradle and bound by hand. The hay was cut with a scythe, raked with a hand rake and stacked outside. As machinery was less available at that time, it required a longer period to harvest the grain. Therefore, women took an active part in outdoor work. The wooden bean plow was prominent in those days. There were no pumps nor windmills. The water was carried from the creek or springs, some using buckets, others a yoke. No threshing rigs hummed. Grain was threshed by the use of a flail, later by the horse power. The first windmill was erected on the oldest homestead, and the first binder was also owned and operated on this place. The first hay fork outfits including fork, rope, three pulleys and grab hook to be installed in their barns was purchased for the sum of $13 each by Ole Larson and Ole Anderson.

Livestock was rather scarce. A yoke of oxen was the main means of conveyance and use on the farm with the exception of a few teams. Sheep and hogs ran wild in the neighborhood. As a rule the farmers owned a cow or so, enough for their own use and if they could manage they would churn and sell a little butter.

As to nationality we find that Sour Creek has almost been entirely in the hands of Norwegians, and can say that at the present day there are only Norwegians and all belong to the Lutheran Church. In the early days, the people of this locality had no church of their own but assembled in a school house to worship.

The same in regards to educating their children, they were compelled to send them to distant schools, until in the year 1900 when Sour Creek saw the erection of a small schoolhouse in the heart of the community where the children of today receive their first education.

We, like other communities, have attained several modern developments. In the early days, mail was received once a week at Union Mills while today we have the rural free delivery. Telephones are found in most of the homes. Every farmer has in his possession at least one car, while in the year 1912 the first car was purchased by L. C. Larson now residing at Holmen. Good roads are found throughout. Among other modern improvements found in this locality are radios, milking machines, tractor and an electric light plant.

If our forefathers could have lived to see the things of today, they would have said: Commencing in 1853, hard times and poverty often stared us in the face and sometimes came near looking us out of countenance; yet, through all those long years of failures and successes, of sorrows and of joys, we never lost faith in the future, nor once regretted having made our home in Sour Creek.

Old Days in West Point
Told by Richmond Van Ness, Lodi

Wammus was the name Mr. Van Ness' New England grandmother who came to West Point in 1851 called a jacket.

When Peter Van Ness came to West Point in 1851 he found the log buildings on his farm not to be large enough to comfortably accommodate his family and stock. The house could be used so he started to build his barn first. It was a frame building and the first of

"Grass Fire," lithograph by Arlo Schmitz WHi Image ID 53584

its kind in the neighborhood. A man traveling past noticed the large new building and on arriving in the village of Lodi remarked that West Point was a funny place to be building a brewery.

Mr. Van Ness once asked his grandfather why he came through all the nice prairies on his way from Milwaukee and settled in the barren hills of West Point. The answer was "wood and water." The hilly part of the country presented problems of being hard to cultivate, the problem of eternal soil erosion, and the difficulty of building roads among the hills. The prairies had for their advantage their rich, level soil and the fact that they were well drained; yet the pioneers chose them last in settling.

Settlers in Columbia County found only groups of mature trees here and there. Mostly burr oaks in park areas. These were called "burr oak openings." The rest of the forested area was second growth from 6 to 10 ft. tall.

Breaking was done with plows which would throw 18 to 20 inch furrows. It was said that these plows could turn under anything which the yolk oxen could bend down under their heavy yolk.

Since in the early days there were no fences the cattle usually ran loose all summer on the hills. A farmer would occasionally jump on his horse and ride miles with salt to give to his cattle. Usually by the end of the summer cattle from several herds would be together so in the fall there would be a general round-up and separating of the herds.

Peter Van Ness stopped at Buffalo on his way to Wisconsin partly to outfit for his new home. While there he visited a nursery and ordered over 100 apple trees to be delivered in Madison on an approximate date. He had these sent to Madison because it was the nearest railroad center. He took a chance on their arriving when they were supposed to and drove over rough trails the 25 miles to get them. Fortunately they arrived on schedule.

The reason Peter Van Ness ordered so many trees was because: (1) In the east he was used to having a large orchard and expected the climate in Wisconsin to be about like that in the east. (2) The apple was a very necessary item of their diet, proving a source of minerals and vitamins during the long winters when there were no raw fruits. . . .

One orchard enemy Van Ness feared was the rabbit because it frequently barked young trees in the wintertime. He told his two sons that if they ever saw a rabbit to kill it if possible. He even told them to drop everything else and tend to exterminating the pest. Yet at the time of this pronouncement rabbits were very scarce. Despite their efforts the rabbit tribe increased as civilization spread. This has always been so. The older brothers lived to see rabbits so thick that hunting them in a small swamp during a winters day they would have enough to make a sizeable pile on the ground.

Haug Family History
Told by Lucille Haug, location unattributed

Peter Haug, born in the year of 1822, lived in the Ness village in Norway; he was a coach driver in this village so he had to be ready to drive people anywhere and at any time of day or night.

In the days before the tallow candle was introduced in this village he had to use the following device to get light. He first wound a small stick with cloth; this stick was dipped into oil. They then hollowed out a potato and placed the stick inside of this. The potato served as a protection from the wind.

One year when the crops froze unusually early the people of this village had to grind the bark of a certain tree, which they mixed with a little flour. This was then made into bread.

Ole and his wife landed in Quebec, Canada, in 1851. They then came to La Crosse. They came to La Crosse County because many of their old acquaintances lived here and because they thought this would be a good place to start out in this new world.

When they came to La Crosse they were to be met by Mr. Lars Olstad of Long Coulee. They arrived in La Crosse a day sooner than they expected to so Mr. Olstad was not there to meet them; they then had to start out walking. They had to carry a two-year-old girl named Bertha, who was born in Norway in the year of 1850, and a six-month-old girl named Mary. They soon became so tired that they were forced to seek shelter for rest in a little, old shack along the road. After they had made themselves comfortable and were about sleeping they were awakened by a man who claimed to be the owner of the shack. He chased them out so they had to sleep on the ground the rest of the night.

The next morning they were met by Mr. Olstad, who had started out to meet them. He drove a team of oxen on a crude lumber wagon. Mr. Olstad took this family into his home until they moved to their new home. This farm is now the Ustby farm in Long Coulee.

After a few years he moved to the present Haug farm one mile north of Holmen. On this farm he built a log cabin and a log barn. The only implements he had was the plow and a grain cradle.

History of Cook Creek
Told by Neoma Lindley, Cook Creek

The school in which I have been observing is situated in a beautiful narrow valley.

A creek meanders crookedly down its length.

On either side great rough hills covered with trees seem to keep guard of all below.

In the valley surrounding the school building are lovely old trees. The building itself is not new. Some sixty years ago the people decided they needed a school and the township was divided into four districts. Consequently it made large schools.

This peaceful valley was settled more than seventy years ago, mostly by Yankees and Irish. At the present time there are peoples of a great many nationalities.

Many and hard were the years that the pioneer put in ere he could raise crops sufficient for the needs of family and domestic animals.

The first homes were tiny log houses chinked with mud.

The land was covered with a virgin forest of hard wood. Great piles of logs that today would be worth hundreds of dollars were rolled up in piles and burned to get them off the land.

The first church was built on St. Mary's Ridge and was Catholic. Game of all kinds was plentiful.

The story is told of one man who went to get his calves. On seeing something by the path, thought he had found them. On going closer he yelled, "I'll show ya." The calf turned out to be a bear and not good natured. The man ran through the wall of a shed taking boards and all as he went.

These people churned their own butter when they had any. In summer they had lots of milk but as cold weather came on, with little feed and poor shelter, the cows dried up. From then until spring there was little or no butter.

Money was scarce and there was little or no work to be had.

Consequently these people had a very hard time of it.

The nearest market place was La Crosse, and that many miles away. Sparta was closer but there wasn't much there at that time.

For amusements they had dances where one fiddler furnished the music and the ladies furnished the lunch. In the fall there would be husking bees. And when a new building was needed the men would gather, cut and trim logs. And then roll up the building, notching them in the corners to make them fit.

There was no such thing as finished lumber in those days. For floors they split boards from logs and nailed them together, for shingle they cut a piece the desired length and took a [froe] and wooden mallet and split them.

Today as we go with car the length of the valley and see the cleared, fertile fields and the lovely homes it is hard to believe it was ever a dreary wooded wilderness. In the pastures we see pure-bred stock. And the machinery is modern.

It seems almost unbelievable that that tiny log building over in that coolie by the spring at one time housed a family.

Smith School

Told by Esther Flugstad, location unattributed

A man named Kikoying came from Madison between 1840 and 1850 to select land for himself and his friends who were at that time residing around Madison. He chose plats of land where the Smith School now stands. He returned to Madison after his work was completed, to bring his family and his friends and their families back with him to this new frontier. When they came back, someone else had come and settled the land which he had selected. They were two brothers-in-law, Smith and a Frenchman, Lamois. The people from Madison moved on and found land a little farther south.

Later on, the Irish moved in in great numbers, and Smith and Lamois, with their families, moved on across the Mississippi to the prairies. These Irish were industrious farmers, tilling the soil very well. They became rich, for this virgin loam or prairie soil was of the best to be found in the entire territory which is now the state of Wisconsin.

This rich land attracted others, among whom were the hardy Norwegians. These Norwegians had never seen the like of this wonderful country. It was a strange contrast to their rocky and worn-out hillside soils. They were willing to lay down their lives to gain a foothold here in this land of "milk and honey" for their children. This was in 1854. At that time, more and more Norwegians came, and the Irish moved on to the new frontier which was fast moving westward.

The hardy Norsemen did not take time to build themselves homes before they began tilling the soil. A hastily constructed log hut was good enough for them until they had laid acres upon acres under the steel share of the plow. Although they did the plowing by foot, they used six yoke of oxen on their plows. These oxen stopped for nothing, and it was well that they didn't for there was no dynamite available for clearing the land. At least, these farmers could not waste the money for it when there were other means at hand. They cut down the great oaks, some of them centuries old, close to the ground. Then they hitched six yokes of oxen to their plows and pulled the trees up by the roots when they made their furrows.

There were few social gatherings because people were too busy taking care of the land they had and acquiring more land. Nevertheless, there was a brotherhood and a loyalty of spirit seldom found in this age. These people looked upon every man as his brother and were as eager to help him. They worked every day of the week harder than their sturdy oxen, but on the seventh they rested, for they were God-fearing people. Then they hitched up their ox-teams and went many miles to their simple meeting house to hear God's word expounded by one of their number or by a wandering preacher or layman. There they laid aside their cares and listened with rapt attention to words of peace which were like music to their souls. After the services, they exchanged pleasantries on the crops and the weather with their neighbors. By the time they came home, there was little time for leisure. It was time for chores and the never-ending tasks of the barnyard, but they never forgot these times of rejoicing for their souls.

The wagons they rode in were not designed for comfort. They were made of rough boards with the ends of a log sawed off for wheels. They were as sturdy as the oxen which pulled them.

It took a long time to drive a mile, but the changes were that they would not get stuck in a snowdrift or a mud puddle.

School was held during the winter months when there was nothing for the children to do at home. The schoolhouse was a simple building of logs, as simple as their homes. Rude benches were made of logs by sawing the log in two. The children sat on the sawed side. Paper was scarce and every child had to bring his piece of slate and piece of hard chalk. The schoolmaster was probably a farmer of a little more learning than the rest. He would know how to read, write, and figure simple and practical mathematical problems.

The school would be divided into two or three divisions, the primary classes, the intermediate, and a few who were more advanced.

"Heritage," wood engraving by Frank Utpatel WHi Image ID 53587

Very few went long enough and learned rapidly enough to reach the advanced grade which was about the limit of the schoolmaster's knowledge. Discipline was maintained by means of the birch rod, and it often happened that a school won a reputation of being "tough" by overpowering the schoolmaster and throwing him out. Although a school of this kind was hardly of the type which could be called advantageous for higher learning, there were many lessons of heroism, right living, and right thinking taught if the schoolmaster himself was truly high minded. However, times went on, and these farmers gained earthly goods. Conditions improved, and educational advantages became greater. Today, Smith School has one of the best school systems in Vernon County. There is little to indicate the early practices.

These are but a few of the interesting historical episodes of those early times. Most of the early pioneers are dead, and their children do not respect the memory of that thrilling past as they should. They, too, are busy gaining more land and more wealth and in their hurry and rush to become prosperous they forget the lofty ideals which their forerunners set up. They have more leisure and yet they have less time for their Lord and Master, and more time to seek their own pleasures, which is after all but a poor means of satisfying their souls.

Town and Village Stories

Oconomowoc

I have heard the following story as to how Oconomowoc got its name. In the early days there was a white settlement where the city now stands. A white man and an Indian were accustomed to hunting and trapping together. It so happened that an old coon proved elusive numbers of times by getting out of traps and avoiding being shot. Finally one day the Indian came into the settlement with a coon, in fact *the* coon, and taking it to the white hunter he smiled and said, "Old coon no more walk." From this sentence a contraction was made and we have Oconomowoc as a result.

The First School Houses in Boscobel
Storyteller unattributed, Boscobel

The first school house on the site of Boscobel was a small building of rough logs, lighted by one small window and with rough boards for desks. A second school of the same character was built in 1852, near a cemetery. The teachers were men hired for their muscular strength as well as their ability to impart learning. "It is not incredible that the graveyard was started with the small boys killed by the teachers or the teachers killed by the big boys. Some of the affairs in the winter schools must have approached homicide. The summer schools were taught by young women and were more serene. One young lady teacher is said to have improved the quietness so as to make up sleep lost by the too great demand for her company at night by the young men who came to court her." There were some rough times in the schools when the boys decided to "throw out the teacher."

Poynette

The village of Poynette should have been called Pacquette, after Pierre Pacquette, the noted early Indian trader and strongman of the Wisconsin portage. Through an error in spelling, it became changed to its present form. Pacquette was the son of a French officer and a Winnebago mother. He was the interpreter of the treaties with the Winnebago at Green Bay in 1828 and at Prairie du Chien in 1835.

He was active in raising a company of Winnebago to participate with the Americans against the hostile Sauk in the Black Hawk War in 1833. He fought at the battle of Wisconsin Heights. He was a powerful man, and stories of his feats of strength in moving teams and supplies across the portage are recorded.

He was shot and killed by a drunken Indian in September, 1836. Pacquette was highly thought of as an honest man and a patriot.

Near Poynette is the State Game and Experimental Fur Farm, the leading institution of its kind in the nation. A total of 40,000 pheasants were released from this farm in 1935 and with the aid of cooperators a thousand black raccoons freed in 1936. The farm specializes in bird and animal rearing and laboratory.

Chief Kewaskum

Storyteller unattributed, Kewaskum

The village of Kewaskum received its name from that of Kewaskum, a quite noted Potawatomi chief of early days of settlement who once had a village, or encampment, on the Milwaukee River at this place and who is reported to have been buried here. The significance of the name is explained as derived from the Indian word *giweskam* ("his tracks are toward home").

Kewaskum had villages at other places in southern Wisconsin— on the shore of Lake Koshkonong (1850), on the Rock River near Rubicon, and at Pike Lake near Hartford (1849). Kewaskum was well known and well liked by the early white settlers. The story is told that when he had a camp at Lake Koshkonong a settler had a field of watermelons which he allowed the Indians to have, and they loaded their ponies to the full extent with them. Several of the biggest melons were reserved for Kewaskum and his family. As a return gift he sent the settler a gift of muskrats which his people were then smoking and packing for winter use.

Hales Corners

This small settlement near Milwaukee was once a famous horse and cattle trading and buying center. Farmers and horse traders came for many miles to engage in trades. There were several tavern hotels, the bars of which were always well patronized. Gamblers and card sharks were sometimes about. Stories were told of farmers who came to buy a team and who returned home without horses or money.

Voree

Storyteller unattributed, Burlington

Near Burlington a small colony of Mormons established themselves in 1846. This settlement they named Voree. The colony did not remain long in Wisconsin but removed to Beaver Island, Michigan. Their leader was James Jesse Strang, known as King Strang. While at Burlington they published from September 1846 to September 1847 the *Times Herald,* which name was changed to *Zion's Reveille* and then to *Gospel Herald.*

Cudahy

Cudahy was platted in 1892 and 1893 and the large Cudahy Brothers Co. meat packing plant located there. Mr. "Pat" (Patrick) Cudahy was the fat and genial head of the plant. Every morning the millionaire

"Hamburger Joint," woodblock print by Edward L. Jansen WHi Image ID 53593

packer rode from Milwaukee in an early train which also convoyed the workmen and surveyors and others to this town site, mingling freely and swapping jokes with all. Everybody liked Pat Cudahy.

In these years three professional baseball players established a large chicken farm at Cudahy and engaged in raising chickens. They invested a lot of money in the adventure and expected a golden return. Meat scraps and bone from the packing plant were to provide some of the food. But the rats of the country round gathered near the farm and these and other destructive causes made away with so many of the chicks that the venture was soon an utter failure. Their golden dream had vanished.

Beetown Hotel

Storyteller unattributed, Beetown

In 1844 there was only one hotel in Beetown (originally Bee Hollow), and that had the sign of a Scotch (straw) beehive. Twelve or fifteen persons were boarding there. All those people, wrapped in Mackinaw blankets or buffalo robes, slept in one large room. The room below was a sort of store where a few groceries, overalls, cider, whiskey, and playing cards were sold. It was frequently used at night for gambling purposes. When one of the miners got "broke" he usually took a tallow candle and went upstairs and peered into the faces of the sleepers to see if he could find a friend who would lend him a sovereign or two or a few five-franc pieces, as a stake, so that he could renew the contest. This was often done four or five times in a night.

Egg Harbor

This town takes its name from an incident which took place near here in the summer of 1825. Four large Mackinaw boats belonging to Mr. Rolette, a prominent and extensive Indian trader, were proceeding from Green Bay to Mackinaw with the returns of the year's trade. When the boats were abreast of Egg Harbor, one of the boats

"Old Sturgeon Bay Wis.," depicting Sturgeon Bay as it looked in 1900, in a 1941
etching by Charles Clark Reynolds WHi IMAGE ID 104870

attempted to take the lead of the Rolette boat and a friendly battle of eggs (of which there were a large quantity on board the boats) took place. The battle kept up for some time, but at length the commodore's boat triumphed and the other boat was obliged to fall behind.

Sun Prairie

The early extensive and beautiful prairie lands of southern Wisconsin are commemorated in the names of a number of cities and villages, Prairie du Chien, Prairie du Sac, Rolling Prairie, North Prairie, Prairie Farm, Pleasant Prairie, Star Prairie, and others.

In June, 1837, a party of thirty-six workmen under the leadership of Commissioner Augustus A. Bird traveled by teams from Milwaukee to Madison to erect a capitol building. They were ten days on the way, making their road as they came and crossing swamps much of the time in a drenching rain. As they reached a point nineteen miles from Madison the sun came out and revived their drooping spirits. This place has ever since borne the name which they then gave to it—Sun Prairie.

The cornerstone of the first Madison capitol, which they built, was laid on July 4, 1837. "There was no lack of eloquence to celebrate the event."

Brule Portage

Storyteller unattributed, Solon Springs

An ancient Indian portage connected the Upper Lake St. Croix and the Brule River. Over this portage Indians, voyageurs, explorers, missionaries, traders, and pioneers traveled from the waters of Lake Superior to the Mississippi. They carried their canoes and supplies. The French used it as early as 1680.

In the year 1886 the last Indian party (Sioux) to pass over this portage camped on the shore of Lake St. Croix. The Chippewa called this trail Misakota and the Sioux, Nemetoakouat. The French called it the Bois Brule portage.

Boulder monuments now mark the ends of this historic aboriginal travelway. These were erected by the D.A.R. in 1933.

Turtle Village
Storyteller unattributed, Beloit

The Winnebago Indian name for Beloit was Kichunk (Turtle). It took its name from Karamaunee, or Walking Turtle, an Indian chief of considerable prominence, who had a village here. This village in 1823 numbered some thirty-five lodges with six hundred inhabitants.

Karamaunee is described as a stalwart Indian with a broad pleasant countenance and as a worthy man. He was a principal chief of his tribe and was known in 1832 as the "Councellor." He fought with the Indians under Tecumseh in the War of 1812 and was by his side when the famous Shawnee chief fell at the battle of the Thames, October 15, 1813. In 1790 he went with this chief on a mission to the Indians in New York. He signed the Indian treaties of 1816, 1825, 1829, and 1832. J. O. Lewis painted his portrait at the Little Butte des Morts treaty in 1827.

Vita Spring
Storyteller unattributed, Beaver Dam

The region around Beaver Dam had always been a favorite Indian hunting ground of the Winnebago in the early part of the nineteenth century and, later, of this tribe and the Potawatomi. In 1848 the chief of the local Winnebago was Wiscopawis, a rough character but said to have been a mighty hunter.

Vita Spring, in present Vita Spring Park, was well known to the Indians as a sacred spring, or "healing spring." Muchkaw, the great medicine chief of the Winnebago, continued to visit it until he died, in about the year 1860. It was a past custom of the Indians to cast into this spring—as an offering to a spirit which was supposed to inhabit it—human and animal bones, many of which were found when it was once cleaned of debris. Other relics found were arrow points, gun barrels, and gun stocks.

From this spring a trail ran to the Beaver Dam River and down the riverbank to the Mud Lake region.

The Lost Tribe

Storyteller unattributed, Grantsburg

Living on the banks of the St. Croix River and in the surrounding counties are a band of Chippewa Indians who became known as the "Lost Band" or "Lost Tribe" of this nation. When reservations in northern Wisconsin were set aside for other Chippewa these Indians refused to settle on any of these, so they were not provided for by the government.

For many years they have not been disturbed in their occupation of the unoccupied lake, river, and forest lands in northwestern Wisconsin. In recent years much of this region has been occupied by summer resort colonies and estates, and the Indians are no longer welcome to occupy these regions where they formerly camped, fished, and hunted unmolested. One of their villages was at "Dog Town" on the St. Croix River. An effort is being made to provide other lands for them.

Prairie du Sac Bear Hunt

Storyteller unattributed, Prairie Du Sac

The present site of Sauk City and Prairie du Sac on the Wisconsin River was in 1840 the place of residence of the romantic pioneer character Count Agoston Harazthy. A native of Hungary, he had come to the new world full of enthusiasm for adventure, sport, commercial enterprise, or whatever the unknown land might offer.

Tales abound of his distinguished appearance and noble lineage,

of the courtliness of his manner, of his prowess as a hunter and particularly of his fruitless efforts to establish a large city on the shores
of the Wisconsin.

One day during the count's life in this region Judge Irwin was
holding court in a frame building in Prairie du Sac. While the court
was in session an individual shouted through the open door in a loud
voice, "Bear in the village." In a twinkling every man in the court
room was on his feet and judge, jury, lawyers, and prisoners joined
the spectators in a mad rush to hunt the bear. All seized weapons as
they ran. The count, who happened to drop into the village at this
time, snatched a large cheese knife from the village grocer and joined
in the bear hunt. The bear was quickly run down and killed, and the
village enjoyed a feast of this favorite delicacy.

Ghost Towns
Storyteller unattributed, Janesville

Along the course of the Rock River between Beloit and Lake Koshkonong are the sites of no less than ten "ghost" towns. They were
once known by such names as Carramana, Newburgh, Warsaw, Kus-
kanong, and Wisconsin City. These phantom municipalities were laid
out by land speculators in early years of the state's history. Their owners hoped to reap a harvest of golden shekels from the sale of building
lots in these paper towns of their dreams. Attractive maps and plots
were prepared to engage the interest of investors. On these sites, lots
were often set aside for a "university," an "academy," and one or several churches. Many persons in the East purchased lots in these town-
sites which were never settled. They are dead towns. . . .

There are many lost towns in Green County. Where the Pecatonica forks there was a village called Otterbourne, founded somewhere
around the late '70s and early '80s. No one remembers it nor knows
why it was founded nor why it was abandoned. Wiota was the second town to be founded in the county and it was originally known
as Winnoshek. Buckhorn was the name of a village which was where

the Illinois Central and Milwaukee roads now join. It is now known as Dill and has a post office. Exeter was on the old lead trail which went to Mineral Point and was founded by the erection of a smelter. When the mining was abandoned years ago the town disappeared with the smelter. Decatur was a little village west of where Brodhead now is. It died when the railroad came through and Broadhead was started. Cadiz was a little village south of Browntown. It was started when a man started a sawmill there and made staves. When he died the town and business were things of the past. Polk is in Jefferson County but it was quite a thriving little community with a post office, creamery and a number of homes. All have gone except the church which is still in use. It was located near Twin Grove.

Richland City
Storyteller unattributed, Gotham

On the banks of the Wisconsin River in the sixties and seventies, in the old lumber-rafting days, was the flourishing river town of Richland City. This town was a stopping place for rafting crews. Here they tied up their rafts while they went ashore for food supplies or liquor.

A "Whiskey Jack" of this place says that a raft crew of which this fabulous river character was captain once landed here. All were thirsty but no one had any money. One man went ashore with a bundle of laths, which he traded to the tavern keeper for drinks. On leaving, he was told to leave the laths outside the rear door. This he did and returned to the raft. Another raftsman then went to the rear door, took the bundle, entered the front door, and also traded it for drinks. This stratagem was worked until the entire crew had had their liquor. After the last man had left, the tavern keeper looked out to see his accumulation of lath bundles and found not a single one; the last man had taken the bundle with him.

Richland City is now a "ghost town." Only a few houses remain there; when the Chicago, Milwaukee & St. Paul Railroad built its line on the opposite bank of the river the fortunes of the town began to decay. Houses were moved to the other bank and many people left the place. River floods of recent years have carried away large areas of the river bank. Today most of the original site of Richland City is in the bed of the Wisconsin River.

Monroe

Told by Emery Odell, Monroe

Abraham Lincoln camped with his company of soldiers on what is now known as the Montieth farm in Adams township, Green County, when the Blackhawk War was being fought. The soldiers used a spring for their supply of water. Many years later when the spring was cleaned out it was found to contain lead, showing that there was a vein or deposit upon the property.

In 1921 when some streets were being repaired in Monroe some digging was done on the south side of the square, off the business sections, in a declivity. The workmen ran into some huge buried logs. After some inquiries it was found that in the early days of the city there used to be a corduroy road over that section of ground. In 1930 when the present Goetz theater was being built and the cellar excavated an old wooden bridge was found about six feet under the soil. In the early days of the community a stream called Thunder Creek had flown through the town and at this particular spot had been spanned by the bridge. Later the stream dried up but its course is now used for a storm sewer and is called the Thunder Creek Storm sewer.

In 1835 the first house was built in Monroe and that house is still standing on the south end of 17th Ave. and is owned by Thomas Niles.

Occasionally people have found pockets of copper in and about Monroe. Much excitement has been caused but nothing but the pockets have ever been discovered. If large deposits could be found the property owner would indeed be wealthy as copper has and still does bring a very good price.

In the village of Twin Grove in the late '40s and '50s there used to be a pottery factory which was owned and operated by Joshua Sanborn, who hauled his product as far as Milwaukee. Mr. Dunwoodie as a kid used to go there and make marbles. The factory no longer functions nor stands.

In my interviews with people I have always managed to mention the wild pigeon, which has been extinct now for about 50 years. Many interesting additional facts have been contributed by each person interviewed. Mr. Dunwoodie said that one of his chief occupations when a young boy was to go with the men who trapped the birds and pinched their heads when they were caught. The men used a unique system of catching the huge flocks that migrated northward in the spring and south in the winter. One wild pigeon was caught and stitches taken in his eyelids so that he could not see. He was then tied by a string to a pole. This bird was used to decoy the others into a trap. He was called the stool pigeon and Mr. Dunwoodie firmly asserts that this is where the name "stool pigeon" originated. The trap consisted of a long bed of green grass which covered a big net. When the pigeons landed the net would be sprung and all entrapped. The birds then had their heads pinched, were plucked and cleaned and shipped to New York.

Jacob Regez, who was a cheese maker in Monroe, was always raving about how good the imported cheeses were. Finally one time when he was in New York he selected an imported cheese with great care and brought it home with him. When he arrived home he invited his choicest friends in to have some of the particularly delectable cheese. When they had arrived he opened it and there beneath all the fact[ory] wrappings was the mark of his own cheese factory. He had bought one of his own cheeses.

Mr. Dunwoodie's daughter lived in Muscatine, Iowa, for some time and the man who had been the Swiss counsel under the Cleveland administration occasionally ate at her house. Once when she expected him for a meal she had her father send down some Swiss cheese from Monroe. The ex-counsel took a bite of the cheese and immediately wanted to know who had been at the house who had just returned from Switzerland. He was much surprised to learn that the cheese came from Monroe.

Mr. Dunwoodie was asked one time when traveling in the eyes how the holes got into the Swiss cheese. His retort was that the eyes in the cheese depended upon how sharp nosed the wife of the cheese maker was. The sharper the nose the smaller the holes.

Wooden Shoes
Storyteller unattributed, Kiel

At Kiel there is a wooden shoe factory. The shoes manufactured there are such as were worn in their home countries by peasants who came to settle in Wisconsin from agricultural regions in Germany, Holland, Belgium, and Switzerland. These are now worn by some men employed in cheese and butter factories. Such shoes were in former years seen hanging from a nail or hook in pairs in general stores in many parts of eastern and central Wisconsin.

The Saukville Flood
Storyteller unattributed, Saukville

Saukville takes its name from the Sauk Indians, who in early years traveled over the Old Sauk trail, the lakeshore trail running from Green Bay to the present sites of Milwaukee and Chicago. This picturesque little hamlet is located on the west bank of the Milwaukee River twenty-eight miles from Milwaukee.

In the spring of 1881 a spring flood occurred, the river rising to the highest point ever known and overflowing the country for several miles on each side of its banks. The village was inundated from two to four feet and a great many families were forced to abandon their homes and find shelter with neighbors who were fortunate enough to have homes located on elevated land. Chickens, pigs, and cows were swept away by the flood. Some wag afterwards said that meat prices came down in Milwaukee after the Saukville flood.

Brodhead Pearls

Told by Jake Benkert, Monroe

One summer sometime in the late '80s the people in and around Brodhead and Albany, where the Sugar and Pecatonica Rivers are, found that the clams in those rivers had pearls in them. For three months practically every man, woman, and child spent time getting the clams out of the streams, opening them, and praying that there would be pearls. It was a miniature '49 rush. Men and women would wade into the streams with rakes and rake out the clams onto the banks. The dam at Brodhead was even opened once to let the water out so the people could get the clams above the dam. People would buy and gather loads of clams, take them home and carefully open each one. Some very good specimens were found but there was no local market so a few local men with some capital started buying pearls on their own. Mr. Benkert was one of these. He owned a merchandise store in Brodhead. The perfect pearls were sold according to weight. One grain bought $1, two grains $3, three grains $6 and 10 grains $20. Pearls are formed by a grain of sand or some small irritating particle getting inside the clam shell. The clam gives out a secretion which covers the foreign substance. This is added on layer by layer, the pearl getting larger and more valuable with each additional one. One pearl which Mr. Benkert bought weighed 32 grains, which is exactly a carat. Mr. Benkert bought up some pearls for which he paid $300 and sent them to New York to the man from whom he bought merchandise and men's goods and told him to get what he could for the pearls and to let him know what and how he should buy and give him some information on pearls and he would keep him supplied. On the first group he bought he lost $75 but on the next he more than doubled his money. He was told to buy for lustre, not color, for size and perfection. Pearls who were disfigured and uneven were called slugs and sold for pearl buttons. So many clams were dragged out of the river that they were sold and shipped to pearl button companies.

Mr. Benkert bought pearls in Argyle, Pearl City (named after the rush on pearls and located northwest of Freeport). He had quite a few on hand when Mr. Upmeyer of Bundi & Upmeyer of Milwuakee came up and wanted to buy. He showed them to him and he bought all, including slugs, for $5 a grain. Mr. Benkert had bought a carat pearl for $600 at Winslow and sold that to Upmeyer for $1500. This same pearl he saw on exhibition at the first World's Fair in Chicago some years later when he visited there.

One man had a large pearl at Argyle, but because it was blistered he was unable to get anything for it. Mr. Benkert bought it after Mr. X had refused to buy it. He peeled off the blister and then put the pearl in acid vinegar to take the gloss found between the layers. He then sold the pearl to Mr. X for $500.

It was rumored that there were bigger and better pearls near McGregor near Speck's Ferry, so Mr. Benkert went there to see if he could buy some. There were absolutely none to be had for none had been found. Many people went there hoping to dig clams with pearls.

A year after this pearl craze Mr. Benkert went on the road for the firm from whom he had bought his merchandise. He went through Iowa and Nebraska and there he found a few pearls which he bought. These he took to Bundi & Upmeyer and tried to sell them, but met with very little enthusiasm, so seeing a very beautiful gold watch in the case he said he would trade the pearls for the watch, which was marked $125. The trade was made and he had paid $25 for the pearls. Two years after that he bought the last pearl he has ever bought and it weighed six grains.

Friends of the family often asked his wife why she didn't wear pearls. Her reply was always because her husband didn't give her any. She went on a trip to some relatives during this pearl period and Mr. Benkert traded some of his pearls for a very beautiful diamond which he had put in a gold ring of his wife's. Thus his wife wore some pearls and the granddaughter now wears that ring. Many thousands of dollars exchanged hands due to the finding of these pearls and no one has since found anything comparable to those found then. I believe it is now against the state law to take clams for pearls but I am not sure.

I heard from the owner of the Eugene Hotel in Monroe that there are a group of people living on the Rock River near Beloit who make their living from fishing for clams. They catch them with their feet, open them for pearls and then burn and grind them and sell them for buttons.

Lodi

Told by Bert Richmond, Lodi

In 1859 Edgar Richmond and two other men from West Point started for Pikes Peak in a covered wagon. They earned their way as they went along by camping outside the village and giving a musical program at night. They took a dog with them who got lost somewhere in Iowa; sometime later when they returned home—they did not make the complete trip—they found the dog had crossed the Mississippi and found his way home. During their trip west the men encountered two Indian tribes who were at war. One night they were awakened by two Indians who asked in sign language if they had seen their enemies. After learning that the strangers had not come upon the enemy tribe that day the two braves departed without causing trouble.

About fifty years ago Lodi had a band in which big John Frye played the tuba. One time while the band was playing at a lawn party John stopped playing and being asked why he had stopped he said, "I stopped to catch up." The saying has become traditional and is still used especially at local band practices.

In 1887 Lodi had terrific hail storm that broke every window on the north side of town.

In 1882 a fire broke out which swept about a half of a city block. The old "bucket brigade" finding the fire to be beyond their reach enlisted the help of the Madison Fire department. The equipment was hurried up on a railroad flat car.

In 1894 before the time of automatic couplings and air-brakes a freak accident happened in Lodi. A freight train was coming down the hill from Dane. One car had a load of empty egg cases. Suddenly one set of trucks (the wheels on each end of the car are called trucks) under the car containing the egg cases broke loose and rolled off track. About half a mile farther down the track the other truck came out and the car rolled down the bank, into the field, and landed right side up without so much as breaking an egg case. The train proceeded on to the village as though nothing had happened. It stopped in the town, coupled up the space left by the missing car and went on.

When Wm. Rapp took up his claim west of Dane he ran night and day until he reached Mineral Point where he filed the claim to his homestead.

Holmen

Told by Margaret Sjolander, Holmen

In the year of 1857 the roads around La Crosse were not much more than trails through the woods, and much of the journey was made by ox team or on foot; but that seemed only a small hindrance to the settlers who in 1863 came to the town that is now called Holmen.

Funds were collected and the first business place was erected, which was the blacksmith shop. The blacksmith shop was operated by a man named Frederick—usually called Frederick the blacksmith.

The second business place was the flour mill started by Mr. Helgeson. However, before the building was finished, it was purchased by William Pfenig from whom Mr. Casberg bought the mill. Five weeks after he became owner, the mill dam went out and had to be rebuilt. This was just one hardship among the many. A large residence was erected near the mill in which the help roomed and boarded. Later the Casberg family moved to a house on the north side and the "mill house" as it was called was occupied by several families until a few years ago when it was razed and part of it used to erect another residence.

About the same time two young men operated a very small store but soon tired of it and left the place. This store was located in the dwelling, which still stands, behind the present brick store of A. O. Jostad and company.

In the fall of 1870 Mr. Peter E. Sjolander with his wife, Olivia, and son, C. A. Sjolander, moved to Holmen and purchased from Mr. Lytle about one and one half acres of land including the blacksmith shop on the corner where the Jostad store now stands. Mr. Peter E. Sjolander then started and operated a small store in the rear part of the dwelling which was operated as a place of business about two years. In the early part of 1873 the business was taken over by the son, C. A. Sjolander, who rented a building from Harry Mulder standing on the corner where Knudson's store now stands. This was used about a year and a half, when Mr. Sjolander purchased a partially completed frame building, which was then moved to the corner, where the building now stands. Later improvements were made as the business required them. It should be stated that Mr. Harry Mulder also owned a small store for a short time in the same building that Mr. Sjolander occupied.

About this same time the hotel was built and changed hands several times until finally it passed into the hands of Even Casberg, a brother of Carl Casberg, who occupied it for some time. Since then it has changed hands several times.

In 1875 the Holmen Post Office was established. Mr. C. A. Sjolander was the first postmaster. He had to agree to carry the mail free of charge as the government would not pay a salary for a carrier. Such was the mail system for a few years; later a carrier was furnished. For many years the mail carriers had to walk many miles with the mail, through the snow and mud and also many other inconveniences.

In 1886 Mr. C. A. Sjolander established the first creamery in Holmen and operated and managed the same for about three years, when it was taken over by the farmers and has been conducted as a cooperative organization since then. Mr. Sjolander had some difficulties in starting the creamery, insomuch that he had to go from farm to farm each day to get the milk. Although it was hard work he kept trying and finally made a success of it.

I am sure that these people worked hard to make this community a success. Although there were a few hardships they continued their work until they succeeded.

Mayhem and Adventure

The Murder of Catherine Jordan

Storyteller unattributed, Cassville

In the cemetery about 3 miles from Cassville is a tombstone which bears the following inscription:

In memory of Catherine daughter of WM. & Martha Jordan
Murdered by WM. Kidd
June 15, 1868 aged 21 years 3 months and 6 days

Virtuous girl lovely dear
A truthful friend lies sleeping here
We hope her soul is now at rest
And in her saviour's prison held.

The local story is that WM. Kidd was very much in love with Catherine and in a fit of jealousy cut her throat. He escaped to California but was captured and while being brought back he took poison and died. He is buried in one of the other nearby cemeteries. The little frame church in the cemetery where Catherine is buried was built in 1874 by G.J. Foeheringer....

Mr. Kuenster can remember Catherine from when he was a young boy. She was a number of years older and took fiendish delight in frightening people. She used to chase the children with a butcher knife and such things. She was big and stout and unnecessarily rough for a lady.

After killing Catherine, Kidd took one of the horses which he was driving and rode her to Boscobel, where he tied her in a lumber yard, where she was found the next day. He then made his way west and obtained work on a farm. Some local woman found what his name was and where he was from and wrote to a friend of hers about his being in that locality. The sheriff acted upon this information and went to where Kidd was working. He had just come in—it was noon—from threshing and was washing his hands at the bench and did not see the sheriff arrive in the buggy. The sheriff went around the house and came up in front of him and said, "I've got you." Kidd replied, "Maybe you have and maybe you haven't," and he took some poison which he had under his coat and fastened to his shirt and drank it, dying almost immediately.

Family Feud

Storyteller unattributed, Cassville

Two brothers by the name of Young started a store some years ago at Glen Haven. It was not very successful financially and they asked for money to help them from their father. The father always gave to them until the time came when he was pretty well drained and he had to look out for himself and he refused. Albert, one of the boys, threatened to kill him if he didn't give them the money. The father lived on a farm and one day saw Albert coming down the road. The father ran to his room and locked himself in, taking a gun with him. Albert tried to locate his father and finally found him locked in his room. He tried to knock the door down to no avail and threatened to shoot his father if he didn't come out. He did shoot through the door, the father opened the door and they had it out. He shot Albert and Albert fired at him killing him. Albert fled to the timber on what is now Irwin Way's farm and taking inventory of himself decided that he couldn't make it as he was so badly wounded, so he pointed his gun at himself and shot.

The mother and wife Mrs. Young lived for many years with the other son but finally she hung herself in the barn.

The Lost Swiss

Storyteller unattributed, Browntown

A Rip Van Winkle tale is connected with the Swiss cheese region. In this county there lived a young Swiss, recently from the old country, who was employed on the farm of a relative. He was a hard-working young fellow but with a spirit for adventure. When not cultivating the fields or minding the cattle he loved to wander over the wooded hills or down the valleys of the surrounding country.

One day he found a cave in the side of a hill. Its entrance was blocked with fallen rock, earth, and brush. By hard work he removed these obstructions and entered the cavern. When night came and the young man did not return to help with the farm chores, his relatives were worried. He did not return on the following day or on the day after. A wide search was made for him but he was not found. It was feared that he had met with an accident or that he had been killed by Indians or wild animals. Months and years passed, but he did not return.

After fifty years there came to this locality a stranger. He made inquiries for certain people, but most of these had died or left the country. He told his story to others and was finally recognized as the lost farm hand. He had entered the cave and had become lost and wandered on and on in the darkness. At last, weak from the lack of food and several days of walking, he had come to an opening. He crawled out, half-blind, and found himself in a new country and among a strange people. These people were engaged in lead mining. They cared for him and he remained among them. His memory had gone during his hard experience and he could not remember who he was or where he had come from.

After fifty years the lost Swiss' memory had suddenly returned. Like Rip Van Winkle he had set out to find his own countrymen.

Tug-House Tales
Storyteller unattributed, Manitowoc

Ever see a seasick sailor? Salt water men who never suffered *mal de mer* on the ocean frequently become seasick on their first experience on the fresh water lakes. It was so with half of the crew of the schooner *W. B. Allen* when she went down to Manitowoc in 1880.

The *Allen* had been ashore on one of the islands in the lower end of Lake Michigan and when she was taken off in the fall of 1879 it was too late in the season to finish the journey to Chicago and she wintered in Traverse City. The *Allen* was in a leaking condition when the tug *Caroline Williams* put in a line on her in the spring but the pumps were able to keep ahead of the in-flow.

There was a 100-fathom tow line between the stern of the tug and the bow of the schooner. Off Manitowoc a gale came out of the northwest with a blinding April snow storm. The nine on the schooner couldn't see the tug, 600 feet ahead and by the same token those on the tug couldn't make out what was happening on the schooner. Solid seas boarded the vessel and to seal her doom the water swamped the fires under the boilers that powered the pumps.

The first intimation of anything wrong came to the pilothouse of the tug, when it was apparent that the tow boat was running free. That meant that either the tow line had parted or to save themselves those on the schooner had cut her loose. With the pumps out of commission the nine on the *Allen* knew that she never could keep float and had given themselves up for lost.

But they had reckoned without the fortitude of those on the tug. Although it was a dangerous maneuver, to turn and come back in search of the foundering schooner, and the *Williams* leaned on her beams end in coming about, nevertheless she came up on the lee quarter of the doomed *Allen*.

Half a dozen times the maneuver was repeated and each time the tug managed to come close enough to permit one or two to make a leap from the deck of the schooner to the tug. Then with the nine

"Lake Freighter," woodblock print by Beryl Beck, from *Superior Wisconsin in Woodblock*

safely aboard, the tug squared away and headed for Milwaukee, leaving the *Allen* headed for Davy Jones' Locker, long before the lee shore could snatch her.

But it was a sorry bunch of rescued sailors that put foot on the dock in Milwaukee. All of the salt water men were too sick to more than barely stand and some of them vowed never to sail the lakes again.

Hortonville Cache
Storyteller unattributed, Hortonville

The caching of various materials was practiced by the primitive peoples of America as well as those of Europe and of other regions. The usual method employed by the American Indians in securing some of their personal possessions was by burying them. Favorite places of concealment were in the vicinity of village and workshop sites, near watercourses and along trails, at the margins of springs and in caves, the hiding place depending somewhat on the nature of the articles to be secreted. In Wisconsin many caches of stone, bone, shell, and metal implements have been unearthed. One of these, a hoard consisting of a fine copper axe and two harpoons of the same material, was found in 1886 by a man engaged in quarrying limestone at Hortonville. The implements had been carefully concealed beneath several layers of rock slabs.

These implements, hidden in prehistoric time, came into the possession of the former noted Wisconsin collector Frederic S. Perkins of Burlington. No one will ever know why their aboriginal owner hid them as he did.

Badgers and Suckers
Storyteller unattributed, Dodgeville

The existence of lead mines in Grant County became known to the outside world early in the nineteenth century. There were miners

"Dynamiters," lithograph by Arlo Schmitz WHi Image ID 104856

here as early as 1822. The fame of the mines spread and the influx of miners increased steadily. Settlements were started at Wingville, Cassville, and Beetown. Those who came from the states farther south considered the country too cold to winter in and returned south at the beginning of winter, thus imitating in their migrations a fish called sucker; hence, the term "suckers" was applied to these men. But the men from the eastern states and from England and Wales could not imitate this practice and had to winter in the country.

Timber was scarce in some places and the miners made for their winter quarters dug-outs in the hillside, the lower sides built up with sod and stones.

By reason of this burrowing they were called "Badgers," and thus Wisconsin became known as the Badger state. Badgers are and have always been a rather rare animal in this state.

The Rio Wreck

Storyteller unattributed, Rio

On October 28, 1886, the fateful Rio train wreck occurred, resulting in the loss of a score of lives. A switch had been left open by a brakeman on a freight train which had pulled onto a side track to allow a limited to pass. It was going at a rate of from forty to forty-five miles per hour, which was then considered a high rate of speed. The switch light could not be seen by the engineer until he was within a few rods of it, and then it was too late for him to stop the train. The engine jumped the tracks, ran a short distance and stopped against the side of a bank and toppled over. The baggage car and the two regular coaches also left the tracks and were badly smashed. The four sleeper coaches kept to the rails; the last one was uncoupled and drawn away. With this one exception the entire train was burned, fire having started from the stoves and lamps in the smashed day coach. It was a most horrible and sickening spectacle. The night was made hideous by the screams of the burning victims, while the bystanders were unable to render assistance. One woman could be seen stand-

"Railroad Center," woodblock print by Beryl Beck, from *Superior Wisconsin in Woodblock*

ing in the middle of the car while the flames enfolded her. Dr. Smith of Chicago was the only one who escaped from the burning coach, with the exception of two small children whose mother, pinioned between seats, moaned, "For the love of God, save my children. I am hurt and cannot get out. Their name is Sherer, their home is Winona." She then passed them through the window to bystanders who cared for them until their father came to claim them. One was an infant a few months old and the other two or three years old. Though strenuous efforts were put forth to save the mother, it was to no avail, for her foot was caught in the seat and the flames driving about the would-be rescuers forced them to relinquish their hold upon her. She fell slowly back into the fire and perished, as did the other unfortunates, with much groaning and shrieking.

The charred remains of many of the victims of the wreck were buried in one common grave in the little cemetery at Rio where afterwards a small monument was set up by a relative of one of them. The monument may still be seen.

Coon Rock Cave
Storyteller unattributed, Arena

Old timers insist that there is a cache of gold and silver loot deep in the recesses of Coon Rock cave, seven miles south of Arena. It was supposed to have been the hideout of a crew of counterfeiters. The cave had several secret passages and false walls. Behind one of these the makers of spurious coins worked unmolested for several months. Finally the surrounding settlers drove them away. Their coin they transported down the Wisconsin to the Mississippi, where it was passed in river towns and on steamboats.

The descent to Coon Rock is difficult but one may still enter the cave. With difficulty one may follow the passages almost one hundred feet into the side of the bluff. After this distance the passage is blocked off abruptly. Beyond this wall, some say, the gold and silver ingots still lie.

There are other stories about this cave. In the 1870s one of the banks in this vicinity was looted by four armed bandits. Two days later these robbers were captured and shot. The gold and currency taken from the bank was never found. Two young farmers did some quarrying at the cave in an effort to recover the loot but with no success. A small kidnapped girl, Wizena Believer, was also once hidden in this cave by her captors. Here she was later found and returned to her father.

Such are the stories of Coon Rock cave.

Bogus Bluff
Storyteller unattributed, Richland Center

Not far from the river bank near Richland Center is a high, rugged, wooded hill which is called Bogus Bluff. According to a local legend, near the top of this bluff there was a cave which was tenanted in the seventies by a gang of counterfeiters. In the recesses of this cave, which was difficult of access, these men had a printing press. They printed paper money and also coined silver dollars. They had confederates, gamblers and "green goods men," who passed this money to unsuspecting travelers on the Mississippi River steamboats and in river towns.

The gang retreat was finally raided one night by government secret service men. A gun battle took place in which several of the counterfeiters were killed and others wounded or taken prisoners. Only one or two escaped.

At various times since the raid people have searched the cave for hidden silver and other mementoes of the counterfeiters.

The Thornapple Creek Feud
Told by Charles Robert, Holcombe

Around the year 1905 John Dietz bought a piece of land from the Chippewa Log and Boom Company. The property ran through one

"Storm over Wisconsin," wood engraving by Frank Utpatel WHi Image ID 53588

gate of the dam on the Thornapple Creek that was owned by the company. The land was surveyed many times to prove there was no mistake. Dietz thought it no more than right that he should be paid toll for the logs that came down the creek, but the C. B. L. & Co. [sic] consistently refused to do it. Dietz held back the logs for two years, during which time a feud between the family and the Co. raged.

The logging Co., rather than pay the 5 cents a thousand feet asked by Dietz, hauled its logs several miles overland and drove them down another creek at a price of four times what it would have cost to have paid the toll.

At various times shooting occurred when each tried to assert his rights. One time Dietz's daughter was shot in the hip while out getting provisions for the family. Another time the sheriff was killed and Dietz was reprimanded for the murder. Though it was not proven that Dietz killed the man, he was sentenced to Waupun. He served ten or fifteen years there and was finally paroled because of poor health.

When Dietz was sent to prison the C. L. & B. Co. considered they had won the battle and began driving its logs down the Thornapple Creek. According to the belief of some Dietz was right.

Elkhart Lake

Near the Sheboygan marsh near Elkhart Lake was the former cabin home of John L. Sexton, "The Old Hermit," a rather famous old educated recluse who was murdered in his home on the night of June 28, 1911, by Tony Umbreilio, an Italian who thought that he had hoarded money. The first school in the Town of Russell was taught by Sexton, who was, in 1861, also the first postmaster of the town. After his death large stacks of newspapers were found in his rooms. During his life he frequently wrote articles for Sheboygan County newspapers.

In the same region was the boyhood home of Francis E. McGovern, governor of the state in the years 1911–1915. Camp Brosius, on

Elkhart Lake, is the American Turnerbund summer training camp and is named in honor of George Brosius, noted Milwaukee Turner leader and instructor.

Horse Sense

Many years ago, in the vicinity of Ableman, Wisconsin, there was a large cliff that extended quite some distance from the rocks of which it was a part. The highway passed underneath this overhanging ledge. Supposedly to have been there since the beginning of time. People often sought shelter under this rock if a sudden rain or storm should happen. One day while driving his team along this highway a man saw a fierce storm approaching. Hastening his horses onward and hoping to reach the accustomed place of shelter under the ledge he was annoyed when the horses became very restless and it was very difficult to hold the reins tightly enough to make the horses stand. Finally he could no longer resist their pulling on the bits and they ran out from underneath the rocks into the downpour of rain just as the rocks crashed and fell into the road, obstructing the passage for some distance. It is said out of appreciation to his horses for having saved his life this man was unusually kind to them during the rest of their lives. This heap of rocks can still be seen where the man so narrowly escaped death.

Circus Tales

Romeo, the Thief, Is Apprehended
Storyteller unattributed, Delavan

Romeo was an elephant brought from England by the Mabie Brothers, to Delavan, where the Mabie Brothers Circus had its winter quarters. He was not the largest elephant ever to be displayed but at the time was considered the longest. Romeo made his debut into Delavan society some time around the year 1870 and had a reputation of being a "bad actor," due to his proclivities of occasionally getting loose and causing no little disturbance.

On one occasion the cook made several pies and when they were baked put them on a rack on the window ledge made for the purpose of cooling. Romeo, smelling the warm food, lifted the latch of the door in the barn and made for the pies. Everything might have remained peaceful, except for the cook, if the pies had not been hot. Romeo, in his haste to devour as many as possible before being caught, burned his mouth and in his pain and anger began to stampede. His trainer tried to calm him, but Romeo was mad and in no mood to be pampered, so Warren Jenkins was treed. Then Romeo set to work to pull down the small tree and teach his keeper a lesson in minding his own business.

On the property and connecting two buildings was a drop trap built for the purpose of catching animals who wandered from their private quarters. The trap would hold the weight of a man, but a heavy animal crossing it would cause it to drop several feet into a pit. It was across here that one of the men encouraged Romeo to chase him. The elephant fell through the trap as anticipated. They raised him by means of pulleys, and when he was back on level ground once more he was punished with hot irons until he "squealed." This experience kept the big pachyderm tractable for some time after that.

Big Charlie
Told by Colonel George W. Hall, Evansville

One of the interesting elephants of the circus world was Big Charlie, whose home for many years—when he was not on the road—was Evansville. He was owned by Colonel George W. Hall, veteran circus man, who made Evansville the headquarters of his show for fifty-four years. He took his last show out of Evansville in 1898.

Col. Hall acquired Big Charlie from the Ringlings, who let the animal go because he was regarded as unsafe to take on tour. At that time he was a member of the noted Lockhart Group of performing elephants, the first elephants trained to form pyramids in the ring. But Charlie had taken a dislike to his trainer, Earl Saunders, and one day attacked him. He knocked Saunders down, but fortunately for the trainer he rolled under a friendly elephant who protected him until he could escape.

When the Ringlings sold Big Charlie to Hall, he was carrying one thousand pounds of chain. Hall removed the chain and gave him to his daughter Mabel (now Mrs. Campbell of Evansville) to train and handle in the ring. Big Charlie was devoted to Mabel Hall and gave her perfect obedience. Once when the show was being loaded in New York harbor for Havana, Cuba, Big Charlie refused to go on the boat. Mabel was sent for. She walked up to him and said quietly, "Come, Charlie." He followed her onto the boat with the utmost confidence and gave no further trouble. (Mabel Hall Campbell is the first woman ever to have handled elephants and the only woman who ever handled a male elephant.)

Big Charlie was even bigger than the famous Jumbo owned by P.T. Barnum. He was nine feet high and weighed six tons. He became insane, finally, and had to be chloroformed. The colonel buried him on his home farm near Evansville.

A Python at Large
Storyteller unattributed, Evansville

Old Popcorn Hall of Evansville spent one winter in bed as a result of a broken hip administered by the wrath of his elephant, Charlie. Among Hall's circus stock was a 23-foot python and a marmoset, which he kept in the house to keep them warm. The snake was kept in a box behind the stove and woke up about once a month to eat. On such occasions he was fed a few pigeons.

One time the local doctor came to see how "Pop" was progressing. During his call the python woke up. Receiving no attention, he set about to create some. The doctor, hearing a noise coming from behind the stove, saw a blanket rising up over the top of the box. Soon the blanket stretched out over the edge and in a moment the head of the python emerged. The doctor made haste for the first exit and in doing so knocked over the monkey cage. Monkeys are frightened to death of snakes, and this little marmoset set a speed record in alighting on great-grandpop's picture, where he chattered the insult to anyone who would lend an ear. The room was vacated except for "Pop," the python, and the chattering marmoset; and the circus man, not being able to move, could do nothing but call for some of the animal keepers to come to his side. One man heard his calls, but when he found the python loose he refused to assist in re-incarcerating the wanderer. The scene that followed continued to be hectic, with the monkey, who had now transferred himself to chandelier, screaming and chattering as hard and fast as he could and with "Pop" swearing at the keeper, telling that **!!oo+! the snake was harmless, that Lou (his wife) had handled him hundreds of times and he hadn't bitten her. With threats and imprecations "Pop" finally induced the man to get the snake into its box. Picking him up, the snake struck its head against the helper's hand. Thinking he had been bitten, the man threw the snake into the box and ran out the door screaming after the fast departing doctor.

The Circus Parrot

Told by Dave Watt, Janesville

Dave Watt of Janesville, Wisconsin, an old circusman and former employee of the Barnum & Bailey shows, told the following story of a circus parrot:

This bird was Barnum's pet and sat on a perch at the entrance of one of the big ticket office tents. He was considered a valuable bird. One day he got away from the circus, no one knew just how. After his disappearance Dave and another circusman set out to look for him. They had a horse and buggy and drove through the town where the show had a "stand" making inquiries for the lost parrot.

At the edge of the town they heard a flock of crows making a lot of noise in a corn field. Tying their horse to the fence they went in among the corn to investigate the cause of the commotion and noise. There they found Mr. Parrot wrapped around a corn stock with crows flying all about screeching and pecking at him. Above the screeching of the crows could be heard the parrot saying, "Keep quiet! Don't crowd! One at a time please!"

Elephant Tricks Not in the Act

Told by Charles Hampton, "Baraboo Red," location unattributed

When the elephants retire for the night, the herd spreads out to such an extent that often there is not room for all to lie down. When this happens, the one left standing waits until his neighbors are asleep; then he reaches out a sly foot and stamps on the ear of the one nearest him. Up jumps the terrified elephant—and perhaps one or two others roused by the sudden commotion. This gives the guilty party his chance to grab himself a bed and let someone else be "It."

Sunday nights the show stays on the lot and invariably some mischief results in spite of the watchfulness of the attendants. Sometimes two or three elephants pull [up] their stakes and sneak over to the cookhouse where they eat all the bread they can find and any

"Wild Life—Bears," woodblock print by John Liskan, from *Superior Wisconsin in Woodblock*

orangeade that may be left in the barrel. If they are caught in their stealing, they run back to their places with guilty haste—and they usually get a beating.

The night attendants make a bed for themselves by shaking out seven or eight bales of hay to be used the next day and spreading their blankets upon it. They go to bed hoping that the elephants will sleep—so that they can, too. But more than likely they will soon be awakened by feeling their mattress slowly oozing out from under them. As soon as he sees he has been detected in his hay-stealing, the culprit shambles back to his place in the herd.

Coco, a little elephant which the Ringling's acquired with the Barnum circus, was a ringleader in these night pranks, and the cunning he showed was amazing. All elephants, when caught out of order, resume their places as quickly as possible. But Coco was not satisfied merely to be found in his place. He would slip his stake in just where it had been when he had pulled it out, and would even coil his chain around it. Then he awaited developments with the utmost composure.

Coco's superior intelligence was early recognized by his trainer, who taught him to mount a tub seven or eight feet high and stand on it on his hind legs. One day when he was being broken in to this act, Coco slipped and fell from the top of the tub. He lay on the ground dazed, and the man feared for a moment that he had been killed by the fall. But suddenly, Coco jumped up and without waiting for a command, he astonished them all by mounting the tub and doing his stand perfectly. Probably he had feared punishment for his failure; but he was generously rewarded for his success.

Jiggs the Chimpanzee

Jiggs was bought by Dr. C.G. Divigtil, one of the zoo's sponsors, from Ansel Robison, an animal dealer in California. He was one of the finest specimens of his kind that could be had.

Jiggs was about the friendliest animal in the zoo. He was a friend to everyone and could be trusted about the grounds without being chained. During the summer he was allowed to take hold of children's hands and walk about with them. He was an unselfish Chimpanzee except for one greed which caused a few tears among the smaller children, but many laughs from the older spectators—that was that no ice cream cone or candy bar was ever safe if he saw it. To him these delicacies were as much his as his cage in the monkey house and he would snatch them from their owners by fair means or foul.

Jiggs had one particular friend among the small children who were his admirers, and that was a little girl. One time when the child came to the zoo, Jiggs was playing around on top of a tree. It was his habit to go up a tree by way of the trunk, but he would descend on the outside of the tree, swinging from one branch to another. On this occasion Mr. Winkleman took the little girl to the tree and called Jiggs, who came swinging down to greet his friend. When he got to the last branch he hung by his feet and put his hands under the child's arms with the intention of taking her into the tree with him. He lifted the young lady about four feet off the ground, before his keeper interfered. The child was not frightened and would probably have gone on with the lark had it not been for the better judgment of the man.

Charlotte Greenwood

Charlotte Greenwood was a white-headed gibbon with a white face and hands, and known as the lowest form of the ape family. She was called Charlotte Greenwood by the keepers at the Vilas Park Zoo because her unusually long hands reminded them of that actress.

This ape was a male, despite the feminine name, but was called "she" anyway. Charlotte was as tame as her friend Jiggs, and like him was given the freedom of the park. She would walk about taking hold of people's hands and was as gentle as a dog. But after a while children began to tease her and she became cross and untrustworthy.

Charlotte Greenwood was also a performer of note. She had been known to swing around a bar 218 times without a pause, and then stopping for only a second because her attention had been diverted.

Another of her entertaining tricks of which she was quite proud was to sit on her seat and spin around like a top.

One time Charlotte Greenwood took leave of her home about 8 o'clock in the morning and set out on a trip of exploration. As soon as one of the keepers would think he had "treed" her she would jump easily as much as 40 ft. to another tree. It was not until 9 o'clock that night that the ape was caught. By then she had gotten hungry and the offer of a banana was too much for her. A courageous young boy delivered the fruit to the top of the tree and while Charlotte consumed it he got a strong hold on her collar, bringing her down the tree and back to her quarters.

Apes as a rule are hard to keep in captivity and die young, but Charlotte lived to be twelve years of age.

Elephant Annie

When Al Ringling gave the Madison Zoo its elephant, one of Ringling's bull trainers, "Baraboo Red" Hampton, was called over to the railroad siding near Coney Island to load the animal selected for shipment. It had been decided to give the zoo a middle-aged female named Alice and she was separated from the herd and boarded into a boxcar where Hampton left her for the night. The next morning the trainer was called again to come down and see the damage Alice had wrought. As is often the case, she had become lonesome for the herd and had smashed the side of the car and returned to the other animals. Thereupon it was decided that it would be more practical to ship a smaller elephant, and so a young female of sixteen years, named Annie, was successfully loaded and sent.

This was in July 1918. Annie's life story is not one of color and glamour. She was never trained for the sawdust ring, but had a more prosaic duty of pulling stakes and pushing wagons. Yet in the years she has lived in Vilas Park her gentle manners and good humor have given amusement and joy to a legion of annual visitors.

When Annie arrived at her new home she was put in the same

building with the lions and tigers and at first resented their growls and roars, but in time she became accustomed to her new surroundings and even became less lonesome for the herd as the attention of the public took her interest.

At times Annie would lose her good nature and become just a little less friendly to her admirers. At such times she would be given an oil bath in two gallons of oil to soften her skin and make her more comfortable; but though this treatment was soothing it made her cold and she would shiver and shake for a day or so afterwards. In 1924 the zoo solved the problem of keeping Annie completely happy at all times by building a summer yard for her. Here she could dig into the dirt to her heart's content. Every day she would give herself a complete mud bath and rinse herself off with the fresh running water that was installed for her special use. Since this time her skin has become softer than the oil treatments made it and she has not had to run the risk of catching cold due to them.

The only time Annie ever caused her keepers any inconvenience or trouble was one spring when she was to be moved to her summer yard for the season. There is a step down of about ten inches from her winter quarters to the ground and Annie refused to make it. She was coaxed and teased to leave, but would not budge. Finally she was forced out inch by inch with the help of a block and tackle. It was believed that she had stumbled on the step when she was taken inside the preceding fall resulting in her being afraid of it.

During the winter months Annie has a voracious appetite and thinks of nothing else but food. The zoo buys her food in large quantities and the cost of feeding her is about 65 or 70¢ a day. Each day she consumes 100 lbs. of timothy hay, half a bushel of carrots or 16 quarts of ground oats, 10 or 12 loaves of bread and all the peanuts and crackerjack the public will feed her. In the summertime the public's attention diverts Annie's attention from her stomach and she eats a little less.

Despite Annie's few human frailties, she is, in the words of her keeper, "one of the quietest and most agreeable elephants in any zoo."

Lumberjack Lore

Stories of French Canadian "Pea Soupers"

In the early logging days many Frenchmen came down from the Canadian woods to the lumber camps of the States and they were so addicted to their favorite food that "no pea soup, no stay in camp." This diet was for them what beer is to a German.

The following stories, with a few exceptions, have to do with French Canadian characters along the Chippewa waters.

Frank Bussier

Frank Bussier was an old "Pea Souper" from Chippewa Falls. He was a big man with a heavy beard and weighed 240 lbs. He was a very strong man and was characterized by the state of undress in which he generally went about. Sometimes his shirt would be half torn off or maybe one foot would boast a shoe while the other wore only a rubber.

Honesty was a virtue he chose to disregard when it interfered with his business activities. He used to come up the river, cut timber for a raft and make it himself. Then he would cut hoop poles for barrel hoops, pick up scraps of iron, and start down the Mississippi to sell his wares at whatever port he found a market. Where he found his scrap iron mattered not to him, whether it was a useful piece that belonged to someone or a stray piece he picked up. It was against his code to be scrupulous. Or he might steal some fat chickens and compliment the owner the next day on their excellent tenderness and flavor.

On one trip Frank made a raft at Little Falls Dam, near Holcombe. While he was cutting poles he found McCleland's camp with a cook stove in it. He broke up the stove and took it down river on his raft. In the meantime some timber estimators came along and saw him, and reported it to McCleland.

The camp owner met Frank on the street a short time later and said to him, "Frank, I heard that you were up to my camp and broke up my good cook stove."

"Sure, sure, Mr. McCleland. I smash him all to hell. I see your cook this summer, he tell me she no good for bake. She smokeum all the time. Every stove she smoke like that, she belong to Frank Bussier."

Frank Likes the Jail

One time Frank Bussier was jailed for some small offense. Incarcerating the law-breaker, however, didn't give the jailer much satisfaction, for the prisoner sang all day long and banged on the iron bars of the window. Not being able to endure the racket any longer the sheriff went to Bussier's cell and said, "Frank, you can go this morning."

But Frank had different ideas for he answered, "I tell you when I go. I got three day yet, and I play my piano some more."

Frank Steals Some Lumber

The Gilbert Company used to get cribs of lumber together at the mouth of the Yellow River, about five or six miles from Chippewa Falls. Going over the falls at Chippewa they would often lose some because of the rough waters. Frank was always on hand to pick up the stray timber.

When the timber got to Chippewa Falls the Company made Chippewa rafts of it, consisting of four cribs. Sometimes the lumber, shingles, and lathes didn't break up and accumulate fast enough for Frank, so he would put a pile of stones on a Company crib and sink it. Later when the cribs had gone down the river, Bussier would raise his and make a Chippewa raft for himself, take it down the river and sell it.

One time Mr. Gilbert met Bussier on the street and told him the company was losing too much timber and Frank answered, "What I got to do with that, Mr. Gilbert?" Gilbert asked him how much he would take to leave town.

"I don't know. I don't know, Mr. Gilbert."

"Well," said Gilbert, "if you will leave Chippewa Falls, Frank, I'll give you a Chippewa raft."

"My Crass," answered Frank, "what you take me for, Mr. Gilbert? My rotary she cut more than that in one summer. You give me Mississippi raft and I go." (The Mississippi rafts were many times larger than the Chippewa rafts.)

Frank meant when he said his rotary could cut more than that in one summer that he could steal more than a mere Chippewa raft in one summer.

Dipple Arrests Bussier

Though Bussier seldom drank and was never seen drunk, he decided one day he would play a joke on Dipple, the Chippewa Falls constable. He came weaving along the street as if he were drunk as a lord and met Dipple, who said, "You damned Rooster, you're drunk; I'll put you in jail."

Frank didn't resist the officer and they started off toward the jail. Dipple was a small man and as the two walked along Bussier pulled the policeman from one side of the street to another. They came to the basement of the old Tremont House and Frank picked his escort up bodily and threw him into the basement. He left him there and proceeded soberly down the street.

Pennenoe, the Cook

Pennenoe was a cook in a lumber camp and one time when he was in Chippewa Falls he decided to play a joke on Dipple, the city officer.

He pretended he was drunk, and as he anticipated, Dipple arrested him. But the cook was so drunk he couldn't walk to jail and Dipple had to employ a wheelbarrow for a "black Maria" and transport his prisoner to the bastille. Every now and then Pennenoe would roll to one side of the wheelbarrow and tip it over, so Dipple had an awful time to get his "rooster" to jail.

Just as they got to the jail yard, the cook fell to the side of the wheelbarrow again and tipped it over again, but before Dipple knew what had happened, the prisoner jumped up and ran like a deer.

The officer shouted after him, "I'll catch you again sometime, my Rooster."

The above incident happened in the early '80s. Dipple's characteristic phrase was calling everyone his "Rooster."

Mondieux Answers Some Questions

Log jobbers were always responsible for their logs until they got them to the main river. Here the companies took charge of them. Sometimes there would be several drivers on the same creek and some would drive faster than others. There would occasionally be accusations of one taking advantage of another and this sometimes [ended] in a fight or in court action.

One time such a case came to court and a pea souper by the name of Mondieux, who was a fine driver, was called as a witness. He was being questioned by a lawyer who asked him, "How long would it take a man to learn to drive?"

Mondieux answered, "It's just like this, Mr. Green. You know something, you learn pretty fast."

"For instance, Mr. Mondieux," asked the lawyer, "how long would it take a man like me to learn to drive?"

"It's just like this, Mr. Green. You know something and you learn pretty fast, but a man like you, it take a damn long time."

"The Cruiser," woodblock print by Marie Bleck. During the lumbering era in Wisconsin, cruisers scouted for timber throughout the North Woods. WHi Image ID 53594

Old Man Balille

Old Man Balille ran a stopping place near Radisson, at Balille Falls. One time he was coming down the river with a corpse in his boat and two lumberjacks who were sitting on the bank eating their lunch saw him as he rowed by. One called out, "Hello, Mr. Balille, what you got there, a corpse?"

Balille shouted back, "No, by crass, that's a dead Frenchman. That's old French Joe, she's got killed last night; she die this morning, four o'clock."

Balille Can't Log

A cyclone once came through the territory where Old Man Balille lived and pulled up his timber by the roots. At the time Colesh Allen of Chippewa Falls had a mortgage on Balille's cattle. A company man came up the river and stayed all night at Balille's stopping place. The visitor asked Balille, "Are you going to log this winter, Mr. Balille?"

"By crass, no," answered the logger. "The God Almighty, she's take my timber, and the Colesh Allen of Chippewa Falls, she's take all my cattle."

Pete Legault

Pete Legault was an old time logger and though illiterate he left a good sized fortune and a great deal of property when he died.

For a while Pete was employed by the French Lumber Co. The company owned a camp store at Ingram and Pete ran it though he could neither read nor write. When anyone came into the store and wanted something with which Pete was not well acquainted, such as a certain brand of cough medicine, the customer would have to point to the product and tell Pete the price on the bottle.

One time the company sent word for Pete to order several axes and a grindstone. Legault's letter contained a series of pictures describing his needs. For a broadaxe, he drew a picture of a large axe of the broadaxe variety; for an ordinary axe he drew a smaller picture. For the grindstone his artistic ability was limited to drawing just a plain circle. When the order arrived, it was complete except for the grindstone, in its place was a huge cheese.

The Wrong 40

Pete Legault once bought a forty of timber up on the Flambeau River and built a camp on it. An inspector from the Sage Land Improvement Co. was one time making his rounds to see that no timber was being cut on the company's property. He came upon Pete Legault nonchalantly cutting timber on their property.

The inspector said, "Pete, you're not cutting timber on your forty."

"By Crass, if this isn't my timber, then, Jees Crass, where is my pine?" asked Legault.

The inspector explained the mistake to the logger and told him that before he made out his report he would give him time to get to Eau Claire and buy the property on which he trespassed, from the company office. Pete did this and was saved from a grave offense.

The Mail Bag

Pete Legault had a camp out of Ingram and he took a crew of men up with him one fall. They had all their turkeys in the baggage car of the train and when they got off the train the baggage master started throwing them off the train and among them was a mail bag to be put off there. Old Pete Legault picked up the mail sack and started off with it. He couldn't read nor write and didn't know a mail sack from a turkey. The depot agent said, "Hey, where are you going with that mail sack?" Old Pete said, "Crass, that's my sack." The other fellow said that was the mail bag and asked him if he couldn't read "U.S. Mail" on the sack. Old Pete said, "U stands for Pete, and S for Legault."

Logging in Northern Minnesota

Urgel Legault, nephew of the old lumberjack character Pete Legault, ran a hotel in Chippewa Falls and made a neat profit on the side by staking logging contractors.

Bruno Vinette, a logger from Chippewa Falls, and considered a good one, met on one of his visits to Duluth a man by the name of Kennedy, who interested him in the Gibson Co. This concern was logging near Stump River in town 65 range 3E in northern Minnesota. Vinette went up to camp to look over the timber and stayed two days. Believing the proposition to be a good one he returned to Chippewa Falls and went to see "financier" Legault. The outfit and contract could be bought for $8,000. Legault put up the money without looking over the property, trusting the reputation and good judgment of the logger.

Ed LeMay was hired to take charge of logging operations and the drive and the outfit started for camp by boat from Duluth to Chicago Bay on Lake Superior. Men, horses and supplies had to be taken before navigation froze up.

LeMay's first work was to look over the timber so he could lay out the roads for winter operation. He was to locate the best timber first so that the partnership could get some quick cash returns. He started out one morning and when he located the timber he wanted to cut he found himself on a ledge so high he could look down on the roof of the camp below at a 45 degree angle. He saw at a glance that everyone concerned would lose money on the contract because of the high cost of logging such rough country, and wished he were anywhere but there. He returned to camp and asked Legault to go back with him that afternoon. By making some big turns and winding around ravines the two finally got on top of the ledge. LeMay pulled the diagram out of his pocket and showed Legault this was the tract picked to log first.

Legault paced about, scratched his head, and said in his French Canadian dialect, "Ha, ha, sacre goddam. You know, ha, ha, sacre goddam. Oui, oui, I have twenty thousand dollar in cash on bank. I look for hole to put him in. Now I think I have goddam good hole."

The contract called for the logs to be put into Pigeon Lake and it was planned by Legault and Vinette that a camp was to be built at MacFarland Lake and the logs hauled from there to Stump River where they could be driven into Pigeon Lake. LeMay suggested that it would be cheaper to drive them down through several lakes and sluice them into Pigeon Lake, but Legault, who was no logger, was adamant, so the building of the new dam and camp began at Mac-Farland Lake. Help was scarce, lumberjacks not caring to take the job because there was no way to leave camp after winter set in except by snow shoes along a trail of the shore of Lake Superior.

By November 12 everything was frozen up and on that day LeMay sent some men with a four horse team to MacFarland Lake to make a road and build the camp. The men had two tents, one for the horses and the other for the road crew and the cook. They had just gotten the ground cleared and the walls of the cook camp started when, on November 16, the first snow storm came. The snow started around seven in the evening and by morning 31 inches of wet snow had fallen. It broke limbs off of trees; the tents fell down in the night, tangling the men and horses in them.

The crew started back to camp No. 1, taking all day to make it with their teams. By then LeMay was certain it would not pay to go on with the new camp. It took eight days to open the tote road so that a team could get through to Chicago Bay, twenty miles away, and get supplies. By that time the cook was down to a sack of buck-wheat flour.

On the 8th day both Legault and Vinette came to camp and were very much put out to find the camp was not being built. LeMay tried to explain that it wouldn't pay, but all Vinette would say was, "By Crass, young feller, you get discourage too goddam quick. We're going to log."

So the new camp continued to go up and the next week 16 inches more of snow fell. Again LeMay argued that camp No. 1 only should be used and no more teams be hired. But Vinette wouldn't listen and started back to Duluth for more men and teams. He hired a tug boat with a barge, loaded 300 tons of hay and other supplies and started for Chicago Bay. On the way a bad storm came up and the barge had to be cut loose and the hay was a total loss. Vinette returned to Duluth; he hired ten teams of horses to be shipped by rail to the city, got another tug on which he loaded the horses, hay, grain and 5 tons of beef (half the amount of beef would have been sufficient), and started out again, only to run into another storm. This time they went into Two Harbors, Minnesota, for shelter and remained until the storm passed.

Logging was finally commenced at camp, but every other day it snowed and was so deep that an 8 ft. measuring stick would entirely disappear in it.

By January 1 there was so much snow that they had to cease logging. They hauled what they had cut and stopped work all together by the middle of February. LeMay stayed on with about ten men to build a driving camp and make improvements for the next winter.

The drive started about March 20 and the logs were all gotten into the river at a cost of about 16 cents a thousand. This was the only part of the operation that had any money in it and the irony of that was that the Gibson Co. had had about 7 million feet of lumber left to be driven but Legault and Vinette wouldn't take the contract when they were making the deal.

Legault lost his $20,000, while Vinette lost all his money and part of his farm. When Vinette came up to camp in the spring he said to LeMay, "By Crass, I wish I do like you tell me."

Jean Legase and Batiste

Batiste Trodeau and Jean Legase were two French Canadians who were fishing partners in Montreal. Jean thought there would be more money in the States so he came down to the woods and became a lumberjack. Here he remained several years, becoming very much a "Yankee Man."

Years later Jean returned to Montreal for a visit and went to see his former partner, Batiste. Arriving he said, "Hello, Batiste Trodeau."

"Who the hell are you, you know my name so good?" asked Batiste. "I never saw you before in my life. You look just like the Yankee Man. You was got the moustache cut off, the swallow tail coat and the chapeau casteu and the red tie on the throat."

"Why, I'm Jean Legase. I used to be your fishing partner."

When Batiste was convinced it was his old friend, Jean pried him for news on what had happened while he was absent.

Batiste said, "Old Pierre Bevine, she's dead. That old Frenchman, you know. She was 98 years old. Joe Le Courtier and Mac Corterier, she's dead too, and some more old Frenchmen, they ready for die too."

"Well," said Jean, "so that's all the news?"

"Crass, no, hold on, the Queen is dead."

Jean could hardly believe the news, but Batiste assured him it was true and asked if he never read the papers.

"I don't get much time, Batiste, for to read the papers. Say, who take the Queen's place?"

"Well, by Crass, Jean, I can't remember his name, what take the Queen's place. Let me see, that was 1, 2, 3, 4, 5—I think they was call him Henry the Five. Don't make no difference anyway. He was a Protestant son-of-a-bitch."

"Is that all Batiste?" asked Jean.

"Oh, no, hold on, Jean, the Pope is dead, too."

"Well, by Crass, Batiste, I am surprised for hear that. Say, Batiste, who take the Pope's place?"

"I don't remember that feller either what took the Pope's place, but I'll guarantee you one thing—that was no Protestant son-of-a-bitch what took the Pope's place."

"Crass, Crass, Catch 'Em"

With a loading sled with an 8 inch bunk, the lumberjacks were one day loading logs at the stump. They cut a road out to each tree and swung around onto the sled. Then the foreman towed it out into the main road and finished the loading there.

There was a Frenchman there who "couldn't talk English and wouldn't talk French." A big log was being moved in order not to tip the sled; the men rolled a log under the bunks to keep the logs already loaded on from tipping the sled. Charles Lee worked left-handed with his back to the back end of the sled. The ox team was pulling cross ways with a chain, loading on the log, and the French telling Lee when to grab the log with his kant hook, yelled, "Crass, Crass, catch 'em." (Christ, Christ, catch them.)

Then Lee would drive his hook in and set himself against the log. One time he grabbed too quickly and the log rolled too far. The Frenchman grabbed it, but Lee flew through the air into a brush pile on his head. The Frenchman said, "Done well, son-a-bitch, done well, son-a-bitch."

Pelke

The Frenchman who "could not talk English and would not talk French" was named Pelletier, but was called Pelke. He was from Canada and had no education. He was 25 years old at that time, and Charles Lee who worked in the same camp was 18. Near Keystone, where they were camped, there was a school house in the woods and the settlers gathered there Sundays to hear a travelling preacher. The young men of the camp added their lusty voices to the singing.

A cattle driver called "Old Stickney" had a comely daughter of 16 who attended the school and the lumberjacks told Pelke that she was a nice girl and he ought to go to see her. One Sunday they talked Pelke into going; however, Pelke's only pair of pants, a bright blue, were worn across the seat. The men patched these with pieces from a pair of red pants belonging to another jack in the camp. Pelke had a sheepskin hood which he wore every day, but the men thought this not good enough to go calling and found him a small skull cap which fit tightly on the top of his head, and made his face seem larger

"Cant Hook Man," woodblock print by Marie Bleck WHi IMAGE ID 104878

than ever. To complete the ensemble, Pelke had a Norwegian home-spun gray jacket, short enough so that the red tail lights on his pants showed up well. He had belting riveted on his shoes and his tracks were big as he started through the snow to see his girl. But the girl must have seen him coming, and though there were only two rooms in the humble cabin, he never saw her.

Frequently groups would gather in the school house evenings to hold spelling bees. The boys got Pelke to go one night and take the Stickney girl home with a lantern. He did, but the path was so narrow that they had to walk single file and the men never did find out whether Pelke walked behind or ahead with the lantern.

Beliell's Pet Dog

Before the game laws limited the number of deer a hunter could kill, many made a business of shipping venison to various markets during the winter season. Sometimes if one of the deer was wounded a dog capable of tracking it down was used. Such a dog was owned by "Old Man Beliell" of Belielle Falls and was one time borrowed by two strangers who had wounded a buck and were unable to track it down themselves.

Louie Blanchard was hewing a barn with a broad axe nearby when the hunters and dog came by. He had raised his axe and just as he let it fall the dog passed under it and was split in two. The logger swiftly gathered Tige up into a blanket and hastened as fast as he could to an old squaw who was noted for her herb cures. He told her he thought he had killed the best deer dog in the country, but that he was still alive when he picked him up.

Seeing the dog the Indian gasped, "You have made a mistake Mr. Blanchard. You have put the dog together wrong." Sure enough, in his hurry he had put the dog together with two feet on the ground and the other two in the air. However, the herb healer kept the animal for three months and he miraculously recovered. When he was returned to his owner Tige was the best deer dog to be found anywhere because of his great endurance—he could run all day without becoming tired because after he had run for a while on two legs he would flop over and use the other two.

Paul Bunyan offered Beliell $1,000 for Tige to be used in his Lake Superior camp but Beliell wouldn't sell.

Lumbering Lore

Mr. Herbert Hale, clerk of the Federal Court, was in the lumbering business from 1891 to 1922, located at Bayfield, Wisconsin.

Among the well-known lumbering companies in northern Wisconsin were Pike Lumber Company, Knight Lumber Company, Sprauge Lumber Company, Keystone Lumber Company, Cranberry Lumber Company and Dalrymple Lumber Company, also Corcoran Lumber Company.

Mr. Hale explained that the tote roads were those used to haul supplies to the lumber camp.

The logging roads were wider with a gauge of eight feet to be exactly in line with the runners of the logging sleighs. These roads always ran downhill to a loading point.

The lumber camps were always centrally located for convenience of unloading logs and supplies secondary.

One team of horses could haul seven or eight thousand feet of logs in good hauling weather.

When the hauling season began ruts were made and iced to conform with the runners of the big log sleighs. If some places on the steep hills were dangerous there were men placed at these places who would put a certain amount of hay or straw on the track to avoid any danger. These men had to be somewhat skilled. The foreman of this crew was called the "Straw Boss."

The ruts were iced with a tank sleigh all during the hauling season.

All logs were scaled at the end of each day.

The managers of a lumber camp consisted of the Camp Foreman, who was Commander-in-Chief, then the cook, who had complete charge of the kitchen, Timekeeper, Landing Boss, who had charge of the unloading, and top loaders, who generally could arrange logs on a sleigh in a very scientific manner. This work required skill in any man that did this kind of work. There were road monkeys who cared for the hauling roads, tote teamsters who hauled all the supplies of the camp and then the teamsters who hauled the logs to the shipping point.

In Northern Wisconsin years ago, hemlock, hard wood, cedar and pine were cut.

Before the first logs wore hauled to the lake for shipping, large logs called "head blocks" were laid at an angle at the bottom of the lake or river to hold the logs and then when they were to be hauled in the spring these heavier logs in the lake were removed and this forced the new logs into the lake. Sometimes they were dynamited to start them.

Dry ground logging and swamp ground logging were done differently. Swamp logging always took place later in the season.

Years ago generally the same group of men would return year after year to the same camp. The coming of the railroad brought many transients to the camps.

A tug boat can haul a boom of logs measuring about 1,000,000 feet. The speed of a boat hauling a boom is about a mile an hour. There is always an open space in a boom directly back of the boat, and this space has to be watched so as to not become very large, because that will force the logs into the rear of the boom and weaken it. This is regulated by the captain of the tug boat hauling the logs.

Lumber camps used to employ between two hundred and three hundred men. Absolute silence is required in the cook shanty and watched quite carefully in the "bunk house" (sleeping quarters).

The bar tender was considered the best friend of the lumberjacks in years gone by. When the lumberjacks would come to town the townspeople more or less ignored them. Sometimes their clothes were infected with vermin and they were considered more or less of a riff-raff class, or ostracized.

Mr. Hale explained how courageous and upright the real lumber-jack as a man really was. His hard experiences with his difficult labor, the severe weather he had to work in continuously, his loneliness in camps made a real soldier and he was often misjudged. The bartender acted as a banker, adviser in many difficulties, stopped many a man from making a fool out of himself when drinking. The many years Mr. Hale experienced with the lumberjack have given him a thor-ough understanding that outsiders may not have; and many atrocious stories of the lumberjack have been related which should have never been printed and are more or less untruthful, to say the least.

Logging camps were generally started during the first freezing weather and closed down with the first thaw of the spring.

Logging Crews

The size of a logging camp depended on the number of logs that were to be out. A big camp consisted of one foreman, 8 road teams (4 horse), 16 to 20 sawyers, 8 or 10 undercutters, 8 or 10 ox teamsters, chain tenders and swampers, 10 road monkeys, 12 road cutters, 9 loaders, 1 scaler, 1 stamper, 6 landing men, a shanty boss, 1 or 2 cooks, a cookee, a blacksmith, a wood butcher, and a tote team.

> Undercutter—His job was to look over a tree, superintend its cutting and determine which way it was to fall. He could determine within two feet which way a tree would fall.

> Skidding Crew—Ox teamster, Chain Tender, and Swamper.

> Swamper—The swamper cuts the road for the skidding team, puts the bark mark on the log and peels the end of the log that is going to slide on the ground.

> Sawyers—This crew fell the trees. Their tools consisted of axes, cross saws from 6 to seven feet long, a saw wedge and a

saw hammer to drive the wedges. Each sawyer had his small can of kerosene used to keep the pitch off their saws.

Skidding Crew—This crew got the logs from the place they were cut to the logging road where they were loaded onto the sled. Their equipment consisted of a go-devil to lay the end of the log on so that it would not gouge into the ground, a snake chain, bunk chain, and swamp hook. The crew consisted of a swamper, ox teamster, and chain tender.

Loading Crew—Consists of a top loader, ground loader and a tail man. For tools they use 1 or 2 axes, 3 cant hooks, 1 loading chain 80 or 100 ft. long and with a swamp hook on the end, and anchor chain and pulley.

Teamster—The teamster and his sleigh were responsible for getting the load to the landing. The sleigh had 4 corner bind chains on the end of each bunk and wrapper. Later a drop chain was used to fasten one of the corner binds. Then a wrapper chain went around the whole load.

Scaler—The scaler's duty was to scale, measure the number of feet in the logs and number them. Each number had to be recorded in a book.

Landing Man—The landing man had to unload the logs and stamp each one 5 times or more.

Jam Crew—In the spring when the loggers were ready for the spring drive, the dams were opened to give the logs a start down the river. The duty of the jam crew was to see that the logs kept from jamming or piling up in the river.

Rear Crew—The Rear Crew comes behind the drive with the wanigan (camp store) and all supplies.

Bateau Crew—The bateau generally had a crew of 10 men.

Two were boatsmen and the other 8 were peavy men who rolled the logs into the river and broke up the jams.

Scaler—The scaler was the time keeper and also took charge of the wanigan.

Sawyer and Skidder Competition—One or two hundred logs a day was not unusual for loggers to cut. There was always strife between the loggers and skidders to see which handled the most timber during the day.

Characters

Chickee's Pink Pills
Told by Bessie Bentley, Ashland

One evening after supper my grandfather told us the following story about himself and his partner, "Chickee":

We were sitting around the campfire telling stories after a hard day on the trail going from Duluth to Two Harbors. I was talking when I suddenly felt something hit me. I paid no attention to it but kept talking. But again I was hit, and then a third and fourth time. This was too much; I became very angry and jumped to my feet shouting, "Who is throwing things at me?" Bending down I picked up the offending missiles and to my surprise found they were vest-buttons. Perplexed, I looked around to see who could be guilty of throwing them. At once I could see that Chickee was guilty; also I could see that his guilt was unintentional. He had a queer bloated look and seemed in pain. We all immediately began to administer first aid, getting no help from him, for his tongue was so swollen he could not speak. Hours later he seemed to profit by our crude treatment enough to tell us that he had eaten the "pink candy entrusted to his care." At once everything was clear—those innocuous pieces were horse pills being delivered to a veterinary. We were glad Chickee suffered no worse effects, but nothing could stop us from chaffing frequently about the incident.

The Owl
Storyeller unattributed, Prescott

A well-known river hobo was familiarly known as the "Owl." Once when he was drunk, he jumped off the bridge at Prescott, Wis., spreading his arms and saying as he did so, "The 'Owl' has wings and the 'Owl' can fly."

On another occasion the "Owl" and two other hoboes, known as the "Camel" and the "Fox," were in a skiff which overturned and cast all of them into the water. To a party who came to rescue them, the "Owl" said, "Save the 'Camel' and the 'Fox'; the 'Owl' can swim."

The Neillsville Hermit
Storyteller unattributed, Neillsville

It looks like an architectural mishap, that small tarpaper covered hut out north of the "mound" wherein lives a man known to his countryside neighbors as "the hermit." He is an unkempt person, apparently of the most careless habits, and his abode is still less tidy. Yet there lives a man whose environment belies him, for he is a person of unusual attainments. He is holder of two degrees from the University of Chicago and his mental hobby is digging into the ancient classics printed in the original Latin, Greek, and Hebrew.

He lives in his little shack on the bank of a small trout stream three miles northwest of the city and spends most of his time in meditation and study.

He has not always been "the hermit." He came here 14 years ago with his wife and purchased 40 acres of land where his shack now stands and began farming. Shortly afterward his one child died and his wife went away.

The hermit was born in Watertown. He attended Carroll College at Waukesha and from there went to Beloit College and later to the University of Chicago, where he received the degree of bachelor of arts in 1905. A little later he received the degree of bachelor of divinity and took up preaching for a while in the Baptist church.

His devotion to his books is intense. He does much of his reading at night by the flickering light of pine knots burning in an open stove. He has no lantern. The smoke from the knots fills the single room and blackens everything, even the face of the ardent student. Neighbors say that they have passed by the little hut at 4 and 5 a.m. and have seen him still reading by the light of the stove.

Above the small rough table in the hut are a few board shelves and on these are piled the works of Cicero, Virgil, Caesar, and ancient Hebrew authors which he delights in reading. One book, a large Hebrew Bible, is practically worn out. There are other books there, borrowed from the public library and from the libraries of ministers, for, living as meagerly as he does, the hermit cannot afford to buy all the books he likes to read.

If one can engage him in a discussion of those classical works in which he is so interested, he will draw the hermit out of his reticence and will find himself a welcome visitor at the hut. He likes to discuss grammatical constructions and other technicalities of language.

Naturally there has been much conjecture as to the cause of the hermit's retirement from the world at large. Several attempts have been made by his neighbors to determine the reason, but these are all guesswork. Those who know him are certain that the separation from his wife did nothing more than present the opportunity to take up the life he now leads. It really seems most probably that his all-consuming desire to sink deeply into study and meditation over those works of Latin, Greek, and Hebrew led him to shake off the ties of the world and assume his lonely existence.

Bill Nye

Storyteller unattributed, River Falls

River Falls, the present location of a State Teachers College, was the boyhood home of Bill (Edgar Wilson) Nye, famous American humorist of a generation ago. Two of his best read books were his *Baled Hay* and his *Comic History of the United States* (1896). His first published volume was *Bill Nye and Boomerang,* which appeared in 1881.

Even in his boyhood Nye had a rare turn for saying humorous things. As he sat and whittled, his neighbors and others gathered about him to hear his droll sayings and remarks. In an old barn on the Nye farm place Bill Nye, George B. Merrick, and Bill's brother practiced circus stunts.

Nye came to Wisconsin with his parents from Shirley, Maine, in 1854. When a young man, he went to Wyoming Territory and there studied law and was admitted to the bar in 1876. Later he returned to Wisconsin and engaged in newspaper work at River Falls. He once traveled with James Whitcomb Riley on lecture tours. He died at Asheville, N. C., in 1896.

Prescott

This town was the boyhood home of George Byron Merrick, historian of the steamboating period of Upper Mississippi River history. His father, Laban Merrick, agent for the Northern Packet Co., 1855, had a warehouse on the levee. In this warehouse (upper story) George and his brother Sam had their sleeping quarters. There at night the boys slept, keeping an ear open for the arrival of the big and little river boats. They knew nearly every boat by its whistle and bell. George was so fascinated by river life that he took a job as pantry boy on one of the boats (*Kate Cassell*). Later he became an assistant engineer and then a cub pilot. His book, *Old Times on the Upper Mis-*

sissippi, was published in 1909. A state park near Fountain City has been named in memory of George Byron Merrick.

Prescott was also the home (1861–69) of the noted newspaperman Lute Taylor, who wrote the *Chip Basket.*

Hermits
Storyteller unattributed, Mayville

Herman Stroede, 74, and his brother Julius, 70, lived as hermits in a log cabin at the base of a ridge near the Horicon marsh near Mayville for a half century. The house in which they resided was old and rather dilapidated. It was surrounded by heaps of rubbish picked up from dumps and ash cans around Mayville and carted to their home by the brothers.

They died during a spell of very cold weather in January 1930. One fell dead of heart disease and the other died about two weeks later, probably starved and frozen to death. More than $700 was found hidden away on the premises after their death. The floor of their house was covered with corn husks to a depth of a foot or more.

The Giant of Gills Rock
Storyteller unattributed, Gills Rock

Allen Bradley, the so-called "Giant of Gills Rock," a pioneer settler of Door County in the late thirties, was a man of incredible strength. He is described as "a good natured, square-dealing person, more than six feet tall." He measured more than four feet around the chest, had hands as broad as shovels and was obliged to wear moccasins because no shoes could be bought that were big enough.

All of the old settlers knew him as "Old Bradley, the timber chap who lived like an Indian and could cut seven cords of body maple in a day." He was a leisurely fellow, a hunter, fisherman, and maple sugar maker. His feats of strength consisted of dragging heavy fishing boats up on the shore and lifting great rocks, timbers, and heavy barrels. He would allow a man to take hold of his thick beard and walk around a room with him hanging suspended from it. His home was at Gills Rock, formerly known as Hedgehog Harbor.

He enlisted as a soldier in the Civil War. Once he was captured by the Confederates. While being taken to the rear he seized his two guards and carried them back behind the Federal lines.

Bradley died at Sturgeon Bay, February 11, 1885.

Cousin Jack

Cornish emigration to the lead region in southwestern Wisconsin was important during the decade beginning with 1835. The extraordinary development of lead mining in Spain about that time rendered the less productive mines of southwest England unprofitable and drove hundreds of highly skilled pick and gad men to Wisconsin where they became a leading mining element. The "Cousin Jacks," as the Cornish were called, ranked as the most skillful practical miners, making good wages from diggings which Americans were ready to abandon. They gave a new impetus to lead mining. In 1850 there were 311 English (mostly Cornish) in Mineral Point. At Dodgeville one of the most important elements was Cornish.

The stone and wooden cottages built by some of these miners are still an interesting feature of Dodgeville. Many interesting and humorous stories are told in southwestern Wisconsin about the experiences and customs of these Cornish folk.

Mice in His Room

A Cornish miner once spent a night in the old Empire House at Dodgeville. They gave him a room up in the third story. After a while he came down to the hotel office in his night clothes to register a complaint with the clerk.

"There are two mice fighting in my room," said he, "and I cannot sleep." To this complaint the irritated clerk angrily replied, "What do you expect for $2.00, a bull fight?" and the reproved Cousin Jack returned to his bed.

The Last Five Cents

An old Cornish miner living in the Dirty Hollow mining district at Dodgeville was approached by his wife Ann for some money with which to make some small purchase at the store. Sandy was known to be pretty tight when it came to spending money for any purpose. Giving his waiting spouse a hard searching look he queried, "Where is the last five cents I guv you?"

A Rubber 'Art

Old Man Trelawney was a town character in Dodgeville. Nearly everyone knew the old gentleman. He was always ready to talk with anyone whom he met in his daily walks. While he lived, a cement sidewalk was laid in front of a store near his home. It was a very smooth surface. One night it sleeted, and converted this already slippery walk into a regular skating rink.

The next morning Old Man Trelawney, out for his walk, stepped off the adjoining wooden walk on to the new cement walk. As he did this his feet slipped, then slid for a few feet. He tried to recover his balance, and came down in a heap with a thump.

His spinster neighbor, Sally Trewitt, coming along just then, saw the fallen man and tried to assist him to his feet. She pleasantly remarked, "Uncle 'Arry, thee should hav'n rubber 'eels." "Rubber 'eels," growled the unfortunate man, "h'll need hay rubber 'art!"

No Results

Harry was a newcomer in the lead mining region. Having procured a pic, shovel, and crowbar, he was soon digging in a likely-looking knoll near his log cabin to locate some of the lead "hore."

After several days had passed, John, strolling up to the diligent digger, asked how he was making "hout." Harry had already done a big job of excavating, disemboweling the entire knoll with his pits and trenches, without any results other than the finding of a few burned stones and decayed bones. After meditatively surveying this work and its results, John said, "'Arry, m'son, thee 'er a gert fule. Thee'l find naw hore 'ere. 'Er diggin' in un o' those bloddy hinjun mounds 'ere always tellin' abaout!"

The Uncertainty of It

A Cornishman was tramping to town with a bag over his shoulder. He was going to buy supplies. In walking past the home of a settler he was suddenly set upon by a dog who growled and showed his teeth. While he was trying to defend himself against Towser by swinging the bag about, the owner of the dog called out.

"Jack, that dorg won't bite, 'es wagging 'es tail!"

"Hi know that," replied the Cousin Jack. "'E's waggin 'es tail at one hend end barkin' at the hother. Hi dsan't naw which of 'es hends to believe?"

The Mother Bird

Some Cornish folks from the Old Country came to visit some relatives at Platteville. They enjoyed their visit. One day the men decided to go hunting, so they secured an old shotgun which happened to be around the place. In looking for game they at last spied a pigeon seated on the barn roof. Just as one of them was getting a bead on the bird with his gun, a woman rushed out of the house and halted

172

the shooting by calling out, "Don't shoot, Cousin Jack, 'ur is the old mother bird!"

So the life of this pigeon was spared.

Za-ga-ko-min

Told by Bessie Bentley, Ashland

One day Za-ga-ko-min took his grocery order to the trading post. By dint of sign language he succeeded in getting it filled and was turning to go when the storekeeper said, "What name should I put down?" "Za-ga-ko-min," was the answer. Immediately the other replied, "The hell you have a cigar coming."

Honest John

Told by Bessie Bentley, Ashland

An old man saw his chance to get something for nothing one day when the storekeeper stepped out for a moment. Quick as a flash he grabbed a big chunk of pork and, putting it under his blanket, was just leaving when the owner returned. The man, seeing a big bulge under his customer's blanket, jerked it before the other knew what he was doing and said, "So, you're stealing my meat!" "Oh, no," answered the Indian, "I no steal, I'm Honest John."

Lazy Tim Wooden

Storyteller unattributed, Grafton

One of the earliest settlers (1839) of the town of Grafton was Timothy Wooden.

"Tim," as he was familiarly known to the old settlers, was quite a character. He used to say, when asked where he came from, that he didn't come at all but grew up with the country. From the originality of his character and the manner in which he used to thrive without work (he never denied being lazy) many were led to believe that

"Farmer's Holiday," engraving by Frank Utpatel WHi IMAGE ID 53586

he really was a favorite child of the forest. Yet with all his antipathy to anything requiring physical or mental exertion, Tim Wooden did succeed in acquiring considerable property. This puzzling trait in Tim's character is best illustrated in the following little story:

A party of Menominee Indians, who probably understood Tim's character, once enticed him to Menomonee Falls, now Grafton Village. They led him to believe that they wanted his scalp. They bound him to a tree and piled wood around him and with all the semblance of native ferocity made preparations to burn him. Tim was unmoved by these proceedings. The chief then whispered to him that as the whites had once shown mercy to him, he would cut Tim's bonds and release him and let him return to his home. He must promise not to mention his capture to anyone. "Walk twenty miles!" ejaculated the heroic Tim. "If you'll lend me one of your horses I'll agree to it!"

Catherine Stanton
Storyteller unattributed, Chilton

At Chilton was the site of the home of Catherine Stanton, a Stockbridge Indian woman of Narragansett blood. At an early date when the Indians of other tribes were unruly and threatening to burn and destroy the homes and families of white settlers, this Indian heroine mounted a horse and rode through the surrounding country warning the settlers to arm and be on their guard. Happily, the Indians quieted down and the war raid never got started.

Old Lady Fowler
Told by Inez Seston, Mazomanie

Mr. Seston tells about "Old Lady Fowler," who started a school. Tuition—50 cents a month—was charged at the Fowler school. Her husband was a preacher and Old Lady Fowler also preached quite frequently.

One of her favorite songs, which she had her congregation sing over and over, started out, "Can't you hear the devil a-howling, on that great day?" Rest of the song was an exhortation to sinners to turn and repent in order to escape the great fire.

Mrs. Fowler had a powerful voice and could be heard on still nights for miles around when she lifted her voice in song or speech.

One of her boys, John Fowler, became a great violinist.

Reverend Alfred Schuh
Told by Reverend Alfred Schuh, Monroe

Back in the '80s immigrants came to this country so fast that there were an insufficient number of priests and ministers to care for their spiritual needs. A letter was sent to the theological school in Europe to send students to take over parishes as soon as possible. Rev. Schuh came from Alsace Loraine with five other theological students. Upon arriving in Milwaukee he was immediately sent to Elkhart Lake where he stayed for 8 years. He then was called to Monroe and will complete his 41st year in this parish this year. His is the reformed church and he has the largest congregation in the city. When he started here his salary was the colossal amount of $25.00 per month.

So far this year he has confirmed 86, all of whom were in one class, the largest in the State, and he has baptized 104. His church records for marriages, births, and deaths have often been referred to to get pensions for widows from the Civil War up to the World War, for qualification under the Townsend act, to satisfy passport requirements, etc. He has preached 1500 funeral sermons and performed 1000 marriages. There are four generations in his own family and he has three generations in his church which he has administered to. Children which he confirmed are now grandparents, and still members of his congregation. He also has a congregation in Darlington which he has maintained for the past 30 years.

Rev. Schuh's father was a missionary in the Alsace Loraine Society. The society was so poor that they gave him to the Dutch Society

"St. Alban's Church," woodblock print by Beryl Beck, from *Superior Wisconsin in Woodblock*

who sent him and his family to Java. It took them 109 days by sailing vessel around the Cape of Good Hope to reach their destination. They were there for 9 years after which the father was transferred to the French Society again and was sent by them to South Africa for 8 years. Members of Rev. Schuh's family are buried in four different continents. One child in Java, two in South Africa, one in Alsace Loraine, and a brother in Milwaukee. The Rev. has confirmed 27 classes in German. Formerly all his sermons were preached in German but he now preaches only in English.

The Ghouls Club

Told by Charles E. Brown, Madison

Humorous song written by Even D. Flint (Past Redemption Flint), a Milwaukee "poet," rhymster and character of the nineties, sung to a guitar and mandolin accompaniment by members of the Ghouls Club, a quite noted musical and literary club of Milwaukee in those years. Their club rooms were in the old John Callahan building, then located on Grand Avenue (now W. Wisconsin Avenue) between Second and Third Streets.

The gory Ghouls Club has been here
And made a snatch at me.
I wonder why such fiends as those
Won't let a body be?

Don't come and weep above my grave
And think that here I be,
For they haven't left an atom
Of my anatomy.

Doodle

Told by Mrs. J.A. Beck, Location Unattributed

A man lived alone in a little square house on a hill.

The house had one window.

He built on to his house a lean-to.

Southeast of his home there was a pond.

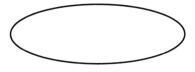

In the pond there was an island.

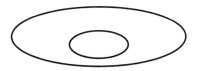

The old man went to the pond to carry water. He would go to the longer path . . .

... and return by way of the shorter path.

There were two tents south of the pond.

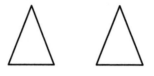

The campers went to the pond to fish, each taking his own path.

The layout looked like this:

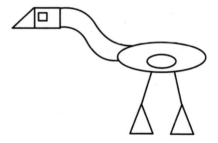

A Town Joke

Told by Bessie Bentley, Ashland

Frank and I were walking home late from the party. Talking about the fun we had had, we were almost to his gate when suddenly he clutched my arm and said, "Look!" pointing across the field. More by guess than knowing the direction, I turned to look and saw a queer light jumping crazily from place to place. Then I was scared because I knew that at last I was seeing a fire-ball. I felt my knees turn to water, but controlled my voice enough to say, "Let's go over and catch it." "Not without a gun," he said and I couldn't help being glad that his voice was as shaky as mine had felt. "Stay here and watch it," he continued, "and I'll get Charley's gun."

Not for anything in the world would I have admitted that I'd much rather go with him and take a chance that the thing would still be there when we returned. Instead, I muttered "all right" and saw him go, leaving me to a terrible fate.

Although it seemed hours to me that he was gone, he returned in about fifteen minutes with two other men. By that time I was nearly beside myself with fright, for each second had added the terrors of imagination of the first fright. Not trusting my voice, I grabbed Charley's arm and started with him towards the awful thing. Never was I gladder for human companionship than at that moment.

As we walked along I gradually regained my self-control even though I knew we were going right towards the danger and Frank, unable to get a gun, had only a heavy club for protection.

No one said a word on the way. As we neared the place we stopped and in whispers decided that two of us should go to the right and the others to the left so we could surround the fire-ball before it became aware of our presence.

By this time the awfulness of the situation was almost gone and I was filled only with great curiosity and a desire to get the whole thing over as soon as possible.

Frank and I, on the right, then proceeded and were getting pretty close. There went the thing way over by the woods and it went in! But soon it came out and—started right towards us. I shivered and felt Frank do the same, but we held our ground. All of a sudden I laughed, for I could see the thing was held by a person. Sure enough—there stood before us Jimmy Felton, the town's practical jokemaster, with a flashlight in one hand and baseball in the other. By this time the other two fellows had come up and Jimmy told us he had been chasing that baseball around for hours trying to get a fire-ball scare out of some of the citizens. We were much chagrined to find that we were the victims of such a hoax and have ever since melted sheepishly from any gathering where the subject has risen.

DAILY LIFE AND CUSTOMS

Oftentimes we take for granted what we eat, how we dress, and the routines of going about the average day. But WPA workers asked a number of interviewees about these topics, and Wisconsinites were more than happy to ply their listeners with a wealth of details about daily life and customs. These accounts cover a wide array of traditions regarding food and clothing, songs and jokes, building families, and burying loved ones.

Not surprisingly, food, being one of life's necessities, was the topic of many anecdotes Wisconsinites shared. Closely intertwined with food were the many feasts and festivals that various ethnic groups observed. Food was normally a part of the celebrations, both sacred and secular, but it was also the cause of merriment as people celebrated the completion of the grape harvest or the gathering of crops in the autumn. Marriage and family life also entailed celebrations and feasts, and an array of customs governed building a home, relating to in-laws, and caring for children.

Whether they fondly recalled the landscape of the old country or recounted how the land shaped work and home life, interviewees provided a compelling picture of the customs that brightened the lives of many Wisconsinites. Combining seemingly disparate elements—work and family, church and school, mealtimes and costume—these accounts showcase the everyday influences upon everyday lives, in the Old World and the New.

Daily Life

Menominee Indian Clothing

Told by Mrs. Angus Lookaround, location unattributed

The clothing of the Menominee before contact with the white traders was made of animal skins, usually with the fur removed. The man's regular costume consisted of leggings, the inner length of which was from crotch to ankle and the outer from waist to ankle, and attached to a belt; a breech cloth like an apron often having tabs both front and back; a coat-like skirt or a vest; moccasins with an ankle cuff or without. Fur caps and mittens, full-length detachable fur sleeves, full-size animal furs for wraps, were worn in winter. The woman's regular costume was a one-piece dress, knee-length leggings, and moccasins. Her winter garb was like that of the man. In summer it was customary for the men to wear leggings only and for the women to wear only a skirt. Children able to walk went naked in summer until approaching adolescence when they dressed like their elders. In winter their clothing was like those of the adults. Infants were wrapped in skins, the traditional rabbit-skin of the old nursery rhyme being an actuality among the Indians.

The leather clothing was not elaborate nor fringed, as commonly thought, for fringe would have been inconvenient on the clothing of dwellers of the forests. Some fringing was done, but most of the ornamentation consisted of dyed porcupine quills and the polished teeth and claws of animals. Embroidery designs were those of leaves and flowers or of figures having religious significance. Bone needles and thread made from fiber and deer sinew were used in the making of embroidery.

It is known that the Menominees made long cross-continent journeys for trading purposes so that metals and blankets and beads from southern and other tribes came into their possession. The earliest white traders brought cloth and the beads called trade beads. The Menominees were quick to make use of both so that the popular conception of an aboriginal costume is a beaded one with beaded belts and hair bands.

The elaborate feathered head dress was not used aboriginally by the Menominees for the same reason that they did not wear a great deal of fringe: i.e., this sort of gear would be an entangling encumbrance in the forests of their habitat. The feather head dress originated with the Plains Indians and was adopted later by the Algonquians for ceremonial and pageantry (commercial) use. It was customary for the Menominees to wear on their heads a band of fur with the animal tail attached and a feather or two according to the rank of the individual in the tribe.

It is said that the Menominees secured copper from the Ojibways of Isle Royale, for these Indians mined it after their own fashion. Copper ornaments were worn by the Menominee, and other ornaments of the trade silver were in use. Elaborate necklaces of animal teeth and claws were worn. Personal adornment was worn to show the wearer's prowess or tribal position and always had some such meaning. Bracelets and earrings were worn by both men and women. Women did not wear feathers unless they earned them, a feather to an Indian being the badge of attainment or of honor, as the medal is to the white man. In the summer women were prone to placing flowers in their braids. They used metal hair ornaments, also.

The leather of the Menominee costume was prepared by the Indian woman after their aboriginal habit of dressing the hides according to age and texture and of removing the fur or not as special uses dictated.

With the introduction of fabrics, needles, and thread by the white traders, cloth garments soon took the place of leather, for the Menominee women found that sewing the calico, linsey-woolsey, and the broadcloth which sometimes came into their hands was much simpler than preparing the hides. Change of clothes took place rapidly during that epoch. Probably moccasins were the last article to be exchanged for a modern one (for, indeed, the older Menominees prefer to this day their moccasins to shoes). While men still wore buckskin leggings, their shirts were often of calico. Women adopted full skirts with ruffles and a sacque-like waist. Children were put into a straight garment of calico. Heavier fabrics were used in the cold months when such fabrics were obtainable. The Indians seemed to have a predilection, however, for the red and green calicoes, regardless of the season. The Menominees, being on especially friendly terms with the *coureurs deu bois* and the *voyageurs*, many of whom had taken Menominee wives, prided themselves on being very up-to-date. This with their inherent conservatism produced some unique costumes, so that, in the early seventeen hundreds, it was not uncommon to see a Menominee attired in moccasins, leather breech cloth, red calico shirt adorned with bear claw necklace and strings of elks' teeth, his hair in braids, and a tall beaver hat, such as the American dandies of the period wore, upon his head. If the weather were cold, he might have a bear or badger skin across his shoulders. Indians prized shawls and secured them in trade in the earliest years of the trading era. Because the Menominees were very dexterous in handiwork and anxious to be "modern," the women were able to make unusually attractive garments of the cloth brought in to them. Today, the Menominee woman considers her tribal costume to consist, not so often of a buckskin dress, as of a full skirted and beruffled gown having a separate sacque of another color, many strings of beads, earrings, bracelets, a beaded head band with a feather, a shawl, and moccasins. The man of the tribe, dressing for a ceremonial, is likely to consider it appropriate to wear "store" trousers, a cotton shirt, an elaborately beaded buckskin vest, beaded and fringed arm bands, a leather breach cloth, feathered head dress, and moccasins, and such trinkets as he happens to possess. Buckskin costumes are much prized, but they are possessed by few Menominees today.

Buckskin costumes and cloth costumes made by the Menominee women in early times may be seen in our museums. They testify to the skill, versatility, and progressive tendencies of the Menominee Indians.

Life in France
Told by Constant and Gustavus Lamboley, Belleville

The trip of the Lamboleys from France was typical of what such immigrants had to forgo. The price for the two adults and four children was about $70. They came on a sailboat and it took 48 days on the water. There was no food furnished and each family had to supply themselves with sufficient to last the entire trip. Cooking was done on the deck. A long trough like a hog trough had coal in it and it was over this that the cooking was done. There was much fighting at every meal time among those who were and those who wished to cook over the flames. Kettles would be pushed aside and often times upset. In their first home in this country they often had to drive snakes, skunks and woodchucks out of the house. When Gus was first married he had absolutely no furniture for his home. Constant made it all from poplar by hand. He was the mechanic of the family. . . .

The threshing was done with a flail by hand. It cost too much to have wheat bread so they would make some of a mixture of wheat and barley or oats or both. . . .

All the people in St. Germain wore wooden shoes even in the coldest and snowiest of winters. The boys learned the art of being able to kick their shoes off so accurately that they could strike almost anything from shins to other targets with them.

Pipes were smoked considerably by the natives and peasants. A flint would be struck against metal to make a spark which would light a rag or tinder held under the metal. This burning tinder would then be transferred to the bowl of the pipe. Tobacco was very cheap in Switzerland, which was only about 47 miles from St. Germain, but it was very high in France due to the import duty. An acquaintance of the Lamboleys would smuggle it across from Switzerland and often hid it in their manure pile while trying to get it further into the country.

The peasants walked everywhere, for only the ministers had horses and carriages. If any of the farmers had the money to own a horse they never had more than the one for the tax on two of any-thing was prohibitive. The farm work was done with oxen which were worked for so long and then sold to be butchered. The cows were also used in the fields.

Hemp was raised, beaten and broken into thread and from this the women made clothes for the entire family. The Lamboleys lived in Hunte Saone, near Lure. The village of St. Germain is not shown on the map. They were a day's walk from Switzerland and 160 miles from Paris.

In this little village of St. Germain the people had their own trades. The cows and other stock were fed by hand and did not graze except if led on a rope by the side of the road. Before the revolu-tion of 1786 the people were all vassals to lords and had no title to their land but had to spend so much time serving the lord in return for having the land, or they had to pay rent in the form of produce. Cruel injustices resulted in the revolution, after which the land on the huge estates was parceled out to the former vassals and they were given title to it, and ownership continued in the family from father to eldest son. The women would sell eggs, raise a hog or two to sell and perhaps a calf, or wheat, potatoes, carrots, etc. They had no corn. . . .

Baking was done in a community oven, which was used turn about. A few had their own ovens.

Wood was obtained by taxpayers only and the more taxes one paid the more wood in proportion was given him. The government owned the woods which were supervised by a supervisor and a local forester. So much brush and log was allotted to each taxpayer. The forester marked and supervised all trees for cutting and each fallen tree was immediately replaced by a young sapling. Every 25 years there is a complete turnover in trees in these woods.

Taxes were big because France had to have a large army and good roads.

Boys had to draw numbers at 20 to see if and what branch of the national defense they had to serve in. Each village had an allotted number which they had to furnish. If there were more eligible than needed the ones who drew the high numbers were exempt. The numbers from the number needed down had to report for service. Those who drew lucky numbers would often sell themselves for service for someone who had drawn a lower number. There were a few exemptions from service, such as the eldest son of a widow woman. Seven years was the usual number for service. Two years would be served the first time and the number would diminish until the man reached 45 and then he would not have to serve any more. After the drawing of the numbers there would be a big celebration and everyone would get very, very drunk. . . .

The people of St. Germain are all farmers and live in little villages from whence they go to tend to their soil and crops and herds. The children take care of the flocks and watch over them.

Three main meals were served a day, but the men took lunches for both morning and afternoon with them to the fields. These consisted of anything from soup through meat and potatoes, fruit and vegetables.

The French had very little meat.

The baking for the household was done outside in brick ovens.

They made their own wine as they had an abundance of fruit. Wine was served daily with the meals except breakfast.

The families made their own cloth and clothes. Mrs. Lamboley's father did the weaving and his wife the sewing.

Wooden shoes were worn in St. Germain. One man in the village would make them and sell them to the rest.

They did not have sheep, so had to buy their wool, but they did raise flax and cotton.

The crockery was much the same as we have, but the spoons were of pewter.

The men were their own barbers and the women did the hair cutting.

There were church services on midnight of Xmas Eve. There were no presents exchanged. Everyone wore new clothes if they could afford them, but their very best at any rate. The celebration was merely in going to church and having a few extra things to eat.

New Year's everyone called on everyone else and wished them Happy New Year.

Children were baptized as soon as possible after they were born.

The French believed that all ailments came from the stomach, so the home remedies concerned themselves with fixing the stomach. Mrs. Lamboley's mother grew many herbs in her garden which she used to brew tea for headaches and colds, etc.

The Swiss
Told by Anna Baumann, Monroe

Bach Canton in Switzerland speak a different dialect. Mr. Baumann, Anna's father, is from Canton Berne, and the house which he was born and lived in was erected in 1604 and is still standing and still occupied. The Swiss built for permanency and durability rather than for appearances and convenience.

The Swiss of a generation or two ago were very superstitious about planting crops and things pertaining to the farm. Potatoes had to be planted at a certain phase of the moon, as did other crops. Sauerkraut had to be made when the moon was waning, otherwise it would rise instead of settle. . . .

In the days before the modern dentist the Swiss had a method, which was quite unique, in extracting teeth. The party afflicted would go to the neighbor's house and sit on a lower step. The neighbor would sit above him, clamp the patient's head firmly between his knees and using an iron hook would pry the offending tooth out, for which he would charge 20 centimes or 4 cents. . . .

A *braenti* is used for carrying the milk down from the alpine pastures. It is shaped much like a flask, except much larger, and has straps which fit over the shoulders and under the arms. It is tin.

The children keep up with their elders in doing the hard work. There is no hectic rush to get things done but the people steadily plod along getting their difficult tasks done by doggedness and determination and a great deal of patience. There are few of the Swiss who ever have nervous breakdowns.

In the fall when the cows are brought down from the pastures the owners are all at the village to meet them, claim and take them home. . . .

Barns were always built onto the houses and the cow and livestock kept in it. The barn and the stock were always immaculate. In this country such a thing is unthought and unheard of.

The two churches of Switzerland, the Catholic and Protestant, were supported by the state and their priests and ministers received their salaries from the state. This permitted and developed a very intensive religious training for the very lowest classes. All were drilled and drilled on the Bible and families always said grace for each meal and had family worship several, if not all, nights of a week. . . .

The lower classes treat their women the same as hired help and sometimes not even that well. The women not only do the housework, cooking and raising of children but have to go into the fields and work with the men at men's work. Some actually help pull the plough. There still are some sufficiently old worldish that they walk behind their husband when uptown with him.

Each community has its own industry. In the Berne mountains one finds very wonderful wood carving. In parts of Appenzell there is beautiful lace making. . . .

Dorothy Potter notes, location unattributed

In Switzerland each canton, of which there are thirteen, has their own distinctive costumes. The many differences between people in the different cantons have arisen from a geographical circumstance—

the same as in Norway. The mountains in the olden days formed barriers which confined people to their own little valleys and communities. They developed their own particular kind of speech, dress and habits. The occupations too differ in the different cantons. Some are herders, others work in the vineyards, others are carvers and so on so the costume also varies with the occupation. A national dress has been considered for Switzerland but it was overruled, as the different dress of the thirteen cantons are beautiful, individualistic and historic, so they have been retained. In the past few years with modern habits making inroads even into the little alpine homes and villages the old costumes have gradually fallen into disuse. A national movement has been started to revive and perpetuate these. They had been degraded to the point where they were being used as costumes for waitresses. The wealthy and prominent Swiss began a campaign to revive the authentic costumes which were being disfigured by incorrect and nonusage. They employed a costume association who hired artists to study and suggest modernization. A national Swiss Costume Festival was inaugurated which is held every five years in a different city in Switzerland. A parade is held in the afternoon in which the cantonal representatives march together depicting, by their dress, the three or four different costumes used in their canton. In 1931 the Festival was held in Geneva. . . .

On a Sunday night in February fires are lit on the heights and hills of Broye which overlook the lake of Neuchatel. This is to celebrate the first movements in the awakening earth. This occasion has been planned for by the cooking in frying pans of fritters and marvels. At dusk, brass bands march by, followed by hordes of children carrying lanterns, repeating the chorus "These are the torches of the town of Yverdon." . . .

In Bern, where Mrs. Schenkel lived, the house and barn are built together and of wood. The basement is used for storing the potatoes, vegetables, apples, schnapps etc. The first and second floors are for the family use and the attic is used for storing the grain after it is cut and before it is threshed. There is too much rain to leave the grain in the fields after it is cut so they stack it in the attic until fall or winter when the men have more time and can thresh it. . . .

Every three months a man comes around and cleans the chimneys whether you want him to or not and if the house is not safe, if it has bad wood around the chimney etc., the owners cannot get insurance, which is compulsory by state law. . . .

Told by Dr. and Mrs. Sylvin J. Francois, New Glarus

Mrs. Francois's father had neglected to keep up his correspondence with his relatives in Switzerland so he knew very little about who was living and what had taken place. He decided to take a trip back there and see who was still alive. He got off the train and started for the place where he had lived and encountered a man with a long gray beard who turned out to be his brother. They went to his home, which had been his father's, and celebrated. They brought from the basement a bottle of wine, which he had won as a boy at a shooting match, which they had put away and said they would not open until he came back. When they had emptied the bottle they filled it with water and put flowers in it.

There is no school on Tuesday or Friday afternoon here either but they do go to school all day Saturday. On the afternoons off they go for a hike with their teachers.

No women take part in the shooting contests which are part of the Sunday recreation.

The house in which her father lived in Switzerland has been occupied by his ancestors since 1700 and up near the caves was painted the family crest. They were millers by trade. Their names were Truttman and their home was in Kussnacht am Rigi from whence came William Tell. . . .

Doctors' wives are considered quite elite and above doing their own work. They have to have two or three maids.

Her father brought over with him a pair of shirt studs of gold with a leaf etched on each which he wore for Sunday and special occasions.

The washing is done about twice a year and 4 to 5 women are hired to help. Two rub while 1 attends to the boiling and the other two do the hanging and taking down when dry. This takes two or three days. When the dirty clothes are put away in hampers they are sprinkled with ashes to kill the odor and prevent mildewing.

A girl has no chance of getting married in Switzerland unless she can furnish all the linen and bring some money. The man makes no bones about asking about this before becoming engaged.

In the last week in June there is a rose carnival in which the girl receiving the most roses is crowned the queen.

Zurich and Lucerne have a celebration on July 4 for the Americans.

They use feather ticks for blankets. . . .

Told by Freda Marty, Monroe

The inhabitants of Appensell Rhoden are so very proud of themselves in character and physique that intermarriage is a common thing. The headdresses of most of the women throughout Switzerland are made of horsehair.

The mountain called Pilatein Switzerland obtained its name from the story that Pilate fled to that mountain after the crucifixion.

In Underwaldner-Trachten, which is the home of William Tell, the costume for the men is the same as history says William wore the day he shot the apple from the boy's head. . . .

Dorothy Potter notes, location unattributed

The Swiss are a very frugal, careful and economic race. They buy with a great deal of consideration and thought and almost always pay cash. They are little given to luxuries. Their homes are very plainly furnished and the homes themselves are never ornate—they are simply plain honest to goodness homes. They are kept immaculately clean as are the clothes and persons of the members of the families. The yards and out buildings and fields of a Swiss family are always tidy and well cared for.

Swiss is still the common language in the stores, banks and on the street. As a whole the people are very kind and willing to help. They are not an emotional people but are neighborly and kindly disposed. . . .

A great many of the Swiss are Masons and Eastern Stars. It seems that almost all who are not Catholic belong to the Lodge.

All the children say hello to you whether they know you or not. The older people will always smile but won't speak unless you do. . . .

In most homes there are an abundance of potted plants. Most of the women have an awful habit of having grotesque bouquets of awful artificial flowers in their homes. Every room in this hotel, which is run by a Swiss couple, has such a floral decoration therein. Ugh. My room is a good illustration of the taste in colors of the average Swiss. The woodwork is painted a delicate shade of blue, the wallpaper is pink roses with blue stems on a cream background, and the floor is covered with a green and brown congoleum with small rugs a different color of green. The curtains are white with yellow dots, a pillow reposes on the chair adorned with all the bright bits of cloth available in this country I am sure, my bouquet is of feathers and leather and crepe paper in a tin vase and the tray is an old fashioned couple doing a minuet or something under a flowering apple tree. I shall bring smoked glasses next time!

Many of the school children speak German very well and in most of the homes the common language is German. . . .

Told by Mary Saxer, Belleville

In Mrs. Saxer's community they only washed twice a year. An extra washwoman would be hired to come and help the women of the household. The clothes would be boiled for an hour before washing. In the city the families would make an appointment with the local laundry house for a whole day. They would then go there with their washing, use the machines and water there and do their washing. They paid so much for this use, and there would be several people there to help with it.

The men wore corduroy clothes and dark shirts.

In some communities one woman would take in washings and another would do the ironing. Another woman would specialize in laundering men's good shirts. These shirts were white with many pleats in the front with stiff collars and cuffs. They were a lot like our full dress shirts. They charged 5 cents apiece for them. Some of the shirts would be made of a soft knit material except for the front, collar and sleeves. Other men would wear just the fronts, collars and cuffs and keep their coats on.

In Belgium

Told by Dr. and Mrs. Sylvin J. Francois, New Glarus

The entire population of Belgium is Catholic and the schools are parochial with separate ones for the boys and girls, who are taught by nuns. They have school on Saturday but none on Tuesday or Friday afternoon. On the afternoons off the children usually go by train somewhere for a picnic. There are few cars in Belgium and most of the traveling is done by train.

There are signs posted in Belgium for keeping off the grass, no smoking etc. and they mean what they say—they are rigidly enforced and violation means a fine. . . .

All the houses are of stone with tile floors. At a certain hour each and every afternoon the women and maids scrub their floors. This is done even on Sunday.

As a whole the Belgians are very thrifty and hard working and most everything is done by hand for there is little machinery. All the sowing and reaping on the farms are done by hand.

The people wear leather shoes for the street but as soon as they get into their home they change to their wooden shoes which they think are very much more comfortable.

The stoves are round and stand on legs. Bundles of twigs, called fagots, are used for fuel. These are purchased from what we would call a fuel dealer.

Each town has a Kermis Day which is a local celebration much the same as our carnivals where there are concessions and entertainment. This lasts several days. . . .

Most of the decorations and niceties of the home are hand made. They have crocheted lamp shades with red and green beads on a white pattern, shopping bags are of cellophane and the curtains have a deep crocheted insertion and then a knit pattern above that.

The pear trees are planted next to the house so that they grow up the side of the building and are wired to it.

All the windows are the French type and open inward.

At specified times the owners of the huge Belgium draft horses bring their horses to the town and show them, running, trotting and posing them. They seem to compete for places. . . .

The clocks in Belgium and Switzerland are numbered from 1 to 24 and all train schedules go accordingly.

The hose is made of artificial silk and does not compare with ours. . . .

In Belgium the clothes are soaked, washed then boiled, rinsed and laid on the grass to bleach. They are then rinsed again and then hung up to dry.

Sweden

Told by Elfreda Zweifel, New Glarus

Women above 75 always wore a square of silk folded over the head under the shawlette for winter wear. It was black. . . .

The mangles which I described in a previous report of an interview with Mrs. Zweifel were often privately owned and the friends

"Spinning Wheel," drawing by Arlo Schmitz WHi IMAGE ID 53585

and neighbors of the owners would reserve certain hours for the use of it to press their linens and would pay a few cents for the use of it.

When it was time to gather the flax the owner thereof would have a bee. It would first be cut and dried and then placed on a stand around which the members of the bee would sit and pound it to get the fiber out. . . .

Usually the Swedish couples are engaged for half a year. They exchange rings, each wearing a plain gold one on their right hand which is changed to the left when they are married. It takes weeks to prepare for a wedding as the whole house has to be scrubbed and enough baking done for the guests, who will stay from 3 to 8 days. The wedding ring is worn on the left hand because it is closer to the heart.

Putting blue paper with white cloth or crocheting will keep it from yellowing and will keep it white.

Czech Lands
Told by Stephen Kliman, location unattributed

Spinning occurs in the winter. The women and girls meet at different homes, much as our American forebears gathered for the sewing and quilting bees.

Each girl sits on a flat board, to which is attached a staff with the hemp or flax tied to it. With one hand she pulls the hemp, twists it into a thread, moistens it with her lips, and winds it on the spindle, a little wheel on an axle held in her other hand. She keeps this up for hours, her tongue wagging incessantly, until she has spun two or three hundred yards of thread. The hemp or flax disposed of, the women turn to the goose feathers, stripping the down from the ribs. The pile of down reaches to the ceiling, a signal for the incorrigible practical joker to blow pepper in the air. A light supper is served, with tea or coffee substitute, made of roasted wheat or corn.

Food and Festivals

Cornish Pasties
Storyteller unattributed, Shullsburg

A girl from the lead regions was telling some associates about how the old Cornish folks in her home neighborhood made the very toothsome and nourishing pasties.

She explained how they cooked the meat and vegetables and enclosed those in pie crust. These pasties, she said, the men wrapped in a newspaper and put in their inside coat pockets when they went to work, to keep them warm. One of the girls who heard this afterward went to Louisiana to teach school. There she told her pupils about these Cornish pasties and how they were made. Later she received a note from the mother of one of the girls asking how to prepare those meat and vegetable pies "which the Cornish miners cook in their shirts."

Watertown Geese
Storyteller unattributed, Watertown

Geese prepared in various delectable ways and dishes have always been a favored food of Wisconsin Germans. Among these are roast goose, goose breast, goose liver, and goose sausage. Over these viands Teutonic epicures smack their lips. The city of Watertown, located on the Rock River midway between Milwaukee and Madison, is widely famed for its geese. These particular birds are prepared for the market by being artificially stuffed and their weight and the fine flavor of their flesh thus increased. Cooked noodles are every day crammed down their throats by their owners, a wooden pestle being used for this purpose. Geese have been hatched and herded at Watertown since the earliest years of its settlement by Germans (1846–47).

This Wisconsin city has also won fame as the early home of the 48er Carl Schurs, distinguished soldier and statesman, and of his wife, Mrs. Carl Schurs, who in the year 1855 established here the first kindergarten in America.

The Nice Old Lady

Years ago Mr. Brown was collecting mushrooms in the woods at the northern city limits of Milwaukee. He had picked up a fine, fresh specimen of the giant puffball and was walking along with it under his arm. On the woodland path he met a very nice old lady carrying a basketful of mushrooms.

When they met she halted him. She noticed the puffball in his hand. She said that she hoped that he was not going to eat the thing he had under his arm—it would make him sick—they were poisonous. She tried to take it from him to throw it away. She only let him keep it because he promised that he would not eat it—he was collecting it for a specimen to be exhibited at the Milwaukee Museum. That satisfied the nice old lady and she went happily on her way. SHE HAD SAVED A HUMAN LIFE.*

Tore His Pants

Farrand Shuttleworth, local attorney, one day found a huge hydnum or spiny mushroom growing high up on the trunk of a shade tree.

He went to the house and told the lady that there was a "poisonous" fungus growing in her tree and asked permission to get it. This she readily granted.

He and his friends had a real feast on this huge white cauliflower-like fungus that night. For several years afterward in the mushroom

---

* The giant puffball is, in general, edible, if prepared at the right time in the mushroom's life cycle.

season this tree yielded other fine specimens of this same fungus, and Farrand got them. One year he tore his new trousers in getting it. Finally the owner had the tree chopped down. Away with Farrand's future golden mushroom dreams.

The Charles Browns

Charles E. Brown knew mushrooms. His friend Charles N. Brown, a botanist, had no knowledge of them.

People began to bring mushrooms to Charles N. for identification. They came in increasing numbers. So Charles N. had to learn about mushrooms himself—he said "in self-defense."

The Expert

George Nelson one day made the mistake announcing that he was an expert on mushrooms. A *Daily News* reporter heard of this and inserted an item in the paper telling of George's gifts. It carried a word of caution and advised all local mushroom hunters to see George before eating any fungi they did not know.

The next morning when George reached his office there were

White mushrooms on the table
Round mushrooms on his chair
Brown mushrooms on the bookcase
And others everywhere.

A woman of foreign extraction was one of his first visitors. Emptying a bag of mushrooms in his lap she said, "I think they must be all right because we ate a lot of them for supper last night and none of us are dead yet."

George's hair stood on end at that.

All day long George received other mushroom collectors, and packages of fungi came by mail and by special messenger. By night both willing George and his stenographer were exhausted. Many telephone messages were also received. One woman wanted George to come out to her home beyond the city limits and see some strange red mushrooms which were growing in her yard. Another had found a mushroom with a green cap, pink gills, and a red stem. "What mushroom could it possibly be?" George was unable to transact any business either that day or the following day.

So he caused a notice to appear in the *Daily News* stating that he was going out of town for a two weeks' vacation. That ended the mushroom expert business for George.

Canned Mushrooms

Mrs. Tonssaint liked mushrooms and would eat and enjoy any that the members of the society brought to her. Doctor Tonssaint never would eat any of them. No wild mushrooms for him—give him the cultivated ones that came in cans. He was passionately fond of them.

Whenever he went down to New Mexico to his silver mines he always took a dozen or two cans of canned mushrooms along.

One day Mrs. Tonssaint received word that the doctor had been very sick. He had, it seems, eaten a can of his canned mushrooms and had had a case of ptomaine poisoning. When he came home the laugh was on him.

He Liked the Pictures

Mr. Loue was a member of the Milwaukee Mycological Society. He had a mushroom book but he had never collected or eaten a mushroom of any kind. He had read his book from end to end, including the recipes—he had memorized most of the descriptions of mushrooms—and he enjoyed looking at the colored and other illustrations of mushrooms—but as long as he was a member of the club he never could be induced to eat a mushroom. His whole joy consisted in reading about fungi.

"Darn"

Mr. W. H. Ellsworth and Rev. Drexel were telling each other at a meeting of the fine mushrooms they had collected. Mr. Ellsworth was particularly enthusiastic. He was unconsciously using a lot of swear words in telling of his collecting success. All of the members were listening. The good priest soon caught his enthusiasm and pretty soon he too was using swear words in describing his own mushroom prizes—such as "darn" and "gol darn," etc.

The members were some of them delighted and some of them horrified at this exhibition.

Morgan's Parasol

Mr. Forsythe, a Milwaukee Road engineer, had collected some big mushrooms in a Waukesha County meadow, near which his engine happened to be.

He brought them to Mr. Brown at the Milwaukee Museum and was told that the mushrooms he thought so delicious were specimens of Morgan's Parasol, an unwholesome species. But he was determined to eat them—they looked good to him. He was shown a picture of them in a mushroom book and the description read to him. He said he didn't care a darn what the book said—he was going to eat them.

He did so and was in a Milwaukee hospital and not entirely recovered from his venture for three months after.

This is the beautiful large parasol mushroom with greenish gills which was so common this autumn.

The Jack o' Lantern

The Jack o' Lantern, a large orange-colored mushroom often growing in clusters at the base of a stump or tree, is an unwholesome species. Many people have become very sick from eating it. This mushroom when fresh and taken into a dark room gives out a phosphorescent luminosity. One can almost read a newspaper by its light. Some other mushrooms are also phosphorescent. This luminosity in some mushrooms is the basis in some countries of fairy stories and superstitions about ghosts.

Mushroom Tests

In America we know that the tests for edible and poisonous mushrooms brought to the United States from Europe are very faulty and dangerous. Such tests as the "onion test," "silver spoon test," etc. are very unreliable. Despite the warnings of mushroom specialists many descendants of European emigrants still rely on these tests.

In Poland I heard of people using the onion test for mushrooms. I had some of the mushrooms and survived. I was hoping as I ate them that they had tried out the variety previously. They seemed to be safe for we suffered no ill effects.

Swiss Food

Told by Anna Baumann, Monroe

The Swiss bread is very much better than that which we have in this country. It is made in large loaves and is very tough and comes in three colors, light, medium and black. It is made of whole wheat flour and is delicious tasting. One loaf lasts a family of four a week. It is very coarse in texture as it is made of homemade yeast.

The Swiss were very poor and ate only the hardier foods and simpler. A hot boiled potato with the jacket on and a piece of cheese is a very old and much used Swiss dish. Up in the mountains where the dishes were very scarce one of the main dishes would be fried potatoes, which would be placed in one bowl and everyone, using their own spoon, would eat from it. . . .

The fruit in Switzerland is very well taken care of, preserved and used in all ways possible. Many of the long winter evenings would be spent by the family gathering around the kitchen table and paring apples, which would then be dried and stored for future use.

Too Much Wine

Told by Mrs. Adolph Abplanalp, Monroe.

It is a Swiss habit to serve wine to their guests and it is very impolite to refuse and the hostess is very much offended if you do. Mrs. Abplanalp served Miss Marty and myself wine, kisses with whipped cream, Swiss cheese and butter, and a fruit jello with cream. Here a Swiss custom popped up. They eat no butter on their bread when they eat cheese with it. Invariably when you spend any length of time in the afternoon or evening in a Swiss home refreshments are served. Cake or cookies are served with the wine. It does get to be a problem how to ward off the wine partaking though; if you make three calls a day and have it offered to you in water tumblers at all three you might readily ruin the reputation of the folklore project for sobriety. I was telling Rev. Schuh, who has a Swiss congregation, my troubles and he told how he avoided it. If he took all the wine offered him at all the homes he visited he would be far from a sober minister, so he goes without any breakfast and uses that as an excuse all during the morning, for one cannot drink wine on an empty stomach. In the afternoon he makes fewer calls and drinks but little at each place and on a full stomach and gets by all right. The editor of the *Evening Times* made another suggestion which does work—eat something very fat before drinking wine and it will not bother you at all.

New Glarus Observations

Dorothy Potter, miscellaneous notes

Swiss women use spinach water to rinse their hair.

Cooked dried fruit is used a lot at meals with meat by the Swiss. Swiss food is highly seasoned.

In Canton Zurich hard cider was used a great deal more than wine.

In this country the Swiss are accustomed to wine daily. Cheese is always served one if not two meals a day.

In New Glarus condensed milk is served unless you specifically request fresh milk. They seemingly are very fond of it and think it nicer and more desirable than the fresh.

Schnapps are made by practically every household. The usual way is to cut up apples and let them ferment in a barrel. At present Switzerland has passed a law which prohibits the home making of intoxicating liquors and distilleries are permitted to sell just so much and if they have more the government buys it at a fixed price. Schnapps can also be made from potatoes, prunes, or any fruit.

Home Remedies
Told by Mary Saxer, Belleville

In the old days families would use home remedies for illness. Herbs were the most commonly used. Tea made from Linder tree leaves and mixed with honey would be used for colds. Goose grease and peppermint would also be used for colds by rubbing it on the chest. Mrs. Saxer's great aunt would always make the children wear the pelt of a cat with the fur side next to their chests for a cold. . . .

On Sundays entire families, and several families, would walk to a nearby town where they would go to what we would call a beer garden and have food and drink. They would then walk home in the evening. . . .

People who were ailing had to drink goat milk.

Coffee and Cherry Whiskey
Told by Dr. and Mrs. Sylvin J. Francois, New Glarus

There is always fruit on the table which one eats before retiring. The strawberries are like small crab apples. They are served whole and each person is given a bowl of sugar to dip them in as they eat them. . . .

The Swiss do not have pies and cakes such as ours but use fresh fruits for desserts instead. They have soup every noon and sometimes for supper too. The wife would cook up enough stock to make soup for three days or more. Wine is served with the dinner at noon and coffee is served an hour later with cherry whiskey in it. Their coffee is drip and very strong. They have no flavoring such as vanilla so they use the cherry whiskey for flavoring. A fruit cocktail is made the night before it is used including bananas and covered with this cherry whiskey. The next day when time to be served the bananas have not even turned brown as they ordinarily do.

Swiss Holidays

Told by Werner Stauffacher, New Glarus

In May, the boys and girls collect eggs with the Queen of the May, who is a small girl enthroned on a hand cart decorated with greenery and flowers. They sing

Eggs are very good
When one adds flower
Eggs are very good
With butter underneath them. . . .

They are given eggs, flour, butter and even sweets at each house they visit, and then some kind person takes their provisions and cooks *croutes dorees* for them, which is the same as our French toast. With this they are given chocolate cream.

In summer is the *abbayes,* counterpart of the Geneva *vogus,* the Flemish *kermesse,* the Fribourg *benichon,* and the *kilby* of German Switzerland. It lasts three days. On Sunday the society members go to divine service where the minister renders a sermon appropriate to the occasion. At mid-day there is an enormous banquet consisting primarily of solid foods. At one *abbaye* in the canton there is always served ox tongue, boiled beef, roast beef, roast veal and *tant*. Speeches follow and then a parade through the village, a reception by the king and queen of the range, and an open air ball on the raised platform. Monday the *abbaye* begins with all the villagers present with their friends. The doors are wide open and the tables stacked with good things to eat. *Boutefas,* a stew, leaven bread, marvels and *tailles* are in the majority. Wine is abundant. To belong to an *abbaye* a candidate has to be balloted upon, is charged a fee of 150 francs and the rights of membership pass from father to eldest son.

At the end of haymaking and harvesting the master gives a feast which is called *Ressat*. Often the last cart entering the village has a bunch of flowers on top of the small ladder which holds up the hay in front.

Before winter sets in there is the gathering of the grapes. Young girls from other parts of the country came in to help and it is regarded as a holiday. The gatherers may take a kiss for each bunch of grapes left on a branch. Through generations the women in the same family go to gather the grapes at the same place.

On the long winter evenings the time is spent nut-cracking. A festivity which is called *Gremaillees*. In the kitchen the men break the shells and the women take out the kernels, from which is made a sweet scented, amber colored oil. There is singing, laughing and bombarding with shells. At midnight a feast is served. . . .

The earliest festivals were also religious ceremonies, to the patron saint of the village or a pilgrimage to the chapels in the higher pastures. It is Catholic and the country is very mountainous. On Corpus Christi, ascension day, everyone dresses in their finest, the men wearing their military uniforms.

These people have a custom of blessing their houses, fields, troops, produce, flowers, the mountains and all that they know are in the hands of God. Their torrents are blessed and some shepherds in the high mountains still conjure the mists.

The Montferrine, Seulatare, and Massacrante are local folk dances of ancient origin. The county is famous for its cheese. The Raclette is a very old but still-used dish. It is made by taking a cheese, not more than three months old, cutting through the middle and holding next to a fire. When it has melted and browned scrape this half melted paste onto a plate, sprinkle with a little pepper, add a steaming potato (*grive*) and wash down with muscatel or Valaisian wine. One of their chief occupations is the making of furniture which lasts for generations.

Ascension, or Corpus Christi Day, is full of ceremony and parading. There is a procession which starts with the ringing of the bells at 8 a.m. The church retinue, women in native garb, men in soldiers' uniforms, children etc. form the procession which winds its way through the town or village to the square where an hour is spent chanting. The flower-decorated altars, doors and gardens are blessed as the procession passes. After this the women sing folk songs to the rhythm of a woman swinging a beautiful porcelain bowl with a silver coin in it.

The costume of the women is recognized by the long wrist fitting sleeves, small fringed shawls, narrow brimmed high crowned hats which they wear. The brims are dark and the crowns a light color. Some wear lace mitts without fingers.

Swedish Wine

Homemade intoxicants are not allowed in Sweden. Each person of age is permitted so much a month to drink. They are given a book and as they buy their drinks it is marked therein. When they have had their quota they cannot get any more until the next month. The only difficulty here is that those who do not drink rent their books to those who do.

Mrs. Zweifel had some very delicious dandelion wine and gave me the recipe, so here it is.

3 gallons flowers
5 gallons water (hot)
*Let soak for 48 hours then strain through a cloth. Slice 5 oranges and
10 lemons and add them. Add 15 pounds of sugar and stir until dissolved. Stir daily. Place in moderate temperature room. In 2 weeks
strain again and place in earthen or glass containers. Place cloth over
tops. Let stand for 2 to 3 months until stops working and then bottle.*

Lingon is a berry in Sweden which is about the size of a blueberry but is red like our cranberries. It is skinned and served with veal. It is very tart and is a relish. . . .

For whooping cough, camphor and turpentine mixed are heated a little and used. The mixture is put in the hand and warmed before a fire and then rubbed on the soles of the feet of the sick person until it is hot. It is done upon going to bed and a little also rubbed on the chest.

Elderberry blossom tea, drunk as hot as possible for colds just before going to bed.

Kerosene or turpentine is rubbed on swollen members.

Diluted carbolic acid is used for open wounds.

Belgian Customs
Told by Dr. and Mrs. Sylvin J. Francois, New Glarus

Their sausage is rolled up on a spindle effect and they enroll it to the number of feet, or rather meters, which you want and cut it with a pair of scissors. It is a pork sausage.

Meat is very much better over there as they age it.

They have beer and wine at all their meals, beer with their dinner.

Their coffee is made thusly—they have a crock with a handle and into the top a bag with a handle fits. The coffee is mixed with chicory, put in the bag and the bag put in the crock. Hot water is then poured over it until the crock is filled and that is the coffee for the entire day. They prefer to drink it lukewarm or cold.

The Belgium pies seem to be a national institution. In each home there is the equivalent of a baker's oven built into the basement and the family does all of its own baking. The pies are made about 14–16" in diameter and 40 to 50 of them are baked at a time. They are made of raised dough and filled with cheese, apples, prunes or whatever happens to be in season. They are open face, having no upper crust on them. These pies are placed on a big platter which is on a low stand with 6 to 7 piled on top of each other, each a different kind and served cold.

They have five meals a day, at 6, 10, 1, 4 and 8.

Their loaves of bread are simply huge being all of a couple of feet in diameter.

Coffee is served after dinner with rum in it. . . .

Fruit is very expensive in Belgium and in the summer the prices are prohibitive. They know nothing about canning of fruit or vegetables. The cherries they make into wine or conserve to preserve them and the vegetables they dry for use in the winter. . . .

When possible all the eating and drinking is done out on terraces.

Christmas and New Year's Day
France
Told by Constant and Gustavus Lamboley, Belleville

On Xmas everyone would go to church. All were Catholic. The people of a farming area would build their homes together forming a village, and many would have to travel quite some distance from it to work their fields. The Xmas celebration, other than attending church, would perhaps be the purchasing of a penny's worth of candy by the youngsters. Presents were not exchanged very often.

On New Years the men and boys would go from house to house wishing everyone a Happy New Year and whistling it. The people so called upon would give each one a couple of English walnuts. The boys would form a crude band to accompany them on their callings. One would play a comb with a piece of paper over it, others would sing and whistle, and sometimes they would shoot at the ground in front of the door of the house they were bound for. This was the day that the boys after wishing a Happy New Year could grab and kiss the girls. They would then be given coffee cake, whiskey and candy. The smaller children would get a penny or two from the neighbors on this gala day. . . .

Presents were never exchanged on Xmas. That was a day of religious observance and piety and an extra fine meal was the only difference from a Sunday.

Presents were exchanged between friends and members of a family on New Years. They were always presented in the morning. The men spent the day going from house to house wishing their friends and relatives a Happy New Year. At each house they would get something to drink; as a result they almost invariably returned home rather drunk.

It was considered a bad omen if a woman was the first caller on New Years. The women did not make calls on this day but occasionally a beggar woman would call asking for food or money and if she was the first caller at that house that day it was an ill omen.

Switzerland
Told by Freda Marty, Monroe

In Switzerland it is an old custom for people before Xmas to send a list of things they want to their friends and relatives. The bride sends out the same thing before she is married and informs friends and relatives what she needs for her new home. This list is called Wunschezdtel and even includes furniture. . . .

The Xmas tree is decorated on Xmas Eve. Cookies and nuts wrapped in gold and silver paper are used for some of the decorations. Presents are exchanged between members of the family and close friends, and they are mostly necessary things. There are always Xmas trees in the school houses and churches. The wealthy people of the community give each child a present which he needs and can use. Among these presents are also distributed a few cookies and chocolate.

December 6 is Santa Claus day. There really is no Santa Claus but occasionally some one of the family will dress up as Santa and go to the neighbors and have fun with the small children asking if they have been good. This is a big market day. The children start at 4 in the morning to form their parade and band, which consist of all the available tins, spoons and jugs with which to make any and all kinds of noise. This noise and parading continue until 9. The people line the streets and throw apples, walnuts, chestnuts, candies from sacks to the children. In the bigger towns there are dances and drinking.

On New Year's people and children go to their parents the first thing and wish them a Happy New Year. Visiting is done only to parents' homes. It is a day of family gathering and a big meal. On Xmas the parents go to the homes of their children. Everyone goes to church in their best and brightest clothes. In one town in which Mrs. Hefty lived the Catholic and Reformed church held their services in the same church. The Catholics would have theirs first and then the Reformed.

At 12 on New Year's Eve the bells in all the towns would ring. In Mrs. Hefty's town it would ring every half hour on Xmas and daily it rings at 11 o'clock. She does not know the reason for this last but says that it is an old, old custom that has been in force ever since the town had bells. In most towns the bell rings at 8 in the evening for curfew and at an earlier time in the winter—according to when it gets dark. . . .

Told by Mary Saxer, Belleville

On Xmas presents are given to members of the family, relatives and friends. They really are exchanged on Xmas Eve. The tree is put up and decorated on Xmas Eve also. In one section of Switzerland *lebckuchen* is used for decorating. It is a flat bread which is bought from bakeries and is cut into many different shapes and figures, covered with bright frosting and sometimes a picture pasted on. The children start collecting these many days before Xmas and then hang all they have accumulated on the tree. It is always open house on Xmas and wine and cake is served to all the visitors.

On Old Year Eve (New Year's Eve) the villagers form a group and go singing from house to house. They carry a basket which is filled at each house with something good to eat.

England
Told by Charles Overndon, Madison

To the children of England Santa Claus is a myth, though they think he comes down the chimney and brings them gifts of candy, nuts and fruits. No other presents are given. Christmas is not commercialized in England as it is in the United States. There are no "Santa Clauses" to be seen about the stores or streets. On Christmas morning the "father of Christmas," a man dressed in a costume something like that of Santa Claus, distributes the candy, etc.

The two main features of the Christmas dinner are the roast beef or roast goose and the plum pudding. The pudding is steamed in a cloth and is in the form of a round ball. Many times the cook will put in three pence and six pence pieces to delight the children.

Bon-bons are another Christmas delicacy. These are small pieces of candy in a wrapper. A child takes hold of each end of the wrapper and pulls. This causes a snap that amuses the youngsters. Inside the wrapper is also a printed motto. . . .

About three o'clock on Christmas morning people are sometimes awakened by bands or orchestras that play in different sections of the city.

Sweden
Told by Elfreda Zweifel, New Glarus

It was believed that Oden, one of the old Swedish gods, used to have a pig for Xmas so the families did too, and even today most Swedish families have a pig for dinner on that day. Oden also had an 8 legged horse which would run until it was tired and then turn over and run on the other four legs. This seemingly could keep up forever.

On Xmas a sheaf of wheat would be put out for the birds and the animals would get an extra portion of their daily feed. If there were ghosts it was thought that they too had to be treated or the Xmas spirit would be lost.

Czechoslovakia
Told by Stephen Kliman, location unattributed

Comes then the Christmas season, again a strange admixture of spiritual habit and mystical custom. Preparations start on St. Lucius Day, about December fourteenth. To exorcise the witches, you begin on St. Lucius Day to build a little stool, working on it day by day until it is finished Christmas Eve. The stool and a bag of poppy seeds you carry with you to mass at midnight. You stand on the stool. If the witches are so bold as to appear in church, at a certain point in the service they turn their backs to the altar and make for you. You throw the poppy seeds about you. The witches must stop to pick them up before they can pursue you.

They may appear, too, in your own garden. So, with one blow each day from St. Lucius Day on, you hammer a good-sized spike into a tough tree trunk. The witches stop to pull out the spikes, break off their teeth, and then can do you no harm.

But otherwise Christmastime is a period of touching naiveté and poignant simplicity. At Christmas Eve supper, dishes are served which are eaten at no other time in the year. Fish is permitted, but no meat nor fowl save the aquatic species, as duck or goose. There is a special bread, made of dough pulled into sticks, cut into blocks, decorated with sweetened water and poppy seeds, and baked in huge ovens. It is piled high on platters and wreathed with garlic and onions. Sauerkraut with dried mushrooms. Wafers of unleavened dough baked in sheets in waffle-like irons. Honey, jars of apples, nuts, Beer, or wine in the well-to-do homes.

Because no one is permitted to leave the table during the meal, everything is piled on at once. Master, servant, house animals, even the bird, sit at one table. A deeply religious attitude prevails. The head of the house makes a long, wearisome speech, a genesis from Adam and Eve to the present day, and ends with his paternal blessing.

Each helps himself from every dish. But before eating, he puts aside a little of each dish in a small pile beside his plate. Supper over, the head of the family gathers up the little piles, takes them to the barn, and feeds the cows, the pigs and the sheep. He thanks them for the past year's benefits and asks for increased productivity in the coming year. He calls upon the chickens, then goes into orchard or garden. He digs a hole at the foot of each tree and buries what is left.

And do you know that animals talk on Christmas Eve? Don't be skeptical. Many a girl has learned the name of her future husband from the family *milch* cow.

(I digress to speak of another way to foretell the future. Take an ordinary housekey, pour molten lead through the hole, then cold water from a jug. The lead assumes fantastic, significant shapes, from which you divine your future.)

Meanwhile the children and young people, on this benign, holy eve, escape from the home and stroll from house to house, singing carols under the windows. Housewives shower pennies on the children and ply the young men with wine. Blessings are exchanged, blessings upon every known relative and circumstance. In a short while these blessings may be chanted backwards, whether by reason of sharp memory or potent wine I am not prepared to say.

"Wild Life—Ducks," woodblock print by John Liskan, from *Superior Wisconsin in Woodblock*

The village shepherd assumes importance of almost biblical proportions. In his full regalia, carrying an ornamented whip, he goes back and forth, blowing his horn lustily.

On the Day he is the first to wish the household a Merry Christmas. He carries a basket of birch twigs with woven ends. The housewife selects one, not with her bare hand, goes to the barn and switches each animal, to promote fecundity. If a child under fifteen happens to lie abed at the time, he is switched also. The housewife rewards the shepherd according to the number of animals he takes care of during the year.

It is indeed a season of beneficence. Golden flour, even, has been milled on Christmas Eve. That is, if all religious and superstitious requirements have been met. These date as far back as the Day of the Three Wise Men, occurring in January, when the miller pours water or honey from a jug in a circle around the mill, to ward off evil spirits. The old-fashioned grist mill is located a mile or two away from the village, near a romantic spot in the woods, where the gnomes and spirits of the spring keep guard over it. On Christmas Eve absolute silence must reign in the mill. The master mill turns the machinery backward. He sends his apprentice helper to midnight mass, and outside the church door stations his journeyman helper (a roving miller who goes from mill to mill and in his wanderings gathers a store of gossip and folk tales).

When the priest elevates the Holy Host, the apprentice gives a sign to the journeyman, who runs back to the mill. The master turns on the water. And golden flour comes.

But once upon a time an avaricious journeyman, seeing the golden stream, cried out: "We'll be rich by morning!" There was a crash. Evil spirits swarmed over the mill and destroyed it. In the morning the journeyman was found two miles away with the print of a big hand on his cheek. The master miller was beaten and the golden flour turned into fertilizer.

Easter and Other Religious Observances
Switzerland
Told by Mrs. John Hoerler, Belleville

On Easter the children would have Easter eggs colored and chocolate rabbits. Presents would be exchanged among families and friends. Young girls would usually exchange handkerchiefs. The entire school would assemble at the school and go singing all the way to the church and then sing in the church itself. This would occur in the morning. There always was a big dinner on Easter.

France
Told by Mrs. Shepard, Belleville

On Easter the children rolled eggs. Each child would have two or three, at the most, boiled eggs which were brightly colored. A board would be placed so that one end was higher than the other. Two or more children would enter the contest. One would place his egg at the bottom of the board and another would roll his. Whoever had his egg cracked would lose his egg to the child whose egg had caused the cracking.

Sweden
Told by Elfreda Zweifel, New Glarus

In Sweden there is a church called Jeder Church, a postal card of which I sent the museum in June. Before the church was constructed one of the women in the neighborhood baked bread on Sunday. Her neighbors told her that that was a sin. The women said that if it were a sin the loaf would turn to stone. The round loaf (limpa) which she was baking did turn to stone and that is masoned in the wall of the Jeder Church. Mrs. Zweifel's mother saw it.

Non-Religious Observances, Feasts, and Celebrations
Switzerland

Told by Freda Marty, Monroe

In Zurich March 21 is considered the first day of spring and is celebrated as such. The celebration starts at 6 in the morning. There is a historical parade and an effigy of winter is the central and most important figure. At the end of the parade the effigy is taken to the middle of a meadow and burned. In this parade the guilds exhibit their customs and costumes too. Switzerland is considered the fatherland of guilds. . . .

Told by Mrs. John Hoerler, Belleville

If a woman wishes a man Happy New Year on New Year's Day he is considered very unlucky. . . .

The Swiss girls many years ago had an extra outfit which to wear on special and important occasions. It was the equivalent of the Norwegian National Costume. Each one differs in each county—each county in Switzerland has its own style and kind. The following is a description of the ones worn in the county from which Mrs. Hoerler comes. The skirt was red, green or black wool with fine pleating down each side. Over that was worn a silk apron with silver ties which tied around the waist. There was a silk collar which was pleated and heavily embroidered. A black vest was worn over a white blouse with puffed sleeves.

The vest had stays in it and silver buttons which were laced about with a silver cord. The ends of the cord hung down at the side. The hat was like a bird's wing made of lace and a wing stretching out on each side. These costumes cost about 1000 franc and only the very wealthy could have them.

The men from the farm wore a national costume too. Theirs consisted of short pants, just below the knee, short coat and a very tight shirt waist and coat, a red or black bow tie and a leather cap. The cap would have designs cut out of it and be lined with a bright colored piece of wool so that the color showed in the open work. They also wore red stockings and black shoes with large silver buckles on them. . . .

Dorothy Potter, miscellaneous notes

Geneva was the last canton to enter the Swiss confederation, and also is the smallest. It was the route taken by nobility and royalty for social or political reasons and much pomp attended their journeys. The citizens took part in the feasts and processions which were given in honor of their famous guests. For such guests verses called histories were written. On December 11, in hymn, song and an annual festival (called Escalade) the Kings of Savoie, former frequent visitors to the city, are made much of within the celebration commemorating the failure of an assault planned by the Duke in 1602, Dec. 11. On that evening the people sing an old song which voices their thanks for the preservation of their independence due to that failure, and the bells of St. Peter repeat the song each hour during the month of December.

Kilby

Dorothy Potter, miscellaneous notes

On Sunday and Monday, September 13 and 14, the Swiss of New Glarus celebrated Kilby, in the modern manner with ball games and dances, for which the community has become famous. Kilby (*Kerchwert*) originated about 100 years ago in Canton Glarus, Switzerland, as the occasion for dedication of the Reformed Church. This custom soon spread to other cantons, and whenever a new church was constructed, its formal dedication was postponed until the last Sunday in September, and then year after year a repetition of this dedication would be held. In New Glarus the festival opens with a religious service on Sunday morning, with more secular activities in the afternoon. The celebration is continued on Monday evening by dancing. After the services, one in German and the other in English, and hymns sung by a men's choir in German, Mr. Jacob Figi calls the confirmation classes starting with that of 1860 as none are alive from the first 10 which started in 1850. None answered their year until 1866 when one person stood. As their year is called those who were confirmed in that church in that year stand. This ceremony occurs only once a year and then on Kilby. . . .

It might well be added that the dances Monday night always have fights thrown in for good measure. Too much liquor and the masculine weakness of showing off is the usual cause. William Tell Hall boasted of six separate and distinct fights this year. The older married people always go to Salerno's dance as they prefer the old dances and the young people patronize the William Tell Hall.

The district in and about New Glarus seems to go in quite strongly for what they call Field Days. Anyone, or any group of people, who think it would be a good idea to have one get one going. Tugs of war, baseball games and concessions are the usual features. Sometimes a boxing match is thrown in and the evening always has a dance. They are usually given at some very small village or perhaps on a farm. The tug of war teams are very proud of their abilities and are always willing to compete with their neighboring townships and villages to determine who is the best puller. At the last one I heard that one of the pullers fainted from his exertions and was unconscious for two hours. These festivities are most common in the fall when the grain and hay and corn are all in and the farmers have a bit of leisure time.

Fosnacht
Told by Mrs. Fred Hefty, Belleville

In February there would be held Fosnacht Masquerade. This is a rather new custom. On this day there is a parade in which all current people and things are satirized and burlesqued. It is the last celebration before Lent begins. There are no police who preside and it is followed by a dance at which everyone is masked. The masks are removed at midnight. Mrs. Hefty tells a story of what happened to a couple from her home town who got mixed up in the masquerade of a neighboring town. Mr. Smith decided that he would like to go to a neighboring town that was having a masquerade and finally persuaded his wife that it was all right for him to go. After he had left on the train she decided to go too. They were both costumed and masked, but she recognized him at the dance because of his height.

They danced together and he started making love to her. Things advanced fairly well until 12 when all unmasked. The fight which ensued made local history.

France
Told by Constant and Gustavus Lamboley, Belleville

August 1 was the date for a local celebration in their particular village. There would be dancing, much drinking of wine and a merry-go-round to make the affair very festive. A beef would be butchered for the day and made into soup for everyone. Before being killed the animal would be inspected by doctors who would pronounce it fit to eat; if so, the mayor would have some part in the preliminaries and then the beef killed. Wheat would be gleaned by hand so that it could be ground and cake made for the occasion.

It was only the very wealthy families who could afford to butcher meat for their own consumption. The Lamboleys butchered a hog when they came to this country and that was the only time. The families who did kill their beef would hang it in the sun for days until it became very ripe. Meat in that section of France was very different from what we have. It was much more tender and had a sweeter flavor. This was due to the fact that the stock was fed on potatoes and meal and only pastured along the sides of the road on the end of a rope. The peasant families, of which the Lamboleys were part, were exceedingly poor and they had to exercise great thrift to be able to get even a bare living.

Land and Law

The English Countryside
Told by Charles Overndon, Madison

The County Sussex is especially noted for its downs. These downs are chalk hills 600 or 700 ft. high. There is about 6 inches of sod covering the chalk. On the hottest days in the summer one can find a cool breeze on top of the downs.

Birds of many varieties, especially the skylark, build their nests in the grass on the downs.

Walking through the country in England, one does not follow well marked highways as he does in America, but rather follows paths through fields and woods. Every fence has a stile or gate. There are two kinds of stiles used, the stile with steps or the hog-stopper. The latter has two curved posts that serve to keep cattle and hogs out of the neighbor's field by means of two curved posts placed closely together. When the animal attempts to pass thru this stile he gets caught and is forced to back out. The hiker surely can open the small gate between the two posts.

Another means of passing from one field to another is the "kissing gate." This is constructed so that when two people pass through the gate at the same time they are forced to face each other. These gates are popular among the young people.

Many of the fields in England are surrounded by hedges rather than fences. The hedges are kept neatly trimmed and present a pleasing appearance.

Wild flowers grow in abundance in England. One must not step from the path to pick any bouquets because of trespassing on the owner's property, but all the flowers one can easily reach from the path may be picked.

Among the flowers that grow most profusely are the primrose, nettle, dog rose, heart's ease, thistle, hedge parsley or rabbit's meat, scabious, jack-in-the-pulpit, and white and blue violets.

Sussex is known for its oak trees. Charcoal is made from these trees and most of the gallant old battleships were fashioned from the oak trees of Sussex County.

The Swiss Alps
Told by Mr. and Mrs. Fred Hefty, Belleville

The Swiss use the word "Alp" as the Norwegian does *saeter*. It refers to the pasture land on the mountains upon which the herds graze in the summer. Every four years in Switzerland each village auctions off its Alps. Each village usually owns two or more and each one is auctioned off separately. They go to the highest bidders. Those who have rented an alp then rent cows from the other villagers for the summer for a specified amount and take them to the mountains to graze and make butter and cheese from their milk. People having young stock which they wish to have grazed must pay the renters of the Alp so much per head. The village limits the number of head that can graze on each Alp, the smaller the Alp the fewer are permitted and vice versa. Each citizen of the village owning the Alp gets about 30 pounds of butter free during the summer months. The government has a particular store in each village where it sells salt to the inhabitants and at this store the butter is distributed. A citizen can obtain it all at once or ration it over a regular period of time. This butter is furnished by the people who have obtained the Alps for the four years and is part of the rental though the price bid at the auction is paid above the furnishing of the butter.

Each cow that goes to the Alps in the summer has a bell and a name on the collar holding the bell so that her name and owner is

Untitled engraving by Frank Utpatel WHi Image ID 104875

known. The herds are assembled the last of May and remain in the mountains until the first of October or when the snow forces them down. The night before the herds are to go to the mountains they are brought in from the surrounding country to the village. The herders make a gala occasion of it yelling and whooping and they all sing. Sometimes the number of cows from the local village does not equal the limit set on the Alp so neighboring counties send their cows. In the spring the cows seem to know their own way over the pass and into the village from which they are to go to the Alp. And in the fall they know their way home equally well. The entire herd moves off in the morning and if anyone is late his cow cannot go to the Alp. They have to be there on time and all have to go at once. Only men go up to the Alp. The herds are moved upward on the mountain in periods of four weeks. They start grazing on the lower pasture of the Alp, in four weeks are moved to the next pasture and then again in four weeks to the topmost and then they move down again as the weather gets too cold and the pasturage less.

The herders do the milking and make the milk and cheese on the Alp. The cheese is kept until the fall and a cheese buyer goes around from Alp to Alp buying it up. A special frame was used to carry the cheeses down the mountain side, it resembled a legless chair and the back would be strapped on the man's back. Three cheeses would be placed on the seat part and thusly carried to the village. This has been improved a bit by the men using a wooden sleigh or sled with wooden runners which is pulled by hand. If the grass is a little wet the sled goes very fast and the men have a difficult time keeping up with it and steering it. 180 pounds at a time would be hauled on the sled.

There is some pasturage which cows cannot get to because the mountain is too steep. This also belongs to the towns and each town owns and keeps about 100 goats. Daily the boy who is the goat herder takes the goats up to these spots and brings them down again in the evening. He has a horn and every morning at four he blows it and the goats come from their various homes and he takes them up the mountain. In the village where Mrs. Hefty came from the goat herder one day took off his vest in which was his watch and chain and laid it down. When he returned a goat had eaten it and they had to kill and open it up to retrieve the lost time piece and chain.

High up on the mountain the village owned land which was too steep for the cattle and presumably too good for the goats. Mr. Hefty and his brother would get up at two in the morning and climb for five hours to get to these spots hauling their sled with them. They would cut all day long and then tie their hay into a canvas with four ropes, pile it on the sled and take it home. An entire day's work would not net more than 180 pounds. Upon his recent visit home in '30, Mr. Hefty saw his neighbor and son do this but they rolled theirs down the mountain after they had it securely tied.

The following is a story about an Alp. A young man was a cheese-maker on an Alp for the summer. His mother came up to visit him one day and he was very chagrined and short with her because he wanted his bride-to-be to come. He was so rude that his mother, after having climbed all that distance, took leave in a few minutes. She had been gone only a few minutes when the sweetheart did arrive. It was muddy around the cheese house so the boy took out cheeses for her to walk on. In a few seconds a landslide came down from the mountain and buried the two of them and the cheese house. The mother was unharmed. . . .

When a young boy, Mr. Hefty recalls having to learn so many verses from the Bible each day and at specified times the students were expected to recite 100 of them and if they made three errors they had to stay after school and learn them until they made no errors. . . .

Told by Anna Baumann, Monroe

Alpine roses seem to be natives on the Alps only. They grow above timberline on a low shrub, which has a tiny slip of a green leaf and small rose colored blossoms which resemble in both color and shape our roses.

The Edelweiss, national flower of Switzerland, is greatly prized by the Swiss. It grows way out on the crags, in all the most inaccessible places and many lives are lost yearly in trying to pick it. The flower is like a star and feels like felt. The foliage is a greyish olive color.

The chamois is a wild animal like our elk which lives in the very tops of the Alps where neither herds nor herders can go. They are very agile and quick and are much sought after by Alpine hunters. Chamois skin, the name, originated from the name of these animals, as it was their skin which we originally used. They have two small straight horns on the top of their heads.

There is so much land in Switzerland that cannot be utilized, as it is covered with glaciers, above the snow line or too mountainous, that every usable inch has to be used. Even the very steep slopes are used and cared for as well as are the level valleys. Fertilizer is carried to them on the backs of the men and women in baskets and the crops are just as laboriously carried down in the same manner. . . .

The herders who tend to the cattle up in the mountains during the summer months have much time and no one in particular to converse with. The Alpine Horn is their means of talking to other herders on the other alps within a radius of several miles. The horn is made of pine root and is six feet and more long. The end of the horn is about a foot in diameter and is usually rested on the ground when blown, because the entire thing is so long and unwieldy it is impossible for the blower to hold it up. When one of these is blown it's heard for miles and miles and soon another herder will answer by blowing his horn and so it continues. . . .

Told by Mr. and Mrs. Fred Hefty, Belleville

Above Mr. Hefty's native village in the mountains is a lake which has no outlet. An hour below the lake a stream comes out from the rocks and it was thought that that was the outlet to the lake. Legend has it that some years ago a young boy who was goat herder in the pastures around the lake made a bet that he could swim across the lake. He reached the middle and there was a whirlpool which sucked him in and under. He was not seen again. A short time later the boy's mother was getting a pail of water from the stream below and she got her son's head in the pail. . . .

There are absolutely no weeds to be found in Switzerland, for the Swiss cannot spare the ground for them to grow on.

Swiss Law and Government
Told by Mr. and Mrs. Fred Hefty, Belleville

Men who have violated the law of the country are put in the work house. Not so many years ago a man escaped from it and went over a mountain pass. He stopped at a house to get something to eat and drink and while the woman went to get some cider he followed her and killed her. He was caught and hung. (There is very little capital punishment in Switzerland as there are very few murders. Many people were not hung because they could not find a hangman.) No one wanted the job. Finally a railroad crossing watchman wrote in and said he could do the job and offered to be the hangman. He did not get the job and the railroad discharged him as they did not want such a person working for them.

A few years ago a German came to a little hotel up on the mountainside in Switzerland. He stayed a week or so and the family thought that he was awfully nice. (Fuel for stoves is made of small bundles of twigs and branches tied together. The housewife puts one in at a time when she is cooking.) The woman of this house was putting one of the bundles in the stove one day and the German shot her with a gun which he borrowed to go bird hunting with. She was killed. The man went into the bedroom where the little girl was sleeping, put a cloth in her mouth, found the money hidden in the house, and left. In those days there was no telephone but the brother of the woman who had been shot lived next door and he rode a horse into the village and telegraphed from the depot to the next village and the man was caught. The German killed himself finally and saved the state the job. . . .

Told by Freda Marty, Belleville

Miss Marty while in Switzerland witnessed a Langsemann in either Glarus or Appensell, which are the only two cantons which have it. It was in Appensell she witnessed the annual meeting, in which the entire municipality votes on old and new laws. It is the same as when it originated in 1413. It is held on a Sunday after church is out, and the people are dressed in their costumes. The voters, who are only the men citizens, as women have not suffrage rights, wear their swords at their left side and press a prayer book to their heart. About 11,000 men take part. The chiming of the church bells starts the meeting. This is followed by the firing of some guns. A group of men dressed as spearmen and carrying those weapons escorted by a fife and drum corps, dressed in black and white, enter the arena from the court house. They meet the government officials who arrive in a carriage. They are dressed in black and white also—black on one shoulder and white on the other, and they wear a three-cornered hat. The open carriage in which they arrive is black, as are the two horses which draw it. The horses are led by the spearmen at the head of the fife and drum corps, who escort them to the center of the ring to the tribune, on which there are no chairs. The officials are considered no better than the voters and since the latter cannot sit the officials cannot either. The meeting is then opened by a prayer and then all sing:

All life proceeds from Thee
And produces in a thousand stanzas.
All creation Thine handiwork are we
That we feel that we exist
And Thou oh great our Father called.
Oh we bend our heads before Thee
In unendable ecstasy.
What unboundable comfort
That as the mild ray of the sun
As Thy future love illumines.

Thy omnipresence be an angel
That will guide us so our weakness lead us from the goal.

This is sung by the voters and spectators with their heads uncovered. All the past laws are taken up and voted upon by the people and they register their vote by merely raising their right hand. Four times a year each taxpayer gets an exact accounting of how the money has been used and the balance. The acceptance of past laws is followed by affirmation of the council holders. A head of the council is proposed and finally after seven had been suggested by the voters all but one of these was eliminated by voting. Each time a man is selected and elected to a position the men standing about him signify his position by raising their swords in the air. The fife and drum corps come over and escort him to the tribune. He is immediately sworn into office. There are seven on the council and one of them officiates as *land-weibl* or clerk. He is elected yearly. The previous one in this council had held office for 38 years and death was the only thing that prevented his reelection. Five candidates are chosen and they had to give a speech about themselves, life history, qualifications, experience and ability. One is finally elected and immediately vested with the triangular hat which is the badge of his office. The whole thing lasts only from three to four hours and is closed with a prayer. A male chorus then serenaded the military guests and federal officials who were present.

Marriage and Family

Marriage Customs

France

Told by Constant and Gustavus Lamboley, Belleville

It was customary for the young man to ask his girl's parents, her father first, for the hand of their daughter. He would ask for their consent and blessing. To be married in the church they had to have a gold wedding ring. The consent granted there would be an official calling upon the bride to his family by the young man's family headed by his father. There would be a little reception and a little lunch served and something to drink....

Told by Mrs. Shepard, Belleville

Until the babies are a month old they are enclosed in a white cloth. This cloth is white, is shaped to the infant's body and is wider at the top than at the bottom. There are eyelets on the edges, which meet on the front of the baby, and through these a ribbon is strung fastening and making the cloth tight about the body. The arms and legs of the baby are straightened out before they are put in this.

The violins used in the early days of St. Germain had only one or two strings. These and accordions were used for the music at dances and festive occasions. All music was played by ear in the small communities, no one could read a note....

Told by Mrs. Constant Lamboley, Belleville

Mr. Lamboley and Mrs. Lamboley and their parents both came from St. Germain, France, though they did not know each other, until they had come to this country and settled in and around Belleville.

In France when a girl becomes engaged she gets a plain gold ring to wear on her engagement finger. The same ring serves as her wedding ring after she is married, and it is worn on the same finger.

The bans are announced in church so many days before the wedding. The wedding cannot occur on Sunday nor during Lent, and should be performed in the morning.

The bride does not wear colors for her wedding but should not be dressed in black. Mrs. Lamboley's mother did wear black to her wedding, as she was still in mourning for her mother who had died five years previously. I could not find out how long mourning is supposed to last. The bride wears a white veil which is a sign of her virginity. Most French are Catholic and hence the rituals and ceremony were much the same as they are now in that church. The bride carries a prayer book but no flowers.

Switzerland

Told by Freda Marty, Monroe

If a professional man marries he brings his wife a professional title such as Herr Frau Doctor, Herr Frau Architect, as do those who bear a political title. . . .

When a couple were married they hired, if they did not own, a rubber-tired carriage with a coachman, and drawn by two horses, for the day. The bride would be dressed in her wedding gown, the groom in his best plus his tall silk hat, and they would be accompanied by their witnesses. After the wedding they set forth in the carriage and spent the rest of the day driving about and going places.

The mother takes her child to be baptized the first day she is out of confinement. The child is not taken from the house until this occasion. In the carton of Berne each child has two godmothers and two godfathers. . . .

Told by Mrs. John Hoerler, Belleville

Babies were carried on a pillow, a huge one, for three months after they were born. They simply were not lifted nor carried anywhere except on that pillow.

Babies were baptized during the first two weeks. The mother would still be in bed but there would be a big celebration. When the child was born friends and neighbors would bring in gifts for the child; they were mostly clothing. The wealthy families, when a child was to be baptized would have a dinner at a hotel which would include the family and relatives and the godfather and godmother. During all this celebration the godfather and godmother would be responsible for the child. . . .

In most every household in which there were children there could be found reposing behind the mirror a small bunch of hazel branches tied together. These were used to remedy the erring of some youngster. The Swiss have a puzzle that goes with this switch:

It's there behind the mirror.
Who gets it will surely know it,
What is it?

Newly married couples usually started out in their own homes. The Swiss took cognizance of the fact that the young and old could not get along together under the same roof. The father was always considered very much the head of the house. The wife had to clean the shoes of the men in the house daily. It was considered a disgrace for children to go to school without shining their shoes at least once a day. It had to be done as regularly as going to church or any of the compulsory duties of life.

Bracelets and chains were often made of hair. A very fine present from a girl to her boyfriend or husband was something which she had made from her own hair. . . .

Told by Mary Saxer, Belleville

When a girl became engaged her fiancé would give her a plain gold band which would be worn next to the little finger on the right hand. When married the ring would be changed to the left hand, the same finger.

It was the custom for the man to ask a girl's parents or guardian for her hand. Occasionally a couple would run away if the parents did not approve of the match. This was seldom, however, and it was considered a disgrace for a girl to do such a thing.

If the girl and her parents could afford it she was supposed to furnish all the furniture and linen for her new home. She would have dozens of sheets, pillow cases, etc. A proud young wife would also come to her husband with enough clothes for a year so that her husband would not have to buy her anything for at least that long. . . .

Dorothy Potter, miscellaneous notes

A *Chilbi* is given in most of the communities of the canton, the most important part of which is the dancing. The dancers are all escorted home by their partners after the ball. On Saturday evenings young people meet at barns or in the square and they then pay visits to isolated farms in a body. No one knocks but the window panes are vibrated with a moistened thumb and the leader does a lot of complaining, complimenting, and menacing. The door is opened and all enter on the tips of their toes. Music ensues and all dance in their stocking feet so as not to waken the old folks. The girls offer a glass of wine to their friends but it is the custom for no one to get the least bit drunk. In this way young people get to know each other in different parts of the country. If some house is omitted on the rounds it is usually because the young woman has a regular caller every Saturday nite and he calls alone. It was the ancient custom that a man would not marry a girl unless she could give him heirs. The lover or kilter from that same section is left in peace to do his Saturday nite calling but if he is from other parts he is subject to many tricks. He may be plunged into the village trough and if he resists he may have a pole thrust through his sleeves and a bell hung around his neck or elsewhere.

A few days before the wedding the *letzi* is celebrated. The young couple invite all their friends to a sort of farewell ceremony. The couple sit in the place of honor and receive congratulations from the guests and then a simple supper is served with wine. Speeches, dancing, yodeling follow. In gratitude the boys will make their mortars (real or improvised) thunder on the eve of the wedding and woe betide the friend who is too mean to offer his *letzi,* and the couple who for some reason or other is not liked. An appalling din, an infernal shindy with cat-calls will announce the public opinion to the deafest.

Czech Lands
Told by Stephen Kliman, location unattributed

I should like to tell of a charming custom to celebrate the coming of spring. This ceremony had its origin in pagan times, and takes place in the village proper. The girls dress in costumes of vividly harmonious colors. From house to house they carry a statue of Morena, Goddess of Winter, sometimes called Goddess of Death, garbed in richly embroidered robes, singing as they go. The housewives throw pennies to them. The boys follow them. When each home has been visited, the boys seize the figure and throw it into the river. With the proceeds of the procession the young people stage a supper and dance.

St. John's Day, which occurs around June sixth, is also observed with pagan rites. On the eve the girls build a huge bonfire and sing while it burns. The boys demonstrate their bravery and prowess by jumping through and over the flames.

Cupid is indefatigable on this occasion, and many marriages result. But a girl who fails to find her mate on St. John's Eve need not worry, for there is always the marriage broker to arrange an alliance for her, through the medium of her parents. This broker is a most important individual. In his head he carries an index of marriageable boys and girls, with due regard for compatibility; proximity and extent of properties, and harmony of station or employment. When he finds two young people who meet these requirements, he calls upon the girl's parents. He indicates his purpose by carrying a cane with all manner of ribbons dangling from it. The daughter is promptly sent from the room, and for two or three hours the plotters engage in conversation on every conceivable bride. The bridal dress, embroidered in gold, is taken from the chest whence it has reposed from generation to generation. A wreath of wax mock-orange blossoms, ornamented with beads and streamers, is placed upon the bride's forehead and allowed to fall gracefully over her shoulders to her back waistline. More like a headdress, it is a symbol of her chastity. The groom, should his morals have been proved impeccable also, wears a boutonniere to match.

(A disconcerting custom that has not survived the olden days gave further proof of the bride's virginity. Should her maid of honor be satisfied as to her purity, a rooster was led from house to house. But should the maid of honor dispute her fitness, there was no rooster procession.)

The gypsy band strikes up its lilting music. The bride appears. The best man, who acts as master of ceremonies, once more asks the parents for the hand of their daughter and congratulates them upon bringing such a fair flower to maturity.

By twos the procession marches to the church, the gypsy band bringing up the rear. The best man escorts the bride, the bridegroom walks with his prospective mother-in-law. A young man leads the way, carrying a specially baked cake in the form of a wreath, and a jug of wine with its narrow neck thrust through the cake. In the cake are strips of paper with various matrimonial prophesies: you will marry a blacksmith, you will marry a miller; you may not, alas, marry at all.

If that new home is in another village, the youth of her native community accompany the bridal pair. At the churchyard they stop the wagon. Beside the gate, draped in red or blue ribbon, are a bottle of wine, two glasses and the ubiquitous collection plate. The disgruntled youths express their high indignation at the loss of the bride. The bridegroom appeases their wrath by putting money in the plate, which later is spent for a supper and dance. The health of the bridal couple is drunk and they are permitted to go to the groom's home.

Her happy, carefree girlhood surrendered, the young wife takes her place beside her husband in barnyard and field. She cares for the poultry; feeds the livestock with carefully selected weeds; and, except for the seeding of grain and the plowing and harvesting of wheat, tends the crops. She raises four or five crops in a field at once; say, potatoes, beets, beans, corn and poppies along the edges and in the corners. She raises the hemp and the flax. . . .

Midwives, by combining superstitious lore with practical experience, have been known to cure diphtheria, pox, fever and even to set broken bones. There is rarely a doctor in the village. In times of birth, of course, the midwife is competent and indispensable.

When she is called to the prospective mother's home, she hangs before the bed a special piece of cloth which has been used on such occasions in the family for generations. This cloth is larger than a bedsheet and embroidered with the delicate needlework for which Czecho-Slovakian women are famous. The mother stays behind this screen or curtain during confinement and for ten days after delivery, when she receives her church purification.

Each day one of the neighbors brings in beef or chicken soup, honey, a bottle of wine. She is treated with great respect and a strict ritual of etiquette, even when she calls with empty hands, for the guest is regarded as a sacred person.

Upon her arrival she is escorted to the table. On this table is a wooden tray covered with an embroidered napkin. A big, round loaf of bread, in a jacket of homespun, lies on the tray. Its cut side is turned from the door, so the bread won't walk out. A knife, salt on a small platter, accompany the bread. The guest takes the loaf, makes the sign of the cross over it, cuts a small piece, dips it in the salt, utters a wish of good will, and eats it. Only then is she offered a chair.

The newborn child, dressed in special robes, is christened as soon as his godparents are selected, usually three or four days after birth. Frequently he is named for the saint on whose name-day he arrives.

Babies
Sweden
Told by Elfreda Zweifel, New Glarus

In Sweden christening is done as soon as possible after birth. The sponsor is always a woman and one who is old. In the catechism it requires one man and one woman but they do not do it that way. If anything happens to the parents of the child the sponsor has to take care of the child.

Funerals
Sweden
Told by Elfreda Zweifel, New Glarus

In Sweden after a funeral, if the family have any means at all there is a feast. It is just like one given for a wedding—it is in honor of the one who has passed on. At the bottom of the notice sent to friends and relatives of a death there is an announcement inviting the recipient to the funeral followed by O. S. A., which is the Swedish equivalent of R.S.V. P. . . .

Black is always worn at church regardless of the occasion.

Members of the deceased's family are in mourning for at least six months. . . .

"Rural Funeral," engraving by Frank Utpatel WHi Image ID 104863

Veils were worn over hats for mourning to hide the tears. . . .

It was a custom among the Vikings that when they were getting past their prime or when they were taken sick and knew they were going to die, they would go off and kill themselves by their own hand. It was considered a weakness to die in bed; it was best to pass on bravely while yet in their prime. In the saga which Mrs. Zweifel has written in Swedish the old king knows he is passing his prime so he has a huge banquet at the end of which he takes a sharp knife, cuts the runic alphabet on his body and bleeds to death.

Czech Lands
Told by Stephan Kliman, location unattributed

As ceremony attends the coming of a soul, so it accompanies the soul on its departure. When life leaves a loved one's body, the survivor immediately goes to the garden, knocks on the beehive, and informs the bees. He returns to the house, stops the clock, and covers the mirror. Else, in the mirror's depths, he may see death.

Yet these people do not embrace the usual conception of death. Their beloved ones have not departed, they have merely changed their abode. They know what you are doing and they keep an eye on you. They live in their graves, from which they emerge at night and attend church. With the first crow of the rooster they return to their resting places.

And if you are kind, you will take my word for this and not invade the churchyard at night. Except on All Souls' Eve, in November. Then the graves are decorated and candles placed on each one. It is a weird, not unhappy scene. Flickering lights make distorted shadows of the living as they move among the mounds and the cast-iron memorials, until you believe with these sincere, trusting people that there is no real parting; and that the deep love of family and country that weld them into a God-fearing, law-abiding community, persists even after the seeming extinction of physical life.

INDEX